Fall Into Me

K.M. Scott

2013 Copper Key Media, LLC

Published in the United States

Cover Design: Bookin' It Designs
Interior Design: Jovana Shirley, Unforeseen Editing

ISBN: 978-0-9891081-7-1

DEDICATION

To my family for patiently listening to all my story ideas, I say thank you. It must be baffling at times for two men to have to spend so much time in the mind of a romance writer.

To Kelley for the wonderful support, I can't say thank you enough for eating glass and smiling for my work.

And to my readers for their tremendous love of Tristan and Nina, all I can say is you've made writing this story so much fun. Thank you.

CONTENTS

ONE

TRISTAN

"I thought you understood how this had to end."

Looking down the hall at Nina's hospital room, I eyed with suspicion every person who walked in and out. Pressing the phone to my ear, I listened as the man on the other end repeated himself and added, "We've given you more than enough time, Tristan. This has to end."

"I won't do it. I told you that. She's no threat to you, Karl."

"You're not thinking with the right head, son. If anyone finds out about the evidence she has, everything your father worked so hard to attain will be gone. Are you prepared to let that happen? We aren't. Take care of this. Or we will."

"She has nothing. I've checked everything she owns and there's nothing. Let her live in peace."

"With you, happily ever after, like some storybook ending? I told you that we can't afford to have any loose ends. There's proof somewhere. Those of us who supported your father all those years won't be taken down by your schoolboy romantic ideas."

"And I told you there's nothing to prove whatever my father was doing. He's dead and Nina's father is dead. Let whatever happened end with them."

Karl was silent for a long time. "We've told you what we want. You decide how this is going to happen. Or we will."

I pressed End Call and stuffed my phone back into my suit coat pocket, disgusted with Karl but more with myself. How had I let this get so fucking far?

All I had to do was find the papers Karl was sure her father had showing what my father had done. I was still in the dark about what exactly Joseph Edwards thought he'd caught my father doing, but I didn't care anymore. Whether it was some tax scam or real estate deal gone bad, it didn't matter. All I cared about was keeping Nina safe from the likes of Karl and the other board members who thought of nothing but protecting their own hides.

"Mr. Stone?"

I shook off my phone call and saw one of Nina's nurses at my side. "Yes?"

"It's time for her to leave. She's all ready. Her ribs might be a little sore at first when she gets back to her daily activity, but that's to be expected. I've told her to just listen to what her body's telling her and she should be fine. Now we just have to wait for her memory to come back."

Nina appeared in the doorway of the hospital room where she'd spent the last five weeks. Seated in a wheelchair, she wore her black yoga pants and white sweatshirt and had the pink roses I'd given her that morning in her lap. Her blue eyes lit up when I stepped out from behind the wall.

"Hey! The doctor said I'm ready to roll."

Bowing deeply, I looked up at her and smiled. "Your chariot awaits, my lady."

The press was out in full force when I pulled the Jag in through the gate at the bottom of the driveway I'd had installed the week before. Cameras flashed on all sides of us, making Nina bury her head in the space between our seats. Snaking my arm around her to hold her close, I hoped this first introduction to my world hadn't made her wish she'd had anywhere else to go.

I leaned my head down and whispered next to her ear, "Don't worry. We'll be home in a minute and we won't have to deal with them again, Nina."

The gates closed behind us and I raced up the driveway, wanting all that bullshit with the paparazzi left back there in the past. Fucking vultures. Like anyone should want to see pictures splattered all over the gossip pages of a man bringing a woman home from the hospital after a car accident.

Nina lifted her head and sat up straight in her seat to look at the house as I stopped the car. "This is where you live?"

"Where we live," I said, gently correcting her.

She turned her head and the look on her face was a mix of uncertainty and disbelief.

As I shut off the car, I flashed her a smile. "Don't worry. It's cozier than it looks."

"Uh huh." She looked unconvinced.

I grabbed her coat and walked around the car to help her out, watching her crane her neck to take in all of the house as I placed my black leather jacket across her shoulders. Looking up at me with those gentle blue eyes, she asked, "I really live here? With you?"

Nodding, I smiled. "You do. In fact, you like this house more than the other one."

She stopped walking and stared straight ahead. "There's another one?"

I shrugged. "Well, it's a penthouse at the Manhattan property, but you told me you liked this one better."

"Wow. First the car and now more than one house. Jordan wasn't kidding when she said you were loaded." Nina fell silent and grimaced. "Sorry. That sounded worse than I meant it to. She just said you were wealthy."

"Wealthy. Loaded. It's all the same. I just hope you're comfortable here."

With a tiny chuckle, she said, "I can't imagine anyone couldn't be."

Rogers met us at the door and bowed. "Miss, it's wonderful to see you again."

Nina studied him for a moment and then smiled meekly, obviously not remembering him. "Hello."

"Get the bags from the car, Rogers."

As he passed us, she looked up at me and frowned. "I guess I've met him before? I don't remember."

"The doctors said it could take some time. Give it a chance."

Nodding, she tried to put on a brave face, but I saw in her eyes she was disappointed. I stood there staring down at her and wishing I could make things better, wishing I had the power to turn back time to before that night when she ran away and...

I pressed a smile onto my lips and extended my hand toward her old bedroom, my heart heavy from the words I was about to say. "Your room is right down this hall."

Nina looked around the entryway and then at me, her eyes wide. "It's beautiful here, Tristan."

Faking enthusiasm the best I could, I said, "Thanks. Let's get you settled in."

I gently placed my hand on the small of her back, a tiny gesture I did out of habit before I remembered for the first time that day that she and I were basically strangers in her mind. She didn't react as I kept my hand against her and escorted her to her wing of the house, and I wanted to at least believe it hadn't bothered her that I'd done it.

Opening the door, she looked around in amazement at her room, her mouth hanging open, just as she'd looked the first time she saw it all those months ago. "Wow, this is great! I thought maybe you were showing me to the servants' quarters or something, but this is as nice as the other part of the house."

Her words cut like knives. To her, I was just some man who paid her to work for him. She had no idea how much I wanted to take her back to our bedroom on the other side of the house, the one she belonged in. The bed she belonged in right next to me.

"You aren't my servant here. This is your home, Nina."

I tried to disguise the hurt in my voice, but it was no use. She heard it too and turned around from looking out the window to face me. "I'm sorry. I didn't mean to say the wrong thing. I didn't mean to make it sound like you'd treat someone like a servant. This is all so new to me."

"Don't be sorry. I'll leave you to get settled in. If you need anything, I'm just on the other side of the house."

I wanted to reach out to touch her hand, to take her in my arms and tell her how much I loved her, but she wasn't ready. I didn't want to scare her off. I knew I had to be patient and hopefully if I was, when she finally started to remember things, she'd also remember how much I loved her.

My insides felt empty as I walked toward my side of the house, alone again as I'd been for so long. I had work to do, but my heart wasn't in it. I didn't care about reporting to the Board as I had to soon at the quarterly meeting. I didn't care about anything involving Stone Worldwide. What did it matter anyway?

I sat down at the desk in my room and looked out the window at the unseasonably warm December day full of sun. All I could think of was that in just over a week the date I'd chosen for our wedding would pass without mention because she didn't remember the day held any special meaning. Nothing like the biggest day of your life going unnoticed.

"Tristan, I've arranged for dinner at five, as you ordered."

Something in Rogers' voice told me he hadn't come to find me to talk about dinner. Closing my eyes, I leaned my head back. "That's fine, Rogers. Thank you."

My words were met with silence, but he didn't leave. I'd avoided Rogers for weeks, knowing what he thought, but I wasn't going to escape this discussion about Nina. Opening my eyes, I turned to see him standing there staring down at me. "Is there something else, Rogers?" I asked, knowing there was.

"I'm simply wondering what I'm to do regarding Nina."

I hated the way he could refer to a human being in the same tone as he'd use to tell me he believed the gutters needed cleaning. Looking into his dark eyes, I leveled my gaze full of disgust on him. "What you're to do regarding Nina? Speak plainly, Rogers. I'm not in the mood for the butler talk. You've known me since I was five years old, for fuck's sake."

Rogers nodded his head slowly, and when he raised his gaze to meet mine again, it was one of doubt. "Nothing has changed, Tristan. Your father is still the one responsible for her father's death and you're still Victor Stone's son. The son of the man who killed Nina's father. Things are the same as they were the night she drove away from here."

I didn't need Rogers to tell me all of this. None of it had ever left my mind since that day Karl had confirmed what I'd found in my father's secret files. I'd lived with the knowledge that my own father had been the architect of Joseph Edwards' murder just as I'd have to continue living with it for the rest of my life.

"I don't need you to remind me of any of this, Rogers. What the fuck am I supposed to do?"

"About what, Tristan? You can't fix what your father did. No one expects you to."

"I don't care about fixing anything Victor Stone did. I care about taking care of Nina, not because of what happened to her father but because I love her. Why is this so difficult for you to understand?"

Rogers stood there staring at me, his face full of judgment. "Because you haven't loved anything or anyone since the accident."

Looking away, I watched out my window as a porcupine walked slowly across the grass. "I'm not incapable of love because of a plane crash. Are you saying you don't believe I fell in love with her?"

"I have no doubt you love her and she loved you. You've been given a second chance to make things right, Tristan. If you do not, I can't see how your future with her could end any differently than it did before."

"All I need is time," I mumbled as I watched the porcupine continue to make his way across the lawn toward the trees on my side of the house.

"Time for what? You must tell her the truth. If you don't, you'll be making the same mistake again and the outcome will be the same as last time."

Time. If I could find the evidence Karl believed existed, then Nina could be safe and never have to know about my father's heinous crime. Never have to know that I was the son of the man responsible for taking her only parent from her.

Turning back to face Rogers, I stood to get to work. "Thank you, Rogers. That will be all."

I saw the disapproval in his eyes as he turned to leave, but I didn't care. I wasn't going to let Nina find out the truth of her father's death. Her memory loss meant I could spare her that. It was the only good thing to come from her accident, and I intended on protecting it, no matter what.

All I needed was time.

At five o'clock I sat in the dining room waiting for Nina so we could eat dinner together as we had every day we'd been here in this house. I'd had Rogers instruct the cook that tonight's meal was to be duck in the hopes that maybe having that would remind her of the time we spent together at the penthouse. I knew it was probably grasping at straws, but what else did I have?

I waited for twenty minutes, watching the steam slowly fade away from the dishes before I was forced to admit that she wasn't coming. Of course she wasn't. She wasn't coming because she didn't remember that this was something we both looked forward to each day. That too was gone.

Loosening my tie, I leaned my head back and closed my eyes in frustration. I couldn't go on like this. It was like being sent to a country where everyone had forgotten the language except that one lonely soul who kept speaking even though nobody understood him, hoping one day he'd find just one other person to comprehend his words.

I pinched the bridge of my nose and felt the stress ebb away for a moment. Maybe I was just kidding myself. Maybe it was time for me to forget that language too.

If I could forget, I may have tried. But I couldn't. Rogers had been right when he'd said I hadn't loved anything or anyone since the accident. He was only partially correct, though. In truth, I'd never loved anyone before the accident either. Not like I loved Nina.

She was my everything. I needed her like I needed air to breathe. I doubted she'd even known how I truly felt about her before the accident. She was unlike anyone I'd ever encountered. Never before had another human being made me want so much more than the things my money could buy me.

All my life I'd been blessed with everything I could want, and it had made me hard and greedy. Nothing meant anything when you could have it at the drop of a hat. I'd learned that was one of the curses of money, but for a long time didn't care. Cars? I'd gone through dozens with not a thought about why I shouldn't. Homes? They came and went without any feeling or connection to them. Women? I could have who I wanted, when I wanted, and how.

And I did. Victor Stone's money paid for whatever I desired, and it didn't matter how fucked up it was. No worries. Money can make anything happen and then make it go away, if someone chooses. I let my cock lead me to places filled with desire, sex, and whatever else I could want. It was all so easy. How often had I fucked someone merely because I could, not because I felt anything for them?

It always amazed me how eager women were to please when good old Benjamin was sitting in my pocket. All it took was flashing the money clip once or twice.

Running my hand through my hair, I shuddered at how many times it had only taken a few bills for me to get everything I wanted or more, if that was what I craved. It all came so easily. A blonde, maybe her friend or two, and as much blow as I could get my hands on. Then it was just a matter of stuffing the junk up my nose and fucking as many women as I could.

And it had felt so fucking good. Life was mine to enjoy, and enjoy it I did. What's that saying about life and letting the juices run down your chin? I had juices enough to last a lifetime.

Then one day all the good times were gone. I was the lone survivor of a plane crash that killed my family. I'd watched my parents and twin brother die around me, listening to their agonizing cries for help and not being able to help them or myself as I waited to suffer the same fate.

I was allowed to live, and what did I do with that gift? I closed myself off from the world and turned into what I'd never wanted to be. The CEO of Stone Worldwide. Shrink after shrink promised with just a little more therapy that I'd find the answer and realize life was worth living again, as if they feared at any time I was going to kill myself. What they didn't seem to understand was there was something worse than dying.

Living.

Having whatever your heart desired and it never being enough to overcome the emptiness that ate away at you every day and night until you felt hollow inside. Dealing with the guilt that every member of your family had been taken away and you were left like some shining monument to Darwinism, as if being alive was some achievement I'd strived for and attained. All I'd done was sit there in that plane seat. That steel bar that had plowed through my brother's heart hadn't been able to find mine not because I was crafty or clever. It wasn't because I was lucky either.

That steel rod hadn't found my heart because I didn't have one. I'd spent my entire life caring for no one enough to call it love. Why would my heart be anything to pierce, much less damage enough to kill someone like me?

So I lived, a sole survivor with everything he could want. Except the one thing he needed.

That all changed when I met Nina. I hadn't intended on anything happening with her. I'd accepted my life alone as a punishment for all that I'd done for so many years. I didn't expect a reprieve. I didn't deserve one. All I wanted to do was try to make up for what my father had done. That she made some good come alive in me was something I wasn't ready for, but I couldn't let it go. Some small part of me was reborn that night we drove up the Taconic to this house.

So now I had a choice to make. Give up or fight. I let all those times I held Nina in my arms fill me, all those times she made my heart leap with one of her gentle smiles. For someone who had never had to fight for anything, it was strangely easy. Whatever I had to go through for her, I'd endure it.

TWO

TRISTAN

Nina was sitting on her bed when I gently pushed the bedroom door open. She was doing something on her laptop, and I stood there for a moment to watch her. Her brown hair had grown much longer since she first moved here. It hung halfway down her back in soft, natural waves as she sat cross-legged and hunched over looking at something on her computer's screen. The sweet memory of twirling those waves around my finger as she lay in my arms made an ache form in my chest as I stood there.

Not wanting to scare her, I tapped on the door and quietly said her name, but she nearly jumped off the bed from fear anyway. Wincing at my clumsiness, I put my hands up to calm her.

"I didn't mean to frighten you. I'm sorry. I was just hoping we could talk."

Shaking her head, she made her apologies. "No, no. I'm sorry. I didn't hear you there. What's up?"

"I wanted to talk."

She closed her laptop and pushed it aside. "You can sit down, if you like. Or would you rather talk somewhere else?"

What I rathered was taking her back to our room on the other side of the house and showing her all the ways I was crazy about her. Instead, I merely nodded and sat down beside her.

"This is a great room, Tristan. Thanks for letting me stay with you."

I forced a smile at her statement, which sounded like something a long lost relative would say to someone who wasn't thrilled about having them visit. "You're welcome, but this is your home, Nina. You don't have to thank me."

Lowering her head, she looked away from me. "I'm sorry. I can't imagine how hard this is for you. Jordan's told me how crazy in love I was with you, and I get that." Looking up at me, she blushed. "I mean, look at you. Who wouldn't be crazy in love with you? I just don't remember. But I don't want you to think that I don't want to remember. I do."

Nina looked away again, her cheeks red from embarrassment. Maybe that was a good thing. At least she seemed to be attracted to me. That was something I could work with.

I took her chin between my thumb and forefinger and gently turned her head to look at me. She still looked down at her hands sitting in her lap, though. "Look at me, Nina. Please."

She lifted her beautiful blue eyes to gaze up at me, and I swallowed hard, my mouth suddenly dry and my brain devoid of all thought about what I'd planned to say. Licking my lips, I began, hoping the right words would come to me.

"Nina, I know this is probably a confusing time for you. Whatever I'm dealing with is nothing compared to what you're forced to deal with. I don't want to make this worse for you. If I do that, let me know. You never have to be afraid to tell me if you're uncomfortable."

"Okay."

"The doctors think that if you get back to your life like it used to be, you'll begin to remember what we were. We just have to make sure you take care of those ribs."

Nina nodded and pressed a smile onto her pretty mouth. "My ribs feel good, so no worries. I hope that's true about remembering. I had hoped something would seem familiar here, but so far nothing."

Her admission of what I already knew hurt just the same. I'd hoped coming home would stir some memories for her too. I guess we were both disappointed.

"It's okay. No hurry. We've got time."

Time. If that's what we had, then I had to make the most of it.

Nina put her fingers over mine and moved them from her chin. Her touch on my skin sent a rush of electricity racing up my arm, making me want more.

"I do have a question. Is that okay?"

I couldn't help but smile. Same old Nina always with the questions. That was something. "Ask anything you want."

She turned to grab her laptop and opened it to bring up a picture of me with one of the actresses at an event a few months earlier. As I examined the image, all I could think of was how Nina had said I looked like a statue when I was with them. I'd never truly realized it until that moment, but I did.

"You seem to have a lot of girlfriends, but I can't find any pictures of me with you at these parties. Why?"

I blew the air out of my lungs and struggled for the best way to explain why there were hundreds of pictures of me with other women. "They aren't girlfriends, Nina. They're employees."

"And I'm your employee?"

"Yes."

"So they're all like I am to you?"

A groan escaped from my throat. This wasn't going well at all. "No. They're employees paid specifically to appear at events with me because I didn't have a girlfriend."

Nina's eyes lit up. "Oh. So there are pictures of us together at events once we began dating? I guess I just didn't get to those."

"Sure. I'm sure there are."

Arching one eyebrow, she saw right through my lie. "There aren't any pictures of us, are there? Why?"

"Because we only attended one event. I'm sure there are pictures, though."

Her look of skepticism turned to one of hurt. "I don't understand. We were together for six months and you asked me to marry you, but we only went to one event together?"

I knew what she was thinking. That for some reason I wouldn't want to be seen with her like I had with the actresses. This was not going as I'd hoped.

"It's a bit more complicated than that. Those women aren't in a relationship with me and get paid to deal with the press. I didn't want you to have to deal with that."

Leveling her gaze at me, she asked, "And what did I want?"

This was definitely the Nina I knew and loved. Smiling, I answered with the truth. "You were jealous and thought I was ashamed of you until I told you the truth about the actresses. Then you were afraid to go with me to the event we attended, but you ended up loving it. It was one of the best nights I've ever had."

Her expression softened and a smile spread across her lips. "Oh."

I wanted to tell her that the sex we had in the back of the Rolls had been better than any I'd ever had with any other woman. That just thinking of it was making me hard. It probably wasn't the right time, though.

"I wanted to talk about you getting back to doing things you used to do." *We* used to do. "I think it would be good for you to return to work."

"That sounds good. You said I'm your private curator, right? What does that mean exactly?"

"You handle choosing the artwork for the suites and penthouses in my hotels. I give you the assignments and then you present your choices to me."

A look of apprehension came over her face, and she bit her bottom lip. "Was I good at this?"

I'd seen that look before. It was the same one she'd worn that first day I assigned her my penthouse in the city. I'd wanted to take her in my arms and kiss her that day too.

"Very good."

Nina took a deep breath. "Tristan, I'm confused. I work for you as your private curator but I'm also your girlfriend?"

Fiancée.

"You loved the job, so you never mentioned wanting to stop once we began dating and even when you said yes to my proposal."

"So if I didn't want to work as your private curator anymore, you'd be okay with that?"

"If that would make you happy, then I'd be fine with it."

"What if I wanted a different job?"

"I'm sure there's something in Stone Worldwide that would suit you."

She bit her lip again. "No, I meant what if I wanted to work somewhere other than for you? I just wonder how good an idea it is to mix your business and personal life."

"Don't worry. I'm not," I said as casually as I could, hoping to hide how unhappy I was with where the conversation had gone.

"Well, then I'm not sure it's such a good idea to mix those in my life."

Fuck. I had hoped it would never come to the contract again, but I saw she wasn't going to just accept things. "Nina, you signed a contract obligating you to work for me."

The shock at my callous words was written all over her face. "For how long?"

"The initial period was for six months, but there's a provision that in the event you're unable to complete the six months that the contract is extended when you are able."

"What? How long is the extension for?"

"Two years."

She sat there on her bed staring at me with a stunned look for almost a minute before she finally spoke again. When she did, her words were like a sledgehammer to my chest.

Her eyebrows knitted. "So this is your idea of love, Tristan?"

I knew how this all sounded. I came off like the world's biggest dick, both in the boss and boyfriend departments. I knew that. But if I wanted to keep Nina safe, I'd have to deal with her thinking I was an ass, or worse, growing to hate me. I'd rather her hate me than be hurt by Karl and his buddies on the Board.

Her words hurt, though, so before I said something else that further convinced her of my asshole status, I stood to leave and repeated what I'd told her months earlier. "I can give you whatever your heart desires, Nina, but I can only do it this way."

"What if I can't handle this way, Tristan? What happens then?"

Another sledgehammer to the chest, but this time I couldn't stop myself from saying something in retaliation. "Then I guess you get to live rent free and get paid an astronomical salary for picking out pictures for hotel rooms, Nina."

I stared at her knowing that was a shitty thing to say, but I didn't care. I wanted her to hurt like she'd hurt me. If the look in her eyes was any indication, I'd succeeded.

Good for me. At this rate, I was going to have her speeding away in another of my goddamn cars by the end of the week. As I turned to leave the woman I loved and her new hatred for me, I wondered if maybe that was what was meant to be anyway.

I needed a drink, so I made my way to the room where Nina and I had first kissed to pour myself a scotch before I headed back to my room to begin the emotional pummeling I knew I deserved. In the span of less than a day, I'd screwed things up so completely that the woman I adored was likely making plans with Jordan to leave me before I even had the chance to give her a reason to stay.

I let the alcohol slide down my throat and closed my eyes to enjoy it. At least drinking was working out for me. By the time my second glass was empty, I was calm enough to admit that I didn't have a choice as to whether or not this worked with Nina. Even if she hated me, she had to stay. Karl and the others weren't going to spare her, no matter how much she begged and swore she knew nothing about her father's investigation.

I thought about returning to her room and apologizing, but that would have probably made it worse. No, I needed to think. I headed back to my room and relaxed on the bed. Nina's picture hung on the wall across from me, and as I stared at the blues and reds and those light brown smudges she'd said were my eyes watching her, I saw what I needed to do. I had to go back to the person the shrinks and Rogers had always said would never find true love. The woman who'd painted it wanted me to be that man, no matter how much everyone else didn't. I just had to make her want me like that again.

Easier said than done when the object of my affections was sitting on the other side of the house likely planning her escape.

I dozed off staring at Nina's picture as my mind drifted back to that night at Tony's when she said yes to spending the rest of our lives together. A knock on my door roused me from my nap, and I lifted my right arm to see the time. 9:28. Scrubbing the sleep from my eyes, I walked to the door, expecting Rogers to be standing there all dour-faced with something to report like Nina leaving again. I took a deep breath and braced myself for what he had to say as I opened the door.

"I just want you to know that I think keeping a woman prisoner is against the law in New York."

Nina stood there in the hallway dressed in shorts and a T-shirt and looking incredibly pissed off. But at least she was standing there and not driving away at a hundred miles an hour. That was definitely better than her leaving.

"You're not a prisoner." That was the second time I'd had to say that.

Her right hip shot out and her hand landed on her waist. "Then what do you call this?"

"Would you like to come in and talk?"

"What?" she asked with the same pissed off expression that now mixed with what looked like a flash of fear in her eyes.

"Would you like to come in? You slept in here for months, Nina. I promise. You liked it here."

"Do you plan to answer my question if I come in there?"

"Sure."

I opened the door and held my arm out to welcome her to the room where we'd spent hours falling in love. As always, I couldn't stop myself from hoping that she'd remember some shred of our past together.

"Would you like to sit down?" I asked as I dragged the chair away from the desk near the window.

She squinted her eyes at me and appeared to consider my offer of a seat. "I guess it couldn't hurt."

As she sat down in the chair in front of me, I had to fight the urge to slide my hands over her shoulders and lean down to kiss her like every fiber of my being wanted to. I stood for a few seconds wishing so much to touch her until the heaviness in my heart made it hard to breathe and I forced myself to move away. My feet felt like they were wading through wet cement as I came around to sit on the bed in front of her.

"So you were about to tell me how this isn't me being held prisoner," she said sharply as she folded her arms across her chest.

So much for memories of love.

I turned to point at her painting hanging on the wall. "That's yours. You painted that for me, and I loved it so much I had it hung there so I can see it every night before I fall asleep and every morning when I wake."

She looked at the painting and tears welled in her eyes. "I painted that for you?"

Nodding, I smiled. "You did. Do you want to know what you said the colors represented?"

Nina got up from her chair and walked over to stand in front of the painting. She stared at it for a long moment and looked back at me. "Those are your eyes. I've never seen eyes like yours—that color brown. There's no way I would've painted those two brown areas without wanting them to represent your eyes."

"That's right."

Turning back to face the painting, she asked, "What do the blues and reds symbolize?"

"You said they represented the emotions I made you feel."

She looked at me and a look of pain crossed her face. "Like hot and cold?"

"Sort of. I guess I can be difficult to be around sometimes."

Wiping a tear on her cheek, she shook her head and came back to sit in front of me. "I never paint for anyone I'm dating. The only man I've ever painted for was my father. If I painted this for you, I must have..."

She tried to choke back the tears, but she couldn't stop them and as they began to stream down her face, she ran out before I could do anything to make her feel better. I knew how she felt. The frustration. The loss. I didn't know if I should run after her since the doctors had repeatedly told me to give her time, but I couldn't let her sit over in that room alone crying about us when I was feeling as bad as she was at what we'd lost.

When I got to her room, she was sitting on the edge of her bed with her head in her hands, her body heaving from her sobs. Watching her like this broke my heart, and I couldn't stand there and do nothing. Whatever her doctors thought they knew, they didn't understand what it was like to watch the woman you love fall apart.

I sat down next to her and pulled her close to me. She didn't fight me and buried her head in my chest as she continued to cry. Trailing my fingers over her soft hair, I moved my hands to her back and held her to me, never wanting to let her go. She was my Nina.

"I hate this. You don't know what that painting means, Tristan," she sobbed into my shirt. "I never paint for others. I've always been too afraid to. This means I did feel everything Jordan says I did."

Pressing my lips to the top of her head, I kissed her softly and whispered, "Then that's a good thing, isn't it?"

Leaning back away from me, she shook her head. "No, it isn't! We were in love and now it's gone. I can't remember you or anything about this house or what we felt for each other. It's like it's a dark space where so much good is sitting there waiting for me and I can't find it."

"The doctors said it might take a little while."

"I don't want to wait a while! I had a life and now I have nothing. I sit over in this room and feel like I have nobody and nothing to hold on to."

I cupped her chin and smiled down into that beautiful sad face. "You have me. Hold on to me."

"I'm no fool, Tristan. I may not remember things, but I'm not an idiot. I know who you are. I looked it up. You're a bajillionaire. What would you want with someone like me?"

"Bajillionaire?" I asked, unable to stifle a smile.

"It's a word. It means you have more money than I could ever make in twenty lifetimes and I have no business believing you'd ever want me, a wannabe artist and curator."

"It's not a word, and as for me wanting you, you have every business believing it. People don't fall in love in spite of money, Nina. I can tell you I have absolute proof that money can make people very attractive, even when they aren't."

"You're intentionally twisting my words. You know what I meant."

"So because I have money, I can't fall in love? Is that what you meant?"

Nina wiped her eyes and shot me a look of reproach. "What would you want with someone like me?"

26

"Yeah. What would I want with a gorgeous woman who makes me crazy every time she's anywhere near me? Who'd want that?"

"Hmmph. Gorgeous. I probably look like a deranged raccoon right now, and even if I didn't, I don't look like any of those women you go to those parties with. I saw them, Tristan. They look like supermodels."

"And they're as boring as that dresser. They think I'm pretty boring too."

"They don't look bored. They look like they adore you."

"Good. At least I know that's money well spent."

She wrinkled her nose at me, letting me know I was going to have to be more convincing. "Nina, I pay those women very nicely to look happy with me. They want to be seen at influential parties and the board of directors of Stone Worldwide thinks a man should have a woman on his arm at all times. So I do. If it means anything, I had basically stopped going to those events before your accident because I didn't want to go with the actresses anymore."

"I don't understand. If you loved me so much, why didn't you take me? Is it because I don't look like those women?" she asked with hurt in her eyes.

Shaking my head, I couldn't help but smile. This was definitely the same old Nina. "I know you don't remember this, but you asked me the same thing once, so I'll tell you again what I told you that night. You're gorgeous, and I'd be happy to be seen anywhere on this Earth with you. But being in the spotlight like that has never been good for relationships. I didn't want that to damage what we had together. In my defense, I did ask you to come with me once and you didn't want to. I had to convince you."

Nina hung her head and sighed. "This is so hard, Tristan. What if I never remember all of that time you remember?"

"Then we make new memories together."

The look she gave me was filled with fear. "Do you still love me? Am I the person you fell in love with?"

I didn't have to think about my answer. I knew it in my heart. "Yes. I love you, even though you don't remember me or feel the same. And it wouldn't matter if you changed. I'd still love you as much as I did the first time I realized I'd found the person I wanted to spend the rest of my life with."

Wiping the tears from her cheeks, she smiled. "I think I know why I fell in love with you."

Her shy smile made me want to take her in my arms and never let her go. "Yeah? Let me guess. It's the way I wear a suit."

"No, but now that you mention it, you do look good in your clothes."

"My great house and the stoic butler that comes along with it?" I joked.

"No, but the house is great."

For the first time she touched me intentionally, sending a shot of excitement racing up my arm. Every clever comment left my head and I stared down at her wanting to press my lips to hers in a kiss that would take her breath away.

"I bet I fell in love with you because of the way you say what's in your heart."

Nothing could have been further from the truth. Shaking my head, I looked away, unable to face her. I couldn't handle feeling like a fraud at that moment.

"Tristan, did I say something wrong?"

I turned back to look at her and forced a smile. "No. How about we say you'll start work tomorrow morning? Nine sharp sound good?"

"Aren't you the boss? Shouldn't you be telling me instead of asking me?" she asked with a sexy grin that made me want to throw her down on the bed and show her exactly who was boss.

Standing, I looked down at her. "You're right. Be in my office at nine and be ready to work. If you need anything tonight, you know where I am."

I'd been right after all. Whether she knew it or not, she wanted the man I'd been all along. Starting tomorrow, I'd be that man again.

THREE

Nina

Tristan left me sitting on my bed wishing that I'd had the nerve to lean in and kiss him when he told me he loved me. I may not have remembered being with him, but my body reacted every time he was nearby, every inch of me wanting to feel his touch, and just hearing him profess his love for me had made my body launch into overdrive.

Jordan had told me all about him—how much he was worth, how crazy he was about me, how sexy he was—but she'd definitely understated that last part because this guy was off the charts hot. Always dressed in a shirt and tie, he appeared stiff and stuffy, but it hadn't taken me long to fall under his spell, as I guessed many women did. Those milk chocolate brown eyes that always seemed to be watching me made my legs go weak when he stared at me, even if he was looking for something in me that I may never remember.

The thought that he and I had been so in love that we'd planned to get married and now none of that existed anymore made my heart hurt. Every time he was near me I felt his loss. It was like a heaviness that emanated from him. He tried so hard to hide it, but it was no use. It covered every inch of him like a cloak of sadness he couldn't shake.

He was a stranger to me in many ways, but even without a memory of everything we'd been, something inside me yearned to be next to him, to touch him. Maybe there was some memory of him deep in my mind that I hadn't found yet but still knew what he'd meant to me.

I looked around my room and couldn't help admit it was beautiful. Designed with the finest fabrics and furnishings, he'd spared no cost with this room, much the same as with the rest of the house. I'd noticed that my bedroom was nearly a replica of his on the other side of the house. Was this intentional? Had he had this room redone while I was in the hospital or had this room always looked like his?

I padded over to the desk to smell the enormous bouquet of pink roses that filled the room with the most delicious fragrance. Pink flowers had always been my favorite ever since I was a child, and the mere fact that I remembered that made me happy. That I seemed to not be able to remember anything of the last four years was still incredibly depressing, but remembering my love of pink roses was something.

Tristan's remembering made me even happier. I couldn't explain why, but I already felt drawn to him. Was it because I knew he loved me, even though I couldn't say the same? I didn't know, but his thoughtfulness with the flowers made me feel cherished for the first time in a long time.

I hadn't noticed before, but there was a small envelope attached to the white silk bow around the flower stems. Slipping the card out, I read Tristan's note.

All my love,

Tristan

As I stood there holding that card, I had the strongest sense of déjà vu. I closed my eyes and struggled to grasp at a shred of an idea of what it meant, but after a few minutes, I gave up in frustration. It felt like there was something, but I couldn't put my finger on it.

Inhaling the sweet scent of roses one last time, I took the card with me and placed it on the night table, reading it once more before I turned out the light. All my love, Tristan. Rolling onto my back, I stared up in the darkness at the ceiling and thought about how many times I'd wished some great guy would feel just this kind of love for me and nothing had happened. He'd either never noticed I even existed or like others, had taken what they could until they grew tired of me.

Them I remembered. The ones who cared nothing were as clear in my mind as my own name. Tristan left roses and cards professing his love, and he was a total stranger.

Sometimes life sucked.

Reaching over to my night stand, I picked up the card with Tristan's handwritten note and pressed it to my lips. If only I could remember...

Then a thought came to me. Maybe he would know why I'd had that feeling of déjà vu when I'd read his card. I walked over to his side of the house and nervously knocked on his bedroom door. He had said if I needed anything I should find him, so I hoped maybe he wouldn't have a problem with me knocking on his door at night.

Idiot, the man says he loves you. He's not going to mind you coming by.

The door opened and there he stood in nothing but black silk pajama bottoms. I nearly passed out from the sight, and every word I would have wanted to say evaporated from my mind to make room for every sexual thought that could fit. God, he looked incredible!

As my eyes roamed up and down his toned, muscular body, I saw the tribal tattoo that sat above his left pec and traveled down his gorgeous left bicep to his elbow. That someone like him had a tattoo at all surprised me, but with a body like his, he should have had tattoos over every last inch of him.

And then the truth dawned on me: I'd slept with this man. I'd touched that body. There was no way in a just world I'd have forgotten that. No way. God, life really did suck sometimes.

"Nina, is everything okay?" he asked as if he were standing there like he normally did, all dressed and covered and exuding just his normal level of sexy, not the so-sexy-I-wanted-to-jump-him level he had going on at that moment.

My mind was filled with ideas about six-packs, whatever they called that cut near a well-built man's hipbones and how incredible Tristan's pants looked as they sat just under those cuts, and every indecent idea I'd ever had about what I would do with my tongue if I had the chance to touch a body like Tristan's. I couldn't talk. Suddenly, my mouth felt parched, and I licked my lips just to enable me to try to form words. It wasn't going to be easy with him standing there like that.

"I...you...I thought I remembered something," I stammered out.

Smooth. This was why hot guys never wanted me, I suspected.

Through all that super hot sexiness came excitement like a child on Christmas morning. His deep brown eyes lit up at the sound of my words and a genuine smile broke out on his face. "You remembered something?"

Nodding, I lifted up his card. "I think so. When I read your note, I had the clearest case of déjà vu."

He stepped back to let me past, and I walked in to stand in the middle of the room, unsure if I should sit on the bed or on the chair near the window. Tristan stood behind me for a moment, as if he wasn't sure what to do either, and then sat down on the bed in front of me.

"Would you like to sit down?" he asked as he looked up at me with an almost innocent look. Almost.

This wasn't going to be easy. I nodded and sat down beside him, all the while attempting to keep my gaze focused on his face instead of everywhere else on his body. Talk about an impossible task!

"Something in my note made you remember something?" he asked as he took the card from me, his fingers grazing mine and making my skin dance with excitement.

"Yeah. I can't put my finger on it, but I felt like there was something."

Without saying a thing, he stood from the bed and walked over to the dresser to open a drawer. He pulled something out, and I saw as he returned to sit next to me that he had a small stack of papers in his hand.

"These are letters and notes I wrote you."

I took them and opened the one that sat on top of the pile. They weren't in chronological order because the first one talked of my moving into his room. The next one was far more businesslike and talked of my job. Right there on his bed, I sat and read through our past together, not remembering anything more but so wishing I would.

More than anything else, Tristan's notes and letters told me we were happy. Two people in love and happy. His handwritten words touched me. Never as flowery as some women might want, they were very much him telling me he cared.

Finally, when I'd read each letter, some more than once, I looked up and saw him watching me intently. He looked so interested in me and how his letters made me feel. I couldn't figure out if I wanted to smile or cry. They were beautiful and sexy and unlike anything any man had ever given me. So simple yet so personal.

"Did I write you any letters, Tristan?"

He grinned a sexy smile. "No. You preferred to speak instead of write."

"And you didn't? Strong silent type, I guess?"

"I prefer to express myself in ways I can control."

His answers intrigued me, so I pressed further. "And you can't control your mouth?"

His eyes darkened, and he slid his tongue over his bottom lip. "It's not my mouth I can't control."

I had no doubt about that. Even more, I had no doubt that I wanted to know more about his mouth. And every other part of him.

"Oh. So what can't you control?"

"Let's just say you do things that make me not have the control I prefer."

His voice was deep and made me want to hear him speak more. "Tell me about what I was like with you."

My words sounded almost like they were begging. Maybe I was. I wanted to know the person he'd fallen in love with—the woman who had made such an incredible man fall for her. Was I still that woman? Or had she been replaced by some cipher who clung to any shred of thought that could attach her to the present in the hopes that it would help her remember the past four years?

"Honest. I never had to guess how you felt."

That was definitely me. I probably told him I loved him before he told me. Honest wasn't terribly sexy, though, usually.

"Did you like that? I can be incredibly difficult with my honesty, if I remember correctly."

He looked away and then back at me with a changed look in his eyes. "I loved it."

"Don't get too many people telling you the truth, huh? Most people don't like hearing it."

"Most people don't tell me anything."

"What do you mean?"

He seemed to think about how he wanted to answer before he finally said, "My work life is one in which very few people speak to me during the day. Most people who want to get to me instead deal with assistants and managers."

"So there's no one above you at your company?"

"Stone Worldwide has a board of directors, which I must deal with, but other than that, no."

God, that sounded lonely. "What about in your personal life? You have to speak to people then."

"I have Rogers to speak to everyone in my personal life. He handles the cook and all the household help, except for Jensen, my driver."

"So you only speak to your butler, your driver, and a few people at work? Why?"

"I speak to you," he said, sidestepping my question and making me feel his life was even lonelier than I'd first thought.

"Yeah, about that. Why would someone who prefers to speak to so few people not only take the time to speak to me but hire me himself instead of making me go through your human resources department?"

"I liked you. I wanted to be around you. I hadn't planned on..."

He abruptly stopped talking and looked away again. What hadn't he planned on?

I reached out and touched his hand as it sat on his thigh. "Don't stop. I like hearing about us then."

"I hadn't planned on meeting anyone that night at the art gallery."

Tristan seemed so reluctant to talk about anything concerning how we met. I'd asked him a few times in the hospital and he'd glossed over our meeting as if it were commonplace, but something in the way he spoke now told me it was very important to him.

"Tell me about what I was like there."

He shrugged and seemed to be at a loss for words.

"Please. I'd love to know about that time in my life. I'd planned on trying to find a gallery position when I was in college, so that I did is pretty important."

He looked at me and shook his head. "I don't know a lot about that part of your life. I only saw you once in your job at the gallery."

"What was I like?"

"Beautiful."

"That's it? Beautiful?"

"That's all I saw. And those little cocktail franks."

"Little cocktail franks?" I couldn't help but giggle. He had the oddest way of describing things. Beautiful and cocktail weenies. "You sure do know how to tell a story. Remind me to begin writing a journal so if one of us loses our memory again at least we have something to look back on," I teased, hoping to see one of his gentle smiles again.

For a second, I worried I had offended him because his expression hardened ever so slightly, but then he gave me one of those smiles that I was sure could melt the iciest heart and quietly said, "I remember the important things."

"Like?" I wanted to know those important things. I wanted to hear him talk about every single thing that meant something to him.

"Like the first time I kissed you. The first time you begged me not to tease you and how much I wanted to be inside you at that moment. What you look like when you sleep, all curled up next to me. How jealous you get. The feel of your hair against my fingers when I wrap it around them while we lay in bed talking."

As he spoke, I watched that beautiful mouth say words that nearly took my breath away. He said so little that when he finally spoke freely, it was like a dam breaking. He never took his eyes off my face, watching for my reaction, I suspected, even as his expression remained calm.

This was the reality of us. He remembered everything and so much of that revolved around me, while I remembered nothing but wanted so much to experience those moments that were so deeply etched in his mind.

My eyes drifted down over his muscular torso, and I saw the outline of his cock through his pajama pants. I couldn't deny I too was excited by his words. I was pretty sure all it would take was one kiss and I'd be more than willing, but I didn't want to make the move on him and he seemed content with just talking.

"I wish I remembered those things, Tristan," I said apologetically.

He leaned in and I waited for him to kiss me. His face was so close to mine I could feel his warm breath on my cheek. Instead, he took a tendril of hair and wrapped it around his middle finger. "There are always new memories, Nina."

I closed my eyes and willed myself not to react to the sound of his husky voice right next to my ear, but it was a lost cause. An involuntary whimper escaped from my mouth as I waited for him to touch me again. God, I wanted him to do something so we could get started on those new memories right then and there!

"Yes, there are," I croaked out as he sat there still as a statue, his breathing the only sound I heard.

He released my hair from around his finger and repeated the action, twirling the strand from the bottom up to next to my ear. When he stopped, he gently tugged on it, sending a twinge over my scalp and making me flinch.

"I didn't hurt you, did I?" he asked, but I had the distinct impression he didn't care if it had hurt.

In truth, it hadn't. The tiny bit of pain he'd caused by pulling my hair was intermingled with the pleasure he was creating in me just by being so close that I almost wished he'd do it again.

"No. Is this how you used to play with my hair?"

He shook his head, sighing heavily near my neck, and his warm breath flowed over my skin. "No," he whispered. "I'd play as you rested your head on my chest while we lay in bed. This bed."

This bed. As in the one I wished he would lay me down on and make love to me on at that very moment.

"Oh." That was all I could muster as a response because if I'd said anymore I'd have sounded like some drunken prom date looking to give it up easier than the town tramp. He was driving me mad with desire, but until he made the move, I planned to do my damnedest to keep it together.

"It's getting late and you have a big day tomorrow."

I sat stunned as he leaned back away from me and smiled. "Take the letters. Maybe they'll help you remember something."

"Yeah. Maybe. Thanks," I muttered as I stood on shaky legs to go back to my room. After all that, he didn't even try to make love to me. I couldn't tell if I was exhausted because of the emotions I'd experienced that day or because of the rollercoaster he'd taken my body on just waiting for him to make a move.

I opened the door and behind me from his place on the bed he said, "Nina, I'm glad you came over."

Turning around, I saw he was rock hard. His cock was nearly peaking out of his pants. Why was he playing with me like this?

"Yeah, it was nice. Thanks." I pressed a smile onto my lips and hoped he didn't see how frustrated he'd made me. "Have a good night, Tristan."

I slid my gaze over his body one last time and made my way back to my room. As I climbed into bed, I couldn't say for sure, but I didn't think I'd ever been so turned on merely by talking in my life.

If this was what life with Tristan Stone was like, it was no wonder I'd fallen in love with him before. I was halfway there already.

FOUR

Nina

At nine sharp, I stood in Tristan's office on his side of the house ready to get to work, even if I wasn't entirely sure I could do the job. Being a curator was far more than I ever remembered doing, but if what everyone was telling me was the truth, I'd done this job before and pretty well, so all I had to do was remember that and I'd be fine. I had the education and the experience. That was what I told myself about a hundred times over as I'd made my way to see Tristan.

I wore a green cashmere sweater that felt like heaven against my skin, a black pencil skirt, and a pair of black pumps that made my legs look damn good, if I did say so myself. While I may not have been able to remember anything since college, I was sure I'd never worn anything so luxurious in my life as what I was in as I stood there in front of him.

Tristan sat behind his enormous cherry wood desk looking breathtaking in a dark grey suit, black dress shirt, and a stunning red and black tie. After what had happened the night before, I wasn't sure I could work side-by-side with him, and looking like that only made it more difficult.

Why couldn't he work at home in sweatpants and a T-shirt? Who am I kidding? He'd probably still look stunning.

He looked up from his laptop and smiled. "Good morning, Nina. Come sit next to me."

I approached him on wobbly legs and sat down in a chair he slid next to his. As if it wasn't bad enough that I was unsure about my ability to do the job of curator, now I had to deal with him sitting as close to me as he had the night before.

This was going to be a long day.

"Ready to work?" he asked, his deep brown eyes staring into mine.

"Yes, sir," I joked, hoping to ease my jitters with some workplace humor.

He arched one dark eyebrow. "Sir? You don't have to be so formal, Nina. Remember, we're more than just employer and employee."

His deep voice spoke the words that should have put me at ease, but there was a sensual undertone to it that made me need to squeeze my thighs together to ease a desperate, sweet ache that had formed between them the moment I saw him sitting behind that desk.

"Okay. I was just trying to calm my jitters. I'm a little nervous about this," I confessed.

Smiling, he shook his head. "There's no need to be nervous. You're a natural at this. Trust me."

Trust me. He'd said that day after day since I'd met him in the hospital, and I still wasn't sure I could. In truth, it wasn't a could thing. It was an I-was-afraid-to thing. I'd never had much success with men, as far as I remembered, and the memory of what others had done to me was always uppermost in my mind when my heart felt even the tiniest tug in Tristan's direction.

He turned his laptop toward me and began clicking on pictures. "I thought I'd show you the work you'd done already so you could see just how great you've been at this." There was a moment of silence as I focused on the pictures and then he said something in that silky, deep voice that made that ache between my legs rush back with a vengeance.

"Relax. I promise you're great at this."

If only I could focus on the artwork on the screen instead of how close he was sitting next to me.

I took a deep breath and nodded as I examined my previous work, pretending that I wasn't already excited at shortly after nine in the morning. "Okay. These look pretty good, if I do say so myself."

Leaning in next to me, he pointed at a picture full of the color gold. "This one is especially good. I love those owls. Those were a great choice, Nina."

Love. He seemed so comfortable using that word when it came to anything involving me. It was unnerving. Nobody I'd ever dated before had been so free with that word. If anything, the L word was something I was uncomfortable saying, at best.

"Thanks." As I looked at the picture, I couldn't imagine how any art with a few blue and white owls I'd chosen had improved that room so overdone in gold. "That's a lot of gold, isn't it?"

"You should have seen it before the owls," he said with a smile, leaning in closer to my left shoulder. "It's more impressive in person. Maybe we should return to Dallas so you can see your handiwork."

While he spoke, I got lost in the scent of his cologne. I had no idea which one it was, but it was very possibly the sexiest fragrance I'd ever smelled. Fresh, the scent was woodsy and almost citrusy, making him smell delicious. How was I supposed to work like this? While he talked of hotel rooms, my mind was distracted and wondering the name of the cologne he was wearing. He was driving me crazy!

"That will have to wait until after the holidays. I thought we'd stay home for Christmas."

Christmas. The mention of the holiday made my brain switch gears. I hadn't thought much of the holidays because of my accident, but he was right. Christmas was just weeks away.

I turned to look at him and nearly touched his cheek with my lips. Startled, I leaned back away from him and muttered, "Do you do anything special for the holidays?"

A look of sadness crossed his face before he turned to smile at me. "No. I haven't really celebrated Christmas for a long time. I usually work."

"You can't work on Christmas! If any day of the year should be a day off, that's it."

That warm smile he offered far too infrequently brightened up his face all the way to his eyes. "Then I guess I'll be taking that day off this year."

Overcome with enthusiasm for the holiday, I began to tell him all about how I'd always celebrated, complete with tinsel, egg nog, and homemade ornaments. "We can trim the tree on Christmas Eve and make cookies."

Suddenly, as I spoke of all the ways I'd celebrated the holiday with my father, the reality of his death settled into my mind. There wouldn't be any more Christmases with him at home around the fireplace as we opened our presents on Christmas morning. No more holiday dinners with him and my sister and her family. No more surprise stocking stuffers.

"Nina, what's wrong?" Tristan asked as I looked away so he couldn't see the tears in my eyes.

I shook my head as I wiped my cheek. "Nothing. It's just that this will be the first Christmas without my father." Turning to face Tristan, I said in frustration, "Well, not really since he's been gone for four years, but since I can't remember that or anything else that meant so much to me, it all feels like it just happened."

"I know. My first Christmas without my family was hard. I felt like I was all alone, that everyone I'd cared about was gone now. But you're not alone."

I took a deep breath and pushed the sadness away to a place in my head I'd deal with later. "I'm sorry. I shouldn't be doing this during work. It's not very professional."

He lifted my chin with his fingertip and looked deep into my eyes. "You don't have to worry. That's one of the great things about working from home. It's more relaxed."

Jesus, just the feel of his touch on my skin made my heart race! At this rate, I wouldn't get to lunch before I jumped his bones. Leaning away from him, I caught my breath and checked out his relaxed home office look.

"If this is more relaxed, why are you in a suit and tie?" I joked, hoping to stall for enough time to get my bearings.

"I always wear a suit and tie to work, no matter where it is," he said in a fake serious tone I could tell was slightly defensive.

"So you've always worn a suit and tie? I'm trying to imagine you as a twenty year old guy hanging out looking like this."

His brow furrowed, and he shook his head. "Nina, I haven't always been this man you see in front of you. This is the person I have to be now. A long time ago, I was like every other guy you've ever met."

I looked at him as he busied himself with clicking to the next set of pictures he wanted me to see. From those gorgeous milk chocolate brown eyes, to his perfectly shaped mouth, and his ripped muscular body, there was no way he was ever like any other guy I'd ever met. Add to that the money, the houses, and the cars and there was no chance. No way.

A half hour later, even I was convinced I was the right woman for the job as Tristan's curator. The pictures from the projects I'd completed in his hotels showed I knew what I was doing. The colors, shapes, and textures I'd chosen worked well with the decor in the suites, and I'd even come around to believe that those adorable blue and white Mexican owls had done something for the Dallas suite.

I'd also settled down and could focus on work, instead of on the way Tristan looked, smelled, and sounded. The man was indeed the most delicious brand of sensory overload.

Tristan leaned back in his chair and ran his hand through his short dark hair. He had a pensive look on his face and sat silently for a long moment before he turned toward me. "I'm thinking we'll go to Atlanta after New Year's. You can get a head start on that job beginning today."

"Oh. Okay. For a minute there, I thought you were going to say you wanted to go to Atlanta for New Year's Eve." I'd never been to Atlanta, so enjoying New Year's there sounded fun.

"No, we'll do New Year's Eve at the penthouse."

"In the city?"

He nodded. "Yes. It's not as cozy as here, but the views are better."

"Do you have any pictures of that, or didn't I do any work there?"

His voice softened as he spoke of his home in Manhattan. "The penthouse is my home, so it's not like other penthouses at the other properties I own, but you did choose a piece for there."

"You sound like you really love it, Tristan. I look forward to seeing it."

Shaking his head, he twisted his expression into something that looked like he'd tasted bad food. "I don't care about the penthouse. In fact, I've never liked it. The only thing I like there is the print you picked out to cover the bare spot in the bedroom."

"I must have hit it out of the park with that one then."

"It's just what that room needed," he said quietly.

"Can we invite Jordan and her boyfriend to join us on New Year's Eve? I'd love to see her, and because of my memory loss, I don't feel like I know Justin at all."

He seemed to think about it for a moment. "If that would make you happy, then we'll do it. We can have them over for drinks and dinner."

Left unsaid was what would happen after drinks and dinner and after they left. I felt like some teenage virgin who was both anticipating and dreading having sex for the first time. Thank God I'd had sex before the point in time where my memory stopped. Even the memory of bad sex was better than going into it blind.

Not that I thought we would wait until New Year's.

"Thank you, Tristan. It's nice of you to include them in our plans."

He smiled at me and shook his head. "There's no need to thank me, Nina. All I want is your happiness."

I didn't know what to say to that. Everything he'd done from the moment I'd met him as I lay there in that hospital bed all broken and bruised showed me that whatever else I may not know, I could truly believe he did want me to be happy. It didn't matter that I couldn't completely understand why either.

To him, I was his Nina, and every moment that passed, I found myself growing more comfortable with that role. And to my surprise, with each moment I spent with him, I also found myself wanting to make him happy. He had that effect on me. Maybe it was because he was my strength in those times when I needed it every day in that hospital, or maybe it was because he seemed so single-mindedly focused on me. Whatever it was, I was quickly falling for him and honestly wasn't sure I shouldn't be sublimely happy about it.

"This is the property in Atlanta. It's one of the few properties of mine that I've never visited, so when we travel there, it'll be my first time too."

Tristan pointed to the pictures of the Atlanta hotel as he explained that he'd visited most of his properties since becoming CEO of Stone Worldwide four years ago. I had a hard time imagining him as anything like a CEO. He didn't act like someone who ran a worldwide business. As I sat there watching him talk about suites and hotel rooms, he seemed more like someone I might meet at a club.

Except for the idea that he was drop dead gorgeous and likely preferred clubs I couldn't afford to get into. I didn't know which one would have been a bigger impediment to our ever meeting.

"Tristan, do you ever go to clubs?" I asked impulsively, curious to know if my mental ramblings had been correct.

He stopped talking about what kind of art he thought the Atlanta suite could use and turned his head to look at me. There was a devilish look in his eyes that made them seem to dance in the light of his office.

"No. Why? Would you like to go out tonight?"

"Could we?" I asked excitedly, thrilled at the idea of not only getting out after weeks of being stuck in the hospital but also seeing him in a different setting.

He nodded and stood from his chair. As he passed by me without a glance, he said, "Of course. If you'll excuse me, I have to arrange a few things and deal with some work issues, but I'll meet you in the dining room at seven for dinner and we'll go out after that."

His leaving was so abrupt I wondered if I'd done something wrong. He hadn't smiled or even touched my hand as he left. His tone had been decidedly all business compared to just minutes earlier, but I guessed he had important work to do, so I set about studying the Atlanta suite in the hopes that I could add something unique to it.

After I'd done a few hours of work, I headed to my closet to search for something to wear that night. That morning when I'd reached for my work clothes, I'd been so nervous I hadn't paid attention to all the gorgeous clothes that hung next to them. I had no idea when I'd purchased the wardrobe I stood staring at, but I was sure it cost a fortune. Designer names, cashmere and silk, and dresses unlike anything I'd ever owned before filled my eyes.

I pushed each beautiful outfit past me, vetoing some because they were too long and others because they just didn't feel right for the night ahead, until I found a little black dress hidden all the way in the back. I held it up in front of me and measured it against my body. It was perfect. Hanging to about three inches above my knees, it showed enough skin to entice while still allowing me to look classy.

On the floor sat over a dozen pairs of shoes, each one more beautiful than the last. Black pumps, red stilettos, tan patent leather sling backs, but none of them seemed right for that little black dress. Then I spied a pair of gold stilettos on the far right side of the closet, hidden behind other shoes and knew instantly they were the ones.

I wanted this night to be one I'd remember forever. Tristan had repeatedly said we would make new memories, so tonight would be the first of many, or at least I hoped it would. I still wasn't sure how I felt about him, but between the jealousy that had nearly consumed me as I looked at those pictures with him and the women he called actresses and the desire he'd created in me as I sat in his room the night before and in his office that morning, I knew one thing for sure. I wanted to know more about him than the caring boyfriend and the accommodating boss.

I wanted him.

Five o'clock came and I took one last look at myself in the mirror. Smoldering sable eye shadow and the perfect red lipstick gave me the sex symbol look I was aiming for, and my dress and shoes screamed seduction. I just had to hope that Tristan was on the same page and hadn't fallen out of love with me after my coolness toward him.

By the time I reached the dining room, I was a complete nervous wreck. I didn't know how I'd handled the first time with him before, but this Nina felt like she was going to pass out from anxiety as she walked down the hallway from her room. Seduction had never been my strong suit, and an attempt to seduce a man as stunning as Tristan Stone made me feel like I was totally out of my league.

I only hoped that he truly did still love me.

FIVE

TRISTAN

"Dinner will be ready in a few minutes, as you ordered," Rogers announced as he walked into the dining room.

I waited for something else to follow his dinner information, but instead he simply stood silently watching me. "Is there anything else, Rogers?"

He shook his head. "No, sir."

My second sir of the day. Another person in my house who wanted to call me something entirely too formal.

"Sir, Rogers? There's no one but the two of us here, and even if Nina was here, she's heard you call me by my given name before."

"As you wish, Tristan."

Why did I have the distinct impression that my butler was giving me the cold shoulder? "Is there something you want to say, Rogers? And if it has anything to do with our conversation the other day, don't bother. I'm not interested in hearing it again."

"Then I have nothing to say," he said as he turned to leave.

"I do. Make sure Jensen is ready to go tonight. I'm taking Nina to the city."

Rogers stopped his movement toward the doorway and stood still as Nina entered the dining room in a dress that was nothing less than stunning. She wore the gold shoes she'd worn the night of the book party at the hotel and the effect was just as incredible as that night. The memory of our time in the back of my car made me want her right then and there.

As I stood from the table to pull her chair out, I couldn't take my eyes off her. I'd never seen her look so beautiful. "Nina, I'm happy you're joining me."

She twirled around to show off her outfit and tripped over her feet, sending her stumbling into my arms. I looked down to see her face red from embarrassment, but to me she looked more gorgeous than ever.

"Thanks. I'm too smooth," she joked in the self-effacing way she always did when she was uncomfortable.

"My pleasure."

As she stood back up on her feet, she added, "Thank God you were there or I would have landed flat on my butt."

"I'll always be there, Nina."

We took our seats and her eyes lit up when Rogers began to bring the platters of food in. "Is that roast beef? I love roast beef!"

"I know. I thought it might be nice to have one of your favorites tonight."

Nina rolled her eyes and smiled. "I swear you don't miss a trick, do you? I better start learning some things about you so I can do nice things like this for you sometime."

I loved the idea of Nina thinking about me enough to surprise me, even if I hated surprises. That I couldn't express that had nothing to do with her and everything to do with me.

I felt Rogers' stern eyes staring at me as she talked of how excited she was about our planned night out. His disapproval filled the room, threatening to ruin all the happiness she felt and I wanted to feel. I couldn't stand his glaring at me as if I'd done something bad by falling in love with her.

Taking my attention away from Nina, I waved my hand in his direction. "Thank you, Rogers. That will be all for tonight."

He glared at me and bowed in a way that was undoubtedly meant to mock me. "Sir."

I stuffed down my anger at him and turned back to see Nina looking at me with reproach. "Are you always so short with your butler? He might smile more if you were nicer."

"I doubt it."

"Have you tried?" Her blue eyes looked like they were staring into my soul, like they were searching for the answer to her question.

Sheepishly, I answered, "No."

"Well, you can't know if you don't try. How long has he worked for you?"

"He's been with my family since I was a child. He's known me longer than anyone else in the world."

"Oh. Have you always been like this with him?"

I thought back to the countless times Rogers had picked up after me, first when I was an insolent child who cared nothing for his belongings and then when I became an adult and cared even less for the effect of my actions on others. How many times had he cleaned up some mess I'd made, making sure some female was driven home and sworn to silence or whisking me away from someone's apartment before I could get arrested for possession of enough coke for a small town?

"Are you hungry?" I asked, changing the subject.

She grimaced, marring that gorgeous face for just a moment. "Guess we're done talking about your cranky butler. That's okay. I am hungry, though."

"Good. We'll eat dinner and then head to the city."

Dinner was fantastic and by the time we left for the city hours later, Nina was laughing and full of smiles. It took every ounce of restraint on my part not to tell Jensen to forget the drive, sweep her into my arms, and take her back to my room to show her how much I loved her. I wanted to believe she'd worn the sexiest dress in her closet for me, but even if that was the case, we were still playing the game all first time lovers play—a light touch here, a sexy glance there, and no one truly sure of the other person's feelings, even though I'd told her I loved her more than once since coming home from the hospital.

I loathed the idea of going to a club, to be honest. After far too many nights spent in supposedly the best places in the city doing things anyone with a conscience should be ashamed of, I'd sworn off the city's nightlife, except for the functions required because of my position as the head of Stone Worldwide. I never even visited the clubs my company owned, but Nina wanted to go out to a club, so I had little choice.

If it made her happy, I'd go.

Jensen dropped us off behind a club called ETA just outside of the West Village, and we snuck in the back door unseen by any of those leeches with cameras. ETA was an enormous club that claimed to afford a person all the privacy he or she desired as they sat amongst hundreds of other like-minded individuals. Its name meant Estimated Time of Arrival, a not-so-clever ploy to get patrons thinking even more about sex. Years ago, I would have been happy to come all over every square inch of the place, but tonight I planned to find as secluded a spot as possible for Nina and me and hopefully she'd enjoy herself.

We were escorted into a semi-private room off the main club and seated in a dark corner in a booth covered in soft purple velvet. Dim lights flickered around the room and provided just enough light to see who you were with but not enough light to notice their imperfections.

It was the perfect place for people who craved privacy and those who didn't want to face the reality of their night's companions. For us, it hopefully would be secluded enough that no one would notice me and interrupt our time together. In any event, I'd prepared for the worst, but I really hoped we could avoid any unwanted attention and just enjoy being with each other.

The beat of the music thrummed inside my head, making it hard to hear anything else, so I pulled Nina close to me. "What do you want to drink?"

She looked around the room as the place began to fill up and turned to smile up at me. "What are you drinking?"

"Scotch."

"Do I like scotch?" she asked with an innocence that made me rethink that idea of not coming at ETA.

"No, I don't think you do," I answered after thinking about that first night we'd spent together. "Maybe something sweeter?"

"Okay," she said and then bit her lip nervously. "Any ideas?"

"I'll have the bartender make something you'll love. Wait here. I'll be right back."

The guy behind the bar seemed to know exactly what Nina would like although I said nothing more than 'make it something sweet', and I returned to the table with a glass of twelve year old scotch and a chocolate martini.

Nina looked down at the martini glass rimmed with sugar and then looked up at me. "What is it?"

Leaning over to whisper in her ear, I said, "Taste it. Lick the rim and then take a taste of the drink. It's sweet."

She tentatively slid her pink tongue over the frosted sugared rim of her glass and took a tiny sip.

The liquor slid down her throat, and she turned to face me with a smile. "It's chocolate!"

A tiny sugar crystal hung off her bottom lip, so I slid the pad of my thumb across it to clean it off before I licked the sugar from my finger. "Definitely sweeter than I'm used to," I joked as I reached for my drink to wash the overwhelming sweetness down.

Nina touched where I'd slid my finger across her lip and smiled. "You prefer the harder stuff, don't you?"

"I guess I do."

She licked her lips and reached up with her fingertip to touch mine. When she tasted the drop of scotch from her finger, she made a face like she'd just sucked a lemon. "I think I'll stick with my sweet stuff and leave that to you. That's gross."

"It's an acquired taste, I guess."

"Maybe someday I'll acquire it," she said with a tiny smile.

I shook my head. "You're more the sweet kind."

Two hours later, we'd talked little more because the music had become so loud we could barely hear one another over it. Memories of my time at clubs just like this one washed over me, making me wish for somewhere far quieter. Nina seemed to enjoy watching the sea of humanity that flowed past us, but I didn't get the sense she was having fun.

My suspicions were proven correct when she turned to me and said in my ear, "I wish we could find a place just a little quieter. Can we go somewhere else?"

I was thankful to get away from ETA and had a place in mind that would be a bit quieter, although I wasn't sure I should take Nina there. It was definitely more secluded and out of the city, but was Top the right place to take someone like her, even if I was part owner of the place?

Jensen held the door open for Nina and as she climbed in, I said to him in a low voice, "Take us to Top. Do you remember how to get there?"

As stoic as Rogers, he simply nodded his head and waited for me to get into the back seat of the car.

"Where are we going?" Nina asked as we pulled away from ETA.

"A club I know of. We'll be able to talk there. They have a private room we can use."

"Where is it? Near here?"

I shook my head. "Outside the city. It shouldn't take long to get there."

Nina talked about how she and Jordan had always planned a huge celebration for her twenty-first birthday. The sadness at the time she'd lost was clear as her voice dropped and she said quietly, "I wonder if we ever did that."

I texted Top's owner, Chase Mitchell, that we were coming, and almost a half hour later, we were in the suburbs at the club. The facade of the building gave no indication of what Top truly was. An old warehouse, Chase had converted it into a members only club three years ago, and other than an occasional visit now and then, I'd been a completely silent partner in the business. Chase's fetishes weren't my style, but the club had made a handsome profit for both of us, so who was I to look down my nose at one man's turn-ons?

I held Nina's hand as we walked up to the door and as I knocked on it, quietly said, "This place will be more intimate."

Her blue eyes widened and a look of fear settled into them. "What kind of place is this?"

"A private club that I'm half owner of. Don't worry. It'll be fun."

"Okay. Promise you won't let anything happen to me, Tristan."

I squeezed her hand and brought it to my lips in a kiss. "I would never let anything bad happen to you, Nina. Never. You can trust me."

The door to Top opened, and just inside stood Chase with a stunned look on his face. "Holy fuck! I got your text and thought somebody was pulling my chain. Tristan Stone as I live and breathe!"

Nodding, I pulled Nina close to my side as the doorman shut the door behind us. "Nice to see you, Chase."

"You're just in time. The night's just getting started. But I'm more interested in who your friend is."

Chase turned his focus to Nina and extended his hand to shake hers. "Chase Mitchell, owner—well, half owner of Top. What's your name, darling?"

Before Nina could say a word, I pulled his attention back where it belonged. "Remember your place in this, Chase. We want to find a secluded spot and have a few drinks, so how about you show us to one of the private rooms?"

Nina reached her hand out and introduced herself. "Hi! I'm Nina. What kind of place is this?"

Chase shook her hand and looked at her like she was some kind of morsel, ratcheting my anger up a few more notches. "What kind of place is this? Love, this is the finest private club on the East coast."

"Private club?"

"Members only and high rollers. Whatever they want, we have at Top."

Nina looked up at me with a confused look on her face. There was no point in explaining it. This probably hadn't been my best idea, but now that we were there, that was a moot point. I really didn't want to explain anything in front of Chase, so I merely shook my head.

Chase continued to talk, testing my patience even more. "Tristan, I didn't expect to see you so soon after last time. You looking for the same? What can I interest you two in tonight?"

"Interest us in?" Nina asked in a shaky voice as she stared wide-eyed up at me.

"You look like you could be a walking schoolgirl fantasy, my dear. No wonder he brought you here."

We stood there surrounded by an awkward silence as I struggled not to knock Chase on his mouthy ass. He got the gist of my glaring at him in little time, though, and quickly escorted us to a dimly lit private room. Nina took a seat at one of the tables as I excused myself to speak to Chase alone.

Closing the door behind me, I grabbed him by the collar and pasted him against the wall. The bass from the music in the main room of the club began to vibrate the lights that hung near his head and only served to irritate me more. "You have less than five minutes to get me the finest scotch you have in this place and a chocolate martini. And I'm not talking about that bottom shelf shit you try to pass off on the customers."

Chase opened his mouth to protest his innocence, and I pushed him into the wall again. "And one more fucking word out of you and I'll make sure this place is shut down by tomorrow morning. You'll have nothing and I'll be short one pissant fucking club I care nothing about. Do you understand me?"

Chase looked at me with fear and confusion. "What? She seems nice. I was just teasing. Trying to give her a compliment. Is that the one I saw you with at some party a few weeks back? The one who was in the car accident? She's got a nice, girl-next-door look you haven't gone for in years."

"Now you have four minutes."

"How did that couple work out? The ones you took out of here a while back? I never got a chance to hear how that went."

Pushing Chase away from me in disgust, I turned to join Nina, adding, "And have someone else bring the drinks."

I found Nina sitting at a table watching some sex show on a big screen television on the other side of the room. Chase had obviously gotten the wrong idea when I said secluded. I sat down across from her and waited for the inevitable questions.

"What kind of place is this, Tristan?" she asked in a hurt tone. "Do you bring women here all the time?"

I could barely make out the sadness in her face, but it was there. "Don't listen to him, Nina. I barely know him, and he knows nothing of what I feel for you."

"What did he mean schoolgirl fantasy? What is this place?"

"Don't let him bother you. He's an ass. I just helped him get this place off the ground."

"With money?"

"Yes."

"Is this a nightclub? What did he mean when he said it's a private club?"

This hadn't been my best idea. I'd hoped that we could find a secluded spot to talk, but maybe Top wasn't the right place, even if I was the owner.

"The club is sort of a nightclub meets sex fantasy camp," I said, hoping I wouldn't have to go into it more than that.

"Sex fantasy camp?" she asked with surprise in her eyes.

"Yeah. I guess this isn't a place you'd want to be. We can go."

Nina shook her head and smiled. "No. We can stay a little while. I'm curious about this side of you, Tristan Stone. A fantasy sex club seems distinctly un-Tristan."

"It is. Don't get the wrong idea. I'm just a silent partner here."

A waitress dressed in a tight, white T-shirt that left nothing to the imagination and skin-tight black shorts interrupted our conversation to deliver our drinks, and I saw Nina's eyes grow wide in the dim light as the woman ran her fingertips over my shoulders as she left. Looking up, I saw it was a girl named Brandi who'd worked at the club for the last year.

"Haven't seen you in ages, Tristan. Nice to see you back," she purred in a silky voice.

"Do you know her?" Nina asked as she watched her walk away.

"No."

"Well, she knows you. She called you by name."

I didn't exactly know Brandi. She'd been Chase's girlfriend when he hired her, and more than once I'd had to listen to her as she cried on my shoulder about his inability to remain faithful.

"She's just someone who works here," I said casually as I took a sip of my drink.

"Oh. What's her name?"

"Brandi."

"Of course it is," Nina bit out.

I could tell she was jealous, which in some twisted way made me feel good. Her feelings had been relatively tepid since coming home from the hospital, even though I'd hoped she was beginning to feel something for me. Maybe if she was jealous, that wish was already coming true.

Her eyes kept darting to the screen behind me, and I couldn't tell if she was curious or embarrassed by what was playing out on the television. I didn't want her distracted by one of Chase's kinky flicks, though.

There was a lounge area on the other side of the room with couches and chairs, so I suggested we move there instead, hoping to turn her focus back to us. The couches were the best money could buy. Chase was nothing if not eager to spend his investor's money. As we sat down next to one another, her jealousy and my hope crashed into each other.

"These are very nice," she said as she rubbed her palm over the back of the black leather couch. Then abruptly, she said, "I think you know that woman."

"I told you I didn't."

"Then why would she touch you like that?"

"Maybe she thought she knew me or maybe she got the sense that I was available and we weren't together?" I said half-jokingly.

"Why would she think that? I'm just as dressed up as you are and we're sitting here together."

"I think she might be used to something different here. Maybe the women are more obvious with how they feel about the men they're with."

To be honest, I was more than thankful Chase's girl had made that little gesture that I knew she did with every male in the club. At least it had gotten Nina to show something of how she felt. Her jealousy was flattering, but I didn't want just that.

Nina turned her body to face me. "Are you saying that I should be more obvious?"

"When in Rome..." I teased.

I saw a tiny pout form on her lips and then she looked away and sighed. She was silent for a long moment and then stood from the couch and smiled down at me. "Well, then I guess I better act more like the locals."

Nina hiked up her dress and straddled me as I sat looking up at her stunned. My hands instantly found their way to cup her pretty ass, pulling her closer.

"Is this better? I've never been to a club like this, so I'm not sure. Maybe I need to be wearing what she had on. Would you prefer that?" she said in a teasing voice.

My cock was rock hard in five seconds, and I had to rein in my urge to fuck her right there. Struggling to keep my voice calm, I smiled and said, "You look beautiful just as you are, Nina."

"Am I being obvious enough for you, Tristan?"

Her tone was almost biting, as if she was angry. My guess was that she was nervous, but I liked a challenge.

"Just enough."

Nina's mouth covered mine, and she snaked her tongue past my lips to tease the tip of my tongue. Running my hands over her hips, I slid my thumbs along the crease of her legs, dying to know if she was as ready as I was.

She relaxed just a little and lowered herself until she was fully seated on my lap. In her tender way, she looked down at me shyly and whispered, "I didn't think this out completely. Now that I'm sitting here like this, I'm not sure I want to do this here."

I couldn't help but smile. God, she was the same honest Nina I'd fallen head over heels for months before.

Shaking my head, I leaned in and kissed the tip of her nose. "I don't want to do this here either, so don't worry. It's okay. What do you say we go somewhere nicer and get back in this exact same position there?"

Nina bit her lip in that cute way she always did when she was nervous and nodded. Finally, tonight we'd begin making those memories.

SIX

TRISTAN

Jensen followed my orders and got us to the penthouse in record time. Even though Nina and I had begun to get comfortable at Top, we kept it together in the car. I don't know what she was feeling, but it took every ounce of self control I possessed not to try for a repeat of that night in the back seat of the Rolls. By the time we got to the hotel, I wanted her so bad I wasn't sure I'd be able to control myself once we hit the elevator.

We rode up to the penthouse with both of us staring at our reflections in the mirrored walls of the elevator as I slid my arm around her waist to pull her close to me. She melted into my body, and I watched as she closed her eyes and her face relaxed. She was happy, and I planned to make her much happier in just minutes.

The elevator door opened and she stepped out into the penthouse, her head swiveling back and forth as she admired the designer's work that I never cared much for. She turned in my hold and looked up at me with a surprised expression. "This is stunning, Tristan!"

As she ran to look at the view of the city in the living room, I followed, happy that she was impressed.

I wanted her to like everything in my world, even the parts of it I didn't give a damn about.

"I've never seen anything like this! How do you live here and not just stare out the window all day?" she asked as she pointed toward the twinkling lights of the city below.

"I don't really pay much attention to it," I said, remembering how she'd asked me that the first time. "Do you want something to drink?"

"Any chance you know how to make that chocolate drink?"

"No, but I could have the concierge bring one up for you," I offered as I made my way to the bar to find my bottle of scotch.

She walked over and stood next to me, smiling. "Looks like I'm going to have to drink the hard stuff. Well, I'm a tough chick. Hit me with that scotch."

I poured her a glass neat and handed it to her. "You sure?"

Raising her glass to clank against mine, she shrugged. "I guess we'll see, right?"

I tapped mine to hers. "To new memories."

"To new memories." She lifted the scotch to her lips and took a sip. Instantly, her face screwed into a grimace. "Oh, I don't know how you drink this. It's so strong. I can feel it racing through my body already, and I only had one taste. A few more and I'll be no good to anyone."

I took the glass out of her hand and placed it on the bar. "Then no more for you. I want you sober."

"Sober for what, Mr. Stone?" she said with a giggle, the scotch already taking effect.

Snaking my arm around her waist, I pulled her close and buried my face in her neck and whispered, "For when I make love to you, Ms. Edwards."

I didn't want to hold back anymore. I wanted her to be mine again, body and soul. Cradling the back of her head, I drew her mouth toward mine and kissed her with all the desire I'd kept bottled up for all those weeks. Her lips were soft against mine but as eager and passionate as I slid my tongue into her mouth to find hers. When she sighed into my mouth, I couldn't wait anymore.

My hands clawed at the zipper down the back of her dress, but it got stuck an inch from the top. Aching to be inside her, I tore the two halves of the dress apart, ruining the zipper and the dress.

"Tristan, my dress!" she cried as I pulled it from her body.

"I don't care. I'll buy you ten dresses just like it," I panted as I unhooked her bra and slid the first strap over her shoulder. "Same thing with the bra. And if these panties don't come off easy, I'm going to rip through them too."

Nina's fingers tore through my shirt buttons until it hung open, and I quickly shrugged out of it. She was as desperate as I was to be out of those damn clothes. In seconds, she had my belt off and my pants and boxer briefs off my legs, and I had her pushed up against the wall.

As I lifted her off the ground to wrap her legs around my waist, I pressed my forehead to hers and rasped, "I hope you weren't expecting something slow and gentle. I can give you that, but tonight I don't want to wait. I need to be inside you, Nina."

Moaning, she pulled me close, but just then I remembered her sore ribs. Pulling back, I said, "I forgot about what the doctor said. Maybe we should go easy this time."

She dug her heels into my lower back and pulled my mouth to hers in a deep kiss. Her voice husky, she groaned, "Please, Tristan. I'm not a china doll. I'll tell you if something hurts."

I gently slid just the head of my cock into her, still worried I might hurt her if I didn't take it slow. My body was in agony wanting to bury myself inside her, but I didn't want to risk bruising those already sore ribs. I could give her gentle, even if every part of me wanted much more.

Nina pushed her palms against my chest and held me away from her. Worried I'd already screwed this up, I opened my mouth to apologize but she touched her finger to my lips to stop me. "Don't make me wait. I don't want gentle now. I want you...all of you."

Her fingers pressed into the back of my neck as I plunged balls deep into her wet and willing cunt. Nothing in the entire world ever felt better than that moment when our bodies joined together as one again. Her body was hot and enveloped me, taking my body to places I thought only existed in my imagination.

She consumed me, but I would have given my last breath for another moment with her. My mouth plundered hers as my cock pounded into her, each searching for that bliss that only she could provide.

I planted my palms against the wall for more leverage and heard her cry out as I began to thrust my hips faster. She clung to me, hanging off my neck and waist, but I felt nothing except the pure ecstasy that came from being inside her.

Time seemed to stand still, but our bodies were drenched with sweat as we edged one another toward that sweetest moment two people could share. Nina's mouth delivered sensations to every part of me it touched, and I was on fire from her need. I wanted to be the only one to fulfill that need—the only soul who could quench the desire that raged inside her.

"Tristan, faster. Don't stop! Give me what I need. I'm almost there."

Her moans spurred my own excitement on, and I slid my hands down to her waist to hold her fast to me as I inched closer to my own release. "Let yourself go, baby. I want to feel you come all over my cock."

"Oh, God! Don't stop...don't..."

Nina's voice trailed off as I felt the first tender squeeze of her cunt around my cock. She buried her head in the crook of my neck and whimpered as her orgasm roared through her, raking her nails across my back and shoulders while she bucked against me.

Her body milking my cock sent my body into overdrive, and I came with a rush inside her. My legs shook under me, nearly buckling from my release. I clung to her as she did me, panting in her ear as I struggled to form coherent thoughts.

I was sure of only one thing. Nina was mine—truly mine—once again, and I was never going let her go.

"Tell me it wasn't always like that, Tristan," Nina whispered as she rested her head on my chest. "Tell me we weren't always so incredible together."

I trailed my fingers over her hair, twirling a strand around my forefinger as we lay in each other's arms on the floor. "Why?"

She wrapped her arm around me and squeezed gently. "Because if that's the case, I'm even sadder that I can't remember our time together."

"I could lie, if it would make you happy."

Nina looked up at me and twisted her face into a scowl. "No, that wouldn't make me happy."

"Then tell me what would and I'll do it," I whispered as I pulled her on top of me.

"Tell me about who I was. Tell me more than just that I was beautiful when you met me."

When she looked at me with those big blue eyes, I wanted to tell her everything. The truth of what my father had done. The truth of how long I'd known and how long it had been eating away at me. The whole horrible story and how something so beautiful had grown out of something so ugly.

I cradled her face in my hands and kissed her tenderly on the lips. "You were just as you are now. Gentle and kind and more honest than anyone I've ever met. You took my breath away the first time I touched you, and it's no different now."

"I bet it was love at first sight for me, Tristan. Tell me the truth. Was it?"

"I doubt it. I was with the actresses that night, so you probably thought I was some Hugh Hefner wannabe."

She giggled and sat up straight on me. Her light brown hair fell in gentle waves around her face and shoulders, making her look like a mermaid or some kind of angel. "I bet you looked incredible dressed in a suit and looking the way you always do."

I ran my hands over her stomach and caressed the tops of her thighs. She let out a tiny moan as my thumbs slid over the insides of her legs.

"I'm sure I was wearing a suit. I do all the time."

Nina wriggled her ass against my thighs and smiled. "Except now. I like the way you look now too. I don't think I've ever met a man more perfect than you. Successful, wealthy, gorgeous, and a body that looks like a Greek god's."

"I guess all those hours at the gym have paid off. The other stuff really isn't in my control, though."

Her fingers slid over my abdomen and up over my chest to my shoulders. "It isn't a good idea that I adore you so much already, Tristan Stone. No one should be this crazy about another person."

"Maybe it's okay since I'm even crazier about you."

She leaned down and kissed me softly on the lips. "I better find something about you I don't like before I become totally lost in you. Hurry up and tell me one of your bad traits."

There were too many to even get into. I knew that. My past. My family. The club I'd taken her to just that night. But I couldn't tell her about those, and even if I could, I didn't want to. I had my Nina back and I wasn't going to let her go.

"Well, I don't talk much. Some women may think that's a bad trait."

"Yeah, but then you do that strong, silent type sexy guy thing and make even the lack of talking a good thing."

I crossed my hands behind my head and smiled. "I guess I could work on being a bad man. Any suggestions?"

The smile she gave me was so sweet I almost pulled her to me and kissed away anything she could have said.

"I think maybe an eye patch could work."

"An eye patch? That would look great with a suit."

"Mmmm... now that's a man I wouldn't be able to say no to. Sort of a pirate meets a tycoon."

"I'm not sure I can pull off pirate. Something about having to say arrrgh all the time might not work in meetings."

Nina ran her fingertips across my hipbones and grazed the head of my cock. Gliding her tongue over her lips, she looked down at me and smiled. "It's too bad. I could definitely be into a pirate."

"Arrrgh."

"I do love a man who can be persuaded."

Both of us stopped our joking, and her eyes grew wide at what she'd just said, as if she'd let something bad slip. I didn't want her saying she loved me if she didn't mean it. I'd wait as long as it took to have her say those words if it meant they came from her heart.

She rolled off me onto the floor and looked up at the ceiling. "I don't know if I'm in love with you, but I've never felt like this in my life. Well, I don't know. Since I was in love with you, maybe I did feel like this." Turning her head, she smiled at me. "I guess I'm not making much sense, am I?"

I propped myself up on my elbow and nodded. I understood what she was trying to say. "I get it. As long as you're happy, that's enough for me. It's only been a few days since you came home from the hospital, so maybe this is good."

"I hear that thing in your voice, though. I know you wish for more."

I knew the thing she was talking about. I wouldn't have been able to hide it even if I wanted to. A mixture of loss, sadness, and regret, it was in everything I said to her.

Twisting a long wave of her hair around my finger, I forced a smile. "I'm happy, Nina. You do that for me. No one else has ever made me happy like you do. So it's not the same as it was. Maybe this time will be even better."

"It breaks my heart to hear you say things like that. You have everything a person could want. I can't imagine not being happy with money, success, power—all the things everyone thinks ensure happiness."

"All they ensure is that you'll have people wanting you for everything but you."

"Like Chase tonight?"

I gave a snort at the sound of my Top partner's name. "Chase is one of the best examples of the people money brings to you. If I didn't have the money to help him get that business going, I'd be invisible to him. Not that being invisible to the likes of Chase Mitchell is a bad thing."

Nina rolled over and propped her head up on her hand. "How did you get involved with him and that club? You two don't seem a thing alike."

"Chase is a remnant of my time before I took over Stone Worldwide. Remember I told you that I wasn't always the man you see?" For a second, I couldn't remember if I told her in the last few days or before the accident.

She gently touched my shoulder with her fingertips. "No, no. I remember. You said when you were twenty that you would have been just like any other guy I've ever met. And I can tell you that I think you're full of it. There's no way you would ever be like anyone else I've ever met."

"Yeah, well, Chase is from those days. He comes from money. Not as much as I came from, but his family's got some. Not that they would have been interested in giving him a dime so he could set up his club in a sleepy town outside New York City. That's where I came in."

"If you're not into that, why did you agree to be his partner?"

"Silent partner."

"Okay. Why did you agree to be his silent partner?"

"Because I know a good investment when I see one. When he came to me with his idea, I knew it would make money. So I agreed to go in on the club with him as long as he agreed that I'd have nothing to do with the day-to-day operations."

"So you just sit back and collect the money?" she asked with a sly grin on her face.

"Exactly. I prefer to stay in the hotel business and keep my involvement with Top silent."

"Why stay silent about it?"

"I don't care what people like, but there are certain segments of society that wouldn't approve of the owner of the Richmont Hotel chain as co-owner of that kind of place, even if he's a silent partner."

"Doesn't the board of your company have a problem with it?"

Shaking my head, I explained, "They don't know. I financed Top with my own money, not Stone Worldwide's money or credit."

Her eyes grew wide as saucers. "Holy shit! You are loaded!" Instantly, she covered her mouth with her hand and mumbled from behind it, "I'm sorry. That's not the way the girlfriend of someone like you should act."

I pulled her hand away from her face. "It's not a problem. I am. I always have been. Money is something I've been blessed with. I'm not one of those people who thinks it isn't important. It is. But it's not the most important thing in life."

"I always hate when you see wealthy people or movie stars talking about their success in interviews and saying things like the money isn't something they think about or it doesn't mean anything to them. That kind of thing just bugs me. For those of us without money, it's a big thing and we always think about it."

Her honesty washed over me like a refreshing summer rain. This was Nina, and I loved her. "And then you find out they give little to nothing to charity and you wonder what they do with that money they say they care nothing about."

"Exactly!" she said as she sat up. "I hate that kind of hypocrisy."

I suspected she hadn't checked her bank account since she'd gotten home from the hospital and didn't know how much money she really had now. Not that it would matter. I had the feeling that she could have millions and still be the same down-to-earth soul she'd always been.

Running my fingertips over the soft skin of her arm, I continued, "By the way, you act perfectly to be my girlfriend. Don't ever think you aren't exactly what my girlfriend should be."

"Yeah. I'm sure the board of directors of Stone Worldwide would be thrilled to find out you are hanging out with some middle class girl instead of those supermodels they like to see on your arm."

Her comment brought the ugly reality of Karl and the other members of the Stone board to the front of my mind. No matter how happy I was with Nina, I had to figure out a way to convince them that she was no threat to them or whatever my father had done.

"I can see by the look on your face that I'm right, aren't I?" she said sadly. "It's okay. I understand if you have to take one of those women to your events instead of me."

Pulling her down to lay on top of me, I kissed her full on the lips. "Not anymore. If you want to go with me, then I go. If not, then those functions can do without me and my silent as a statue act."

She traced the outline of my lips with her forefinger. "How's the Board going to feel about that?"

"I don't care. You're the woman I'm in love with, so if I'm going, so are you. If they don't like it, too bad."

"You'd do that for me?"

I caressed her cheek and spoke the absolute truth. "I'd do anything for you, Nina. Anything."

SEVEN

Nina

Tristan and I fell asleep right there on the floor of the penthouse's living room with the floor to ceiling windows showing the entire world our lovemaking. Naked and in each other's arms, we held each other close as the nightlife of Manhattan slipped away to allow the business of day to take over, but as I stirred awake, I didn't feel his arms around me. Instead, a blanket kept me warm. Wiping the sleep from my eyes, I looked around and saw no Tristan but an envelope near my head.

Smiling to myself, I opened it and slipped the note from inside. As always, his words charmed me.

Good morning, Nina. I hope you slept well. I realized when I woke up that I did quite a number on your dress last night. You can find clothes to wear in the closet in the bedroom at the far end of the penthouse. When you're ready, simply take the elevator to the garage and my driver will be waiting to bring you to me.

I hope you're in the mood for shopping. It's the least I can do to replace the dress I ruined.

Thank you for giving me another wonderful memory.

Love,
Tristan

A man who wanted to take me shopping? I thought such men only existed in fantasies, like unicorns and dragons. Stretching my arms above my head, I thought about the other ways Tristan was the stuff of fantasies. Had a man ever made me want him like he did? Those stunning eyes, that beautiful mouth, those chiseled abs and strong arms...

Just thinking about him excited me. If only he was there with me so I could show him how much I wanted him. I could only guess that making love with him first thing in the morning would be another delicious experience.

The man had a way of making love that made other men seem like schoolboys. My hand slid between my legs to stroke through my soft folds as I remembered the exquisite sensations his cock had given me just hours before. Kicking the blanket off my body, I spread my legs open wide and let my fingers try to replicate the feeling of Tristan's hands and cock on my pussy. A tiny moan escaped my throat as each stroke brought back the wonderful memories of him.

Just then I remembered that I was lying in front of a wall of windows and giving the entire city a show. Opening my eyes, I saw in horror that it was late enough that the office buildings nearby would have people in them!

Quickly, I gathered up the blanket and ran from the living room to the back bedroom where he said I'd be able to find clothes. Embarrassed, I blushed from head to toe at the idea that some poor secretary just sitting down with her morning coffee had nearly seen me masturbate. I rolled my eyes at my stupidity, wondering if Tristan was as modest as I was or if he routinely paraded around nude for nearby office workers to see.

The closet was in the corner of the room, and I opened it up to see an entire wardrobe of women's clothes alongside all of Tristan's suits, shirts, and ties. As I ran my fingers over each outfit, I wondered if I had always kept clothes here or if he'd had them brought there before we arrived the night before.

I'd learned so much about Tristan already, but at every turn he seemed capable of surprising me.

Grabbing a grey jersey mini-dress and a pair of underwear from the dresser that seemed devoted to my clothes, I wrapped the blanket around me and made my way to the bathroom to get ready. I stepped into the room and stopped dead, stunned at how gorgeous it was. The man certainly knew how to live. Marble and granite covered every square inch of the room, except where an enormous soaker tub sat in front of a narrow floor to ceiling window and a large glass shower, which stood nearby the tub.

I draped my clothes over the tub and got into the shower, still uncomfortable about the window but hoping that my paranoia about being seen by the office workers across the street was just that. Of course it was. This was Manhattan. No one saw anything here, even with eight million people around. God, I hoped that was true or I was giving some unsuspecting souls a peep show as I showered.

I'd accepted the fact that I was going au natural, and I hoped that Tristan was into the pale girl look, but after I dressed I took a chance and looked through the vanity in the bathroom, desperate for at least some toothpaste I could rub across my teeth to get rid of my morning breath. I was stunned to find a toothbrush next to duplicates of every stitch of makeup I regularly used right there for me. It was like this was a parallel dimension that contained everything the other one at the house had. My father's joke about loving Spock and his goatee in the old Star Trek episode ran through my head and I smiled.

My father. I had tried so hard not to think about him being gone, but every so often something reminded me of him and forced the sadness I so wanted to forget back into my mind. His quirky humor. His lectures about working hard so I could do better than he had. What would he think of me now as I stood in the gorgeous Manhattan penthouse of Tristan Stone, CEO of Stone Worldwide and madly in love with me?

Of all the things and people I'd forgotten because of my accident, my father's death hurt the most. I couldn't help but feel it was unfair that I had to go through the pain of mourning him a second time. Why was this happening to me? Wasn't it bad enough to lose your father once? Why did I have to lose him again and feel all the pain a second time?

I couldn't keep doing this, so I pushed the thought away until some other time when I was able to deal with it. Looking in the mirror, I fixed the hair around my face and put on my best supermodel face. Well, I wasn't a supermodel, but I could make their face as well as any of them. That would have to do. A change of shoes from the closet in the bedroom since the gold shoes were definitely not a good look with the jersey dress and I was ready for my shopping trip.

Tristan was as good as his word, and when I exited the elevator, his driver stood waiting for me as if he was a permanent fixture right there in the garage. I approached him and saw he wore a serious expression on his fifty-something face, but he smiled like it was part of his job when I stopped in front of him.

"Miss, if you're ready, we can leave."

"Where are we going?"

"Le Ciel, miss. It shouldn't take long at all."

"Do you have to call Tristan or something to let him know we're coming?"

The driver opened the back passenger side door to the black Town Car and stood back so I could enter. His gaze drifted up toward the concrete ceiling above us. "Not to worry, miss. He knows."

If I thought the man would give me a more complete answer, I would have asked how Tristan knew we were leaving, but something told me he would simply plaster another formal grin on his face and repeat his cryptic sentence. It didn't matter. I could just ask Tristan when we arrived at the store.

I climbed into the car and settled in for the ride, not knowing where this Le Ciel was but happy that it wouldn't take long. The idea of a man taking me shopping had my curiosity piqued. Was it possible

Tristan Stone was gorgeous, wealthy, sexy as all hell, and loved to shop?

No. Even he was a mere mortal man. But that was okay. I was still crazy about him.

As I pondered all the ways Tristan was far more than just a mere mortal, the Town Car weaved through traffic like the driver owned the road. By the time I'd mentally listed half a dozen things I loved about the man who had given me one of the best nights of my life, we'd arrived at a boutique in Midtown. I stepped out of the car and saw even the window showcase was obviously upscale with mannequins dressed in designer names and wearing smug looks that somehow intimidated me, telling me Le Ciel wasn't anywhere I'd ever shop.

As I entered the store, a thin woman with jet black hair and a love of Botox, if her frozen forehead was any indication, approached me with an eager look on the lower half of her face. I guessed my current outfit made it seem like I may have belonged there, but I felt like I stuck out like a sore thumb.

"Miss Edwards, Mr. Stone is waiting for you. Please let me take you to him," she chirped out from her perfect mouth.

I was afraid to open my own mouth, unsure I wouldn't inadvertently say something that would give away the truth of how much I didn't belong in her store. Instead, I silently followed her, catching the price of a few dresses as we passed and mentally adding them up to a ridiculous total on our way to a room at the back of the boutique. I found Tristan sitting with three blondes who appeared totally engrossed in whatever he was saying, each hanging on every word he spoke.

The back room was even more luxurious than the store. The walls were draped in deep blue satin fabric that reminded me of what I imagined a sheik's harem would look like. Tristan relaxed on a black velvet couch, his arms opened wide across the back and his legs spread slightly. He wore his usual suit, that day's a black pinstripe with a grey shirt, and looked so incredibly right sitting there that I felt like I was intruding. He oozed power, and the three saleswomen lapped it up.

They noticed me immediately and straightened their backs when I stepped into the room. Tristan looked over at me with a warm smile and stood to take my hand. "Good morning, Nina. Are you ready to shop?"

I looked up at him and wished we were alone so I could tell him how happy I was to see him. Quietly, I said, "I guess."

"Did you have something to eat for breakfast? I instructed the concierge to give you whatever you wanted."

I sheepishly admitted that I hadn't eaten yet. "I didn't know I could do that."

Tristan leaned down to kiss my cheek and whispered, "I'm sorry. I forgot that you wouldn't know that. I should have remembered."

His voice sounded sad, making me feel bad for not knowing. "It's okay. My stomach isn't grumbling yet, so I'm good."

He slid his thumb over my bottom lip and turned to face the three women. "Ladies, this is Nina and she hasn't eaten breakfast yet. I'm sure one of you can find her something to eat while we shop."

The blonde who stood in the middle nodded her understanding and scurried away, ostensibly to find my breakfast. I gently tugged on the sleeve of Tristan's suit coat to get his attention, and he turned to face me with a smile on his face. "You didn't have to do that. I would've waited."

"Nina, I'm about to leave a nice chunk of money in this store. The very least they can do is run out to the café down the street and pick up some pastries. I just hope you like what she brings back. If you don't, she can go again."

He turned to face the other two women who remained standing there before I could explain that making a salesgirl run out repeatedly to grab a blueberry muffin for me seemed out of line. Neither of the women seemed put off by his request, though.

"Miss," one of the women said, "we can begin anytime you'd like. Do you have a preference for beginning with day or night?"

Confused, I asked, "Day or night?"

Tristan smiled back at me and answered, "Nina will begin with clothes she can wear at night. We have a few celebrations to attend over the holidays, and she's going to need dresses."

The two women sprung into action and dashed out past me into the store. Tristan took his seat on the couch again and looked up at me, obviously satisfied by how it was all going. I remained unsure of what to do, but there was something reassuring about the fact that he was staying. While I was a master at the art of shopping as any woman in her twenties likely was, he fit right in with the ambiance of Le Ciel, while I felt like a fish out of water.

"Should I sit and wait or stand?"

"Do whatever you feel comfortable with. They'll be back in a few minutes, but I'm always a fan of having you next to me."

I took a seat on the couch. It felt like I was sitting on a cloud, and instantly, I felt more at ease. Leaning over, I gave him a peck on the cheek. "Good morning. It's nice to see you. I would have loved to have seen you when I woke up."

"But you got my note, didn't you?"

"I did." Lowering my voice, I whispered, "But it's hard to have great morning sex with a note."

He slid his tongue across his lower lip and smiled. "Ah, now that's true. I'll have to remedy that oversight." Looking down, he ran his finger across my stomach. "How do your ribs feel?"

I couldn't help but smile at how sweet he was. "They feel great. I'm not so easily broken."

The women returned with their arms full of clothes. They appeared far more excited by the idea of my trying them on than I did, although I had to admit I could get used to this kind of treatment. They hung them on movable racks around the room and then took their places at the ends of one of the racks like fashion sentries.

"We're ready when you are, miss."

"Okay. I need to replace a black dress. Is there a cocktail dress in there?" I asked the left sentry.

"Of course!" she answered as she picked out some similar to the one Tristan had shredded the night before. With her arm extended, she held out three gorgeous black dresses and displayed them like she was a game show model. "I think any one of these would look incredible on you, don't you think, Mr. Stone?"

Tristan studied the three dresses for a few moments and nodded his appreciation. Turning to look at me, he leaned his head toward the saleswoman and mouthed, "You're up."

I walked over to the woman and smiled, unsure of where I was supposed to try them on. There didn't seem to be a dressing room in this area of the store. "Hi, what's your name?"

"Regina, miss."

"Hi, Regina. If you can just direct me to somewhere I can change, that would be great."

"Of course. Follow me."

As I walked away, Tristan said, "I'll be out here waiting to see you in them. When Felicia returns with your breakfast, I'll be sure to have her bring it back."

I tried on each dress and modeled them for Tristan, who loved them all. I honestly couldn't choose which one I liked most and told him that when he asked, figuring he'd choose one and make it easy, so he instructed the saleswoman that we'd take all of them. When I protested, he merely pointed at the pastries Felicia had brought back and told me to eat something.

Arguing would have been pointless, so I enjoyed a cheese Danish and thanked Felicia, who seemed surprised by my politeness.

"Next, I thought we'd try something a little different," Regina said in a happy voice. "Mr. Stone mentioned that you're looking for some lingerie."

I looked over at Tristan, who grinned like a cat who'd just eaten a bird. "Really?"

"I think you'll like what I've picked out. I hung them in the dressing room for you," she continued.

"Okay. Lingerie it is," I said as I flashed a smile at Tristan. "But I'm not coming out here to model these."

The dressing room was a well-lit, large room that reminded me of a movie star's closet I once saw on one of those shows about famous people's homes. There were built-in racks along three walls and a large built-in dresser on the wall next to the door. In the corner of the room stood a tri-fold mirror so customers could see how great they looked in any Le Ciel outfit from every possible angle. Positioned in the middle of the room was a large, red padded ottoman directly in front of the mirrors presumably to allow a person to relax in their new outfit while still checking themselves out.

The lingerie Regina had picked out was sexier than anything I'd ever slept in, and as I held the first one up in front of me, I couldn't help but admit that it was nicer than the shorts and T-shirt I usually wore to bed. I slipped out of my jersey dress and slid the white silk lingerie over my head. It shimmied down my body until the hem just touched the floor, and when I looked at how it hung on me, I silently wondered if those high-heel slippers with feathers on top and a long cigarette holder were requirements to wear it.

It fit, so it went on the rack closest to the door and I turned back to grab a much shorter and lacy babydoll set. This one was black and definitely sexier than my usual bedtime attire. I took off my bra and slipped into the babydoll, leaving my panties on instead of trying on the bottoms of the lingerie. Stepping in front of the mirrors, I checked myself out and had to admit I looked good. The babydoll pushed my breasts up until I had some very sexy cleavage and the silk fabric draped nicely down to the top of my thighs.

I heard the door open and was surprised to see Tristan walk in. Closing the door behind him, he slid out of his suit coat, hung it on a satin covered hanger, and walked over behind me. He cupped my shoulders and dipped his head to kiss my neck as he whispered, "You look gorgeous. Do you like it?"

Blushing, I nodded and stared at the erotic scene in the mirror. I looked ten times sexier with him standing behind me nuzzling just below my ear. "I do. It's very nice."

"I don't think you remember, but you've been here before. The day after we were first together, you came here to shop and I called you while you sat in this very dressing room."

His voice was laced with sensuality, and every word made my body come alive. "What did you say?"

Looking up from my neck, he stared at me in the mirror with eyes full of desire. "I'd rather show you."

I didn't answer as he led me to the overstuffed ottoman and dipped his head to place a full kiss on my lips. Releasing my hand, he gently pressed on my shoulders to lower me to the seat, smiling seductively at me as I looked up at him.

"Lay back, Nina."

I did as he commanded, my legs shaking nervously as he slid his palms over my thighs. Right there, in the dressing room at Le Ciel, Tristan was about to go down on me with the saleswomen not more than a few yards away at most. My body was a mixture of pure fear and uncontrollable excitement.

"Tristan, what if the ladies..."

He cut me off with a quick nip on my inner thigh as he pulled off my panties. "Shhh. Don't worry about them."

That was easier said than done. The fear that Regina or Felicia might barge in with some great outfit for me to try on and see Tristan's head between my legs made my stomach knot. I was no prude, but sex in public wasn't something I'd ever done.

At least I didn't think I'd ever done it.

"Nina, relax and enjoy this. I've wanted to taste you since you walked in here this morning. Did you know that?" As he spoke, his warm breath trailed against my skin, making me want him more.

Before I could even get a word out, he slid his tongue up to my clit and did this flicking thing that nearly sent me straight to the moon. My back arched and a moan that came from deep inside me escaped from my throat, but I didn't care at that moment. Whatever fear I'd had about anyone knowing what Tristan and I were up to evaporated into thin air with the first touch of his tongue to my pussy.

His hands caressed my abdomen as his mouth and tongue danced over my tender skin. Every inch of my sex was treated to the most incredible sensations from that expert tongue of his. I'd imagined that mouth that had delighted me with the most delicious kisses would be just as wonderful between my legs, but this was so much more than I could have dreamed of.

Running my hands through his short hair, I pulled him into me. Taking my swollen clit in his mouth, he sucked gently, making me ache for more when he pulled away. Suddenly, I felt cold and alone. Opening my eyes, I lifted my head to see him kneeling there staring at me.

"Wh...why did you stop?"

"Tell me you want me to continue, Nina."

"Of course, I do," I whispered. "Don't tease me, Tristan."

He winced ever so slightly and then that seductive look was back. As he leaned in to go down on me again, he looked up at me with eyes full of emotion and whispered, "I'd never tease you, Nina. Let me give you what you need."

And then he did just that.

As his tongue sent my body into overdrive, he slid one and then two fingers inside me, touching a spot that made me cover my mouth so the rest of Le Ciel didn't hear my cries of delight. Over and over, he stroked in and out of my body with expert fingers as every inch of me craved more of his touch.

The first ripple of my orgasm began deep inside and slowly weaved through me until one last playful flick of his tongue made me come apart. I cried out without any care for who heard me, moaning, "Don't stop," as I clawed at his head to make the feeling continue.

He rode my pussy with his mouth and tongue until there wasn't a tremor left in my body. I was boneless when he moved away, the picture of satisfaction staring down at me. Taking my hands in his, he pulled me up to kiss him, and I tasted myself on his lips and tongue.

"I've wanted to do that for a while," he whispered in a deep voice as he stroked my cheek.

"I can't believe I just had sex in a Midtown boutique dressing room. This is like the on-the-ground version of the Mile High Club," I said with a giggle.

"That reminds me. We're taking a trip after New Year's."

I lowered my head, shaking no. "I could never have sex on an airplane, Tristan. Where do those people do that, anyway? Aren't the bathrooms too tiny?"

"I don't know. I've never been on a public airplane. We'll be traveling on my private jet, so perhaps that will make your initiation into the Mile High Club easier."

I looked up, shocked. He had a private jet? I should have guessed that, but it still sounded incredible that I knew someone with a private jet. That I was dating someone with a private jet.

"Wow. Is there anything you don't have?"

Those deep brown eyes focused on mine. "Just one thing, but I'm working on that."

The idea that all he lacked in his life was my love made me feel like I was the most important person in his world. With every moment that passed, I knew why I'd fallen in love with him and wanted to spend the rest of my life with Tristan Stone.

I just had to let myself go this time too.

"Oh my God! What are you doing here?"

Jordan opened her arms and pulled me into the apartment with a huge bear hug, crushing my face against her shoulder. As she closed the door behind us, she released me just long enough to decide she needed another hug.

"Come here! I've missed you so much."

"I did too. When Tristan and I went to the penthouse last night, I knew I wanted to stop over and see how you're doing."

She released me again and led the way to the living room. We sat down in our usual seats and as she folded her legs under her, she stared at me. "You look incredible, Nina. I know it's just been a few days since we saw each other, but it feels like months."

"It does. I thought it was just because I don't remember anything of the past four years."

She let out a big sigh. "Anything good happening on that front?"

Shaking my head, I tried to hide my disappointment with a smile. "Not yet, but Tristan keeps reminding me that the doctors said it might take a little while."

"How is that yummy man?"

I felt my face warm and grinned. "He's fine."

"Oh, he's definitely fine," she teased with a wiggle of her eyebrows.

Changing the subject, I asked, "So what's new with you? I came here to find out about your life."

"My life is nowhere as exciting as yours. Between that gorgeous man, your gorgeous house, and all the wonderful things that come with both of those things, I wish I had your life."

She wasn't wrong. My life was perfect. Wonderful. Tristan was everything I'd ever wanted in a man. The house was beyond stunning. A driver took me wherever I wanted to go. And my boyfriend loved to spend money on me.

The only problem was that I'd lost four years of my life and no matter what I did, I missed them. I wanted to live in the present, but that void from my past haunted me every moment of the day.

"I know. It's great," I said as I looked away.

Jordan leaned forward and pressed her hand to my knee. "Oh, honey. I didn't mean to say everything was perfect. I was just trying to be positive."

Her frown told me she hadn't tried to be callous. "I know you didn't mean anything by it. I should be happy with everything I have."

"Bullshit. You're allowed to be unhappy about not remembering one-sixth of your damn life. Just know that whatever you want to ask about the last four years, I'm here as your own personal encyclopedia." Tapping her finger to her forehead, she added, "I've got everything stored right up here."

Biting my lip, I considered what part of my past I wanted to know about the most. There was really no question. My father's death.

"Jordan, what happened to my father?" I asked in a quiet voice, as if no one else knew about his passing.

She inhaled deeply and blew the air out of her lungs in a hard wooosh. "Oh, honey. I was afraid you were going to ask that. It was tough on you. I can tell you that."

"What happened? He was so young."

She shook her head and frowned. "You and Kim never found out what really happened. All I know is this. He was in Newark investigating some story and was found dead in a parking garage."

"Shot?"

Nodding, she answered quietly, "Yeah. The police said he was murdered execution style."

Tears welled in my eyes. "Oh my God! Why would someone do that to him? He was a writer who investigated things like small town politics. Who kills someone over nepotism on the town council?"

I couldn't hold back the tears as I had since my sister had told me about my father's death. They poured down over my cheeks as I buried my face in my hands, and my body heaved with each sob. My father was murdered and I'd forgotten the whole thing!

Jordan sat down beside me and took me in her arms. "Let it out, sweetie. You have to let it out or you'll get like you did then."

Another thing I couldn't remember.

I buried my face in her shoulder and did exactly that. I let all the sadness out until I couldn't cry anymore. Until I felt hollow and empty.

Pulling away from Jordan, I asked, "What do you mean I'll get like I did then? What happened to me then?"

She smoothed the hair from my forehead and wiped her thumb under my eyes. "It was pretty bad. You didn't get out of bed for weeks. Thank God your professors were understanding since it was your senior year because day after day, no matter how I tried, you wouldn't do anything but lay in bed. Sometimes you cried. Other times you just stared up at the ceiling or off in the distance."

"For how long?"

"Honey, it went on for a long time. Even after you came back to life, I was worried you might never be the same old Nina again."

"I wish I knew who that same old Nina was now," I admitted sadly. "I feel like I'm missing so much of me."

"You're still you, Nina. It's all in there. It's just a matter of it coming out."

I sat back against the couch cushions and hung my head. Just thinking about my father's death was exhausting. It was like he'd just died that day and not years before. My heart hurt at Jordan's description of his murder.

Looking up, I asked, "Am I really the same? Of anybody, you'd know. Am I? What was I like when I got into that accident?"

"Blissfully happy. I'd never seen you as happy as when you were with Tristan. I mean, I don't want to say it was perfect. Nothing is. But you were as happy as anyone could want to be."

"Is he as incredible as I think he is?"

"Yeah. He is. When you moved in with him, he paid the rest of your portion of the rent for the year. When that weird guy attacked us on the front steps, he let me stay at his hotel in a gorgeous suite for weeks because you asked him to. You were worried for my safety, and he didn't blink an eye. You wanted something and he made it happen."

"Why don't I remember any of that? Why can't I remember how much in love with him I was? Don't you think I'd remember that? I mean, I can understand not wanting to remember my father's death, but Tristan is wonderful. And the rest of those four years couldn't have been all bad. Were they?"

"No. They weren't all bad. We had some really fun times once you got back to being yourself. Two single girls living in New York. Good times."

Her smile faded as the words trailed off. She was hiding something. It hadn't been all good times.

"What aren't you telling me, Jordan?"

"It's not important. Your life was as good as anyone who's just out of college and trying to make it on their own."

"But?"

"But nothing. You were happy."

Everything in her face said otherwise, though. What had been so bad about my life?

"Tell me, Jordan. I need to know."

She got up from the couch and walked toward the kitchen. "Jordan, tell me!" I called after her.

She stopped dead in the living room doorway and with her back to me asked, "Cal. Do you remember him?"

"Of course. I was crazy about him."

Turning around, she looked at me with pain in her eyes. "Do you remember what happened between the two of you?"

I thought about what I knew about Cal. "We broke it off because he had the chance to study abroad in Spain for a year. He was a junior and it was the chance of a lifetime, so we broke up. But it wasn't anything awful."

"That wasn't the end of it. He came back and you two began seeing each other again, but he wasn't the same guy. Whatever he did in Europe, he came back a real asshole."

"What are you saying?"

She walked away into the kitchen, and I followed her, needing to know what the hell she was talking about. Standing with her back to me, she shook her head. "It was bad, Nina. He was a real shit. You were crazy about him, madly in love, and he..."

She stopped and said nothing for a long time.

"He what?" I finally demanded.

She spun around and I couldn't tell if she was angry or upset. "He fucked you up really bad, Nina. You didn't just break up another time. He broke your heart. You told him you loved him and what did he do? He cheated on you that very fucking night!"

My memory of Cal wasn't of a love meant for the ages, but I had no idea what she was talking about. I'd been disappointed when we broke up so he could go to Spain, but I understood why. The person she was describing wasn't the person I'd cared about, though.

"I can't believe that. Cal and I had been fun together. I never thought it was going to be a forever thing, but we had fun. We cared about each other."

"Well, it wasn't like that when you got back together. He was a real dick. He left you in pieces, Nina. Pieces. It was like it was when your father died all over again. Even worse, if you ask Kim."

"Why? What happened?"

Jordan's body sagged under the weight of what she was saying. "You said some things about wanting to die. I don't think you ever really meant it, but it was a lot to deal with. I was afraid for a long time that you might do something."

"Tell me everything. I need to know."

"Honey, it's in the past, and in my opinion, that bullshit can stay there. Don't do this."

I knew she was trying to protect me, but I needed to fill in the huge blank spots in my memory. I needed to begin to figure out why my mind was keeping me in the dark about so much time.

"Jordan, I need to know what my mind's keeping from me. What happened to make me say I wanted to die?"

"You told him you loved him. For the first time, you actually weren't afraid to take that leap. You remember what you were like when we first started school, right? You were always beautiful and sweet, but you never had the guts to go out on a limb and tell someone you loved them. It was probably because of how you lost your mother. And Cal knew that. He knew how much it meant that you were finally able to open up and say you loved him. And what did he do with that gift? He ripped it to shreds."

I did remember being afraid to tell boyfriends how I felt about them. While every other girl in high school had been dying to tell their boyfriends they loved them, I dreaded it. It terrified me. They might leave and then where would I be? I'd never told Cal I loved him.

At least I didn't remember telling him. Now Jordan was saying that the only time she knew of me saying I love you to anyone other than Tristan had ended in disaster. My stomach felt like it was twisting into knots.

She wrapped her arms around me. "Honey, don't get down about it. Cal was an asshole. He didn't deserve you. He deserved the girl who used him and threw him away three months later."

I pushed her away and shook my head. "I need to know what happened. What did he do?"

"Don't do this. It's not going to make anything better."

"Jordan, this is part of my life I don't remember. I have to know."

Sighing heavily, she nodded. "He'd been cheating on you the whole time. We went out for a drink because you were so happy that you'd finally told him how you felt and we saw him with some cheap blonde. It was terrible. You confronted him all in tears, and she was more than happy to tell you how long they'd been seeing each other. He tried to deny it, but it was no use. The proof was standing there in front of you basically throwing it in your face."

God, had I never had any luck with men? Cal had been the one man I'd remembered in all this as a decent person, and now that was all wrong too.

Jordan smoothed my hair away from my face. Her expression was so sad. "You never meant that you wanted to die, honey. That was just something you said because you were feeling down. I know how it feels. It hurts like hell when you care about someone and they betray you. We've all been through it, and sometimes when we're feeling our worst, we say things we don't mean."

"I don't want to die, Jordan. Even when I've felt like I was totally lost these past few weeks, I never wanted to end it."

"I think Tristan's a big part of that, Nina. He's a good man. And I swear to you on a stack of Bibles that he's crazy about you."

"I know. There's no need to sell him to me. I can see it."

She looked away from me and said quietly, "I'm worried you won't give him a chance now."

"Why?"

Turning to face me, she knitted her brows in concern. "Because of what I told you. I don't want you to think you're just unlucky with men."

It was as if Jordan was reading my mind. The only happy memory I'd had concerning the opposite sex, other than Tristan, was Cal. Now that he had turned out to be just like every other male I'd ever been with that I could remember, all I could think of was that I was jinxed in the realm of love.

"Me unlucky? Look at my life. No worries about luck there," I said with as much bravado I could muster, not even convincing myself. I forced a smile as I looked at my cell phone for the time. "I guess it's time to go."

"Okay, honey. Okay."

I knew Jordan didn't believe me, but like the best friend she was, she didn't say a thing. She knew talking about it wasn't going to help now. "Tristan and I would like you and Justin to join us for New Year's. We'll be at the penthouse and it would mean so much to me if we could all hang out."

The darkness that had covered her features lifted and her genuine smile lit up the room. "That would be great! If his penthouse is anything like that suite he put me up in, it'll be incredible."

I couldn't help but grin. Tristan's penthouse was stunning, and I couldn't wait to show it off to Jordan. Just the view was going to blow her away.

"He'll have his cooks make some late night dinner for us and we'll watch the new year come in high above the city. How does ten o'clock sound?"

"I can't wait! It'll be fun!" she squealed as she enveloped me in a bear hug. As she held me, I felt her grow serious. In my ear, she said quietly, "Take care of yourself. I want you to remember something. I don't know if you know what I always say, but it's true. Good things happen to good people, and you're the best, so that means great things are in store for you."

Releasing me, she smiled. "Now promise me you won't forget that."

"Not unless I have another head injury," I joked.

Jordan screwed her face into a frown. "Not funny. Now you go have an incredible Christmas and I'll see you at the top of the world at ten on New Year's Eve."

"I'll be there in sparkles and bangles."

NINE

Nina

I couldn't help but think about everything Jordan had told me as the Town Car rolled over the highway on my way back home. By the time Jensen got me back to Tristan's house, my mind was filled with doubts about love. Why had Cal betrayed me like that? We'd been so close. Or at least I'd thought we'd been. Would I ever feel the same love I'd obviously felt for Tristan before? Or was that a remnant of my forgotten past I'd never have the chance to enjoy again?

God, everything was so confusing! I felt like everywhere I turned were those funhouse mirrors that distorted people and I kept seeing myself in them—stretched out and wavy in one, flattened in another. Now Cal had to be added to the distortion.

But not Jordan or Tristan. Neither one of them ever veered away from what they'd said to me that first time I saw them in the hospital. I was lucky to have two people who cared about me. I knew that.

I put away my new clothes and flopped back onto my bed. As I lay there, I couldn't help but wonder why the memory of Cal was all I could think about.

Listen to what Jordan said and don't be stupid, Nina. You have a great guy here who tells you he loves you all the time and means it. Leave Cal where he belongs. In the past.

I knew I should leave him in my forgotten past. I just couldn't.

Tristan and I had dinner promptly at five, as I'd come to find out was our routine. He smiled when he saw me and said he'd had a great day after our rendezvous, but those sexy brown eyes told a different story about his day. Perhaps after taking off so much time to tend to me after my accident, the work he'd neglected had finally caught up to him. Whatever it was that made him look so exhausted, I wished I could make it all go away.

Pushing his plate away from him, he forced a smile. "How was your day after you left Le Ciel?"

I felt a blush race over my cheeks at the mention of our time at the boutique. "It was good. I went to see Jordan. She said she and Justin would come to celebrate New Year's Eve with us. I think she's looking forward to it."

Tristan reached out his hand to cover mine as it sat on the table. "And are you?"

"I am. I think we'll have a great time."

His smile softened, becoming more genuine. "Good. Any idea what we should feed them?"

"Cocktail weenies?" I said with a giggle.

Raising his eyebrows, he smirked. "I think my chef can do better than that. Perhaps I'll let him run with the menu. I promise you'll love it."

"I'm sure I will...love it," I said as I slid my hand out from under his.

He noticed its movement immediately and looked down at the spot where my hand had sat and then up at my face. "Is there something wrong, Nina? I'd thought after last night and this morning, we'd turned a corner. Was I wrong?"

I didn't know if he was wrong. The time we'd spent together at the penthouse the night before had been incredible. And the dressing room at Le Ciel? Mind blowing. There was no doubt in my mind that the sex between us worked. It worked like with no one before. But I had to wonder about the feelings underneath what we did with one another when we were naked.

"No. It was great. There's no denying that."

Tristan's eyebrows knitted in that look of concern that he seemed to wear a lot, mostly because of me. "But something's wrong?"

I couldn't think of a way to say what was on my mind, so I just went with the straightforward truth. "There's no doubt we rock it in bed. No doubt. But is sex all we are? I mean, couples usually do normal couples stuff."

"Like?" he asked with a distinct edge to his voice.

"Like sit around and watch movies," I blurted out, unsure if that's what I meant at all.

"You want to watch a movie tonight? Is that what you're saying?"

I could tell by the look on his face that he was confused by my attitude toward him. I couldn't blame him. We'd made love over and over the night before, and then the Le Ciel thing had happened, so he had every right to think that I was beginning to feel something for him.

I was. I just didn't know how to feel about that.

"Could we? Did we ever do that, or did we only have sex all over the place?"

On those rare occasions when Tristan really smiled, he was the most incredibly stunning man I'd ever seen. At that moment when I asked if all we'd ever done was have sex, one of those true smiles broke out across his face, lighting up even his tired eyes.

"Yes, we've watched movies before. You tend to like ones I don't and vice versa, but I'm sure we can compromise."

"Good."

Loosening his tie, he focused his gaze on me. "But I want to get something straight with you. Just because we're attracted to one another doesn't mean we never cared for each other. The two things are not mutually exclusive."

"I'm sorry. I didn't mean anything by that."

"I think you have some idea that because I want you that I can't be in love with you. Nothing could be further from the truth, Nina."

This was one of those times I was sure he had some mind reading ability he used on me. Even before I'd realized it, he'd nailed down what had been playing on my mind since Jordan had told me about Cal.

I looked down at my hands as they sat in my lap. "I guess I'm just worried that sex was all there was between us." Looking up, I saw him staring at me with what looked like hurt in his eyes. "Not that the sex isn't great, but was there more?"

"The sex was great—is great—because there is more. Your mind may not know it yet, but your heart does. Listen to it, Nina."

When he looked at me with those eyes that seemed to look straight into my soul, I couldn't help but prayed that he was right. I wanted to listen to my heart. It's just that my head kept interrupting with all those doubts about him. About love. About Cal.

I needed to know why Cal had so easily dumped me for some girl after I'd told him I'd loved him. Something inside told me that if I didn't find out what had happened between us, then nothing would ever truly be right between Tristan and me.

He interpreted my silence as rejection and leaned back in his chair. "I'm happy to give you all the time you need, Nina. All I ask is that you not fight feeling something for me."

"That's not it, Tristan. I didn't mean..." I let my sentence trail off into the uncomfortable feeling that had formed around us right there in that dining room. I felt bad, but I was sure once I found out what had happened with Cal, everything between Tristan and me could be right. Maybe it would be even better than it had been before.

He stood from the table and placed his napkin next to his plate. "Let me get changed and we'll haggle over that movie. Sound good?"

"Sure. That sounds great. Give me a few minutes and I'll meet you in..." I stopped because I didn't know where to say to meet him. The media room? His room? Now that we'd slept together, spending the night with him in his room seemed like the next logical step, but I wasn't sure it meant the same thing to him.

"Let's get some use out of that media room. I'll meet you there in say twenty minutes? I have some work I have to take care of, but I'll tell Rogers to make some popcorn."

His desire to watch the movie not in his room but in the media room confused me. Maybe last night hadn't meant what I thought it had. But then again, he was the one always professing love.

As he left the dining room, I worked to clear my muddled head. It was probably better if we kept our living arrangements like they'd been for a little while more anyway. I needed to find out about what had made the only other man I'd ever said I love you to leave me. Once the past was cleared up, the present could begin to be great.

At least I hoped so.

Tristan's media room wasn't like any room normal people watched movies in. More like a movie theater than a room, it had an enormous U-shaped black chenille sectional couch that felt like heaven to sit on. Extra deep, the seats were almost as big as chaise lounges all around. It faced a TV that was so big it took up almost the entire wall. I felt tiny in this room so full of big things.

Easing back onto the sofa, I let myself enjoy the luxury. He did know how to live.

"Don't get too comfortable," he announced as he entered the room, his arms full with a yellow plastic bowl overflowing with buttery popcorn and a roll of paper towels.

I sat up quickly, unsure what he meant. "Why?"

"We need to have some of this popcorn. Three pans of Jiffy Pop popcorn are here waiting for us to dig in."

He placed the bowl on the coffee table in the center of the sofa and walked back to begin the movie as I took a handful of popcorn. The familiar taste of that buttery and salty snack was delicious, even after our perfectly prepared steak dinner.

Popping another kernel in my mouth, I looked back at him. "I haven't had Jiffy Pop in years! I wouldn't think you'd be a Jiffy Pop guy."

He shook his head. "I'm not. I'd never had it before you asked for it one night when we watched one of your chick flicks."

I twisted my face into a look of fake disgust at his cheap shot at my favorite type of movie. "So when did you run out to get some Jiffy Pop in the last twenty minutes?"

He sat down beside me as the movie began. "I didn't. We have it here all the time since you told me you liked it."

"Oh. Well, that's good to know. You know, just in case I decide I want popcorn at two in the morning."

Tristan's casual statement rocked me. I tried to hide how much it meant to me behind my joking, but I was truly touched by his attentiveness.

"So are you ready for some Iron Man 2?"

"And this is what you call haggling? I'm not getting a chick flick vibe here," I teased.

Putting his arm around me, he pulled me close and grinned. "Yes and no. It's not a chick flick, but it's got great cars and there's a girl."

"Please tell me you at least believe I like this movie."

As the film began and he dimmed the lights, he softly kissed my lips. "You do. Trust me."

I ended up loving the movie, and by the time we fell asleep in each other's arms right there in the media room, I was almost convinced that, in the end, my heart would have the final say instead of my head.

The winter sun warmed my room as it woke me the next morning. I rolled over and focused on the clock. 8:05. Looking around, I saw I was in my bedroom tucked under the covers. I vaguely remembered Tristan carrying me there and putting me to bed after the movie.

As I slowly came back to life, I saw a sheet of white paper on the pillow next to me. As was his habit, Tristan had left me his own version of a good morning kiss. No envelope this time. Just a sheet of stationery.

Dear Nina,

Thank you for the movie date. I'm happy you enjoyed it. I'll be busy all day, but tonight I thought we'd visit one of our favorite restaurants. I'll pick you up at six sharp.

Love,
Tristan

My eyes slid over the words, noting each stroke of his handwriting. I'd grown to love these notes from him, even feeling disappointed when he didn't leave one. As I reread his letter, I wondered what restaurant he meant. I guessed I'd see at six.

After a quick shower, I dressed in a cute navy blue sweater dress and knee-high boots and headed to the kitchen for some much needed coffee. As I sipped the French Vanilla roast blend, I thought about the day ahead of me, nervous about what I'd find out.

"Miss, is there anything you need?"

I looked around and saw Rogers standing in the doorway. His expression was kind, as it had been the day I arrived at this house, but he watched me like a hawk, his dark eyes following every move I made. With his slicked back steel grey hair and long face, he reminded me of a maître d' at one of those exclusive restaurants.

Lifting my mug of coffee, I smiled and shook my head. "Got everything I need. Thanks. I'll pick something up to eat in the city when I go shopping."

FALL INTO ME

As soon as I said the words, I felt guilty, as if going to visit someone from my past was a bad thing. Lying had never been something I was good at. I knew Tristan's butler saw my guilt too. Something in the way his eyes grew wider for just a moment told me he didn't believe me.

He stood silently looking at me, and every second that went by I grew more uncomfortable. I began to fidget and my eyes darted around the room to avoid his stare. Finally, I croaked out, "Well, guess it's time to head out. Have a good one."

Rogers nodded slowly and moved aside to allow me to pass, but I felt his eyes on me the whole time. I couldn't tell if it was my own guilty conscience or his silent judging me about something else, but I felt sick all of a sudden.

"Jensen, I'm meeting Jordan to shop, so feel free to take a break. Get some lunch," I chirped out to Tristan's driver.

He lowered his slightly graying head and smiled. I didn't get any sense that he suspected me of anything as Rogers seemed to have, so I happily marched into Macy's and waited for what seemed like long enough before I ducked out the nearest exit.

Out to Cal's office four blocks away.

I raced up the street, walking as fast as I could in my boots, among the throngs of people headed out on their day's business. As I passed the men and women on their way to wherever they were going, I wondered if any of them was like me—going to talk to a ghost from her past.

Cal's office was on the fifteenth floor of a typical skyscraper in Manhattan. I stepped inside the building and looked for the elevator, eager to speak to him and hopefully find out what about me had made it so easy for him to turn his back on my love. I wasn't sure I wanted to know, to be honest, but I was sure I needed to.

The elevator stopped on his floor, and I stepped out into a greeting area for the firm he worked for as an actuary. I'd found out he worked at Peak International with just a few minutes of online searching, and as I stood behind a gentleman in an overcoat waiting to speak to the receptionist, I began to doubt my initial idea of meeting with Cal.

The reception area was modest, with older chairs and a carpet that reminded me of the cream and burgundy print one my grandmother had in her living room when I was a child. The walls were off white, but I couldn't decide if they'd been painted that shade or aged to that color.

"May I help you?" the attractive Asian woman behind the desk asked.

Torn from my thoughts, I smiled and said, "Yes. I'm hoping to see Cal Johnson. Is he in?"

"Who may I say is here to see him?"

I took a deep breath in and exhaled slowly. "Nina Edwards."

The receptionist nodded. "If you'll take a seat, I'll buzz him, miss."

I sat on one of the upholstered waiting area chairs and smoothed my dress over my thighs in an effort to calm myself and dry my hands drenched with nervous sweat. A hundred recriminations ran through my mind, making me want to bolt out the door, but I remained planted in the chair and tried to focus on the possibility of what Cal could tell me about what happened between us. An elderly couple seated next to me whispered to each other about life insurance as I worked to stay relaxed.

"Nina?"

I looked up at the sound of a man's voice and saw Cal standing at the receptionist's desk. He looked like I remembered—light brown hair, blue eyes that hadn't faded a bit, and an athlete's body visible even under his white shirt and brown dress pants.

"Cal," I said with nervous enthusiasm. "Do you have a few minutes? I was hoping we could talk."

Extending his arm toward me, he smiled and nodded. "Sure. Come with me. We'll talk in my office."

Cal led me to his office halfway down the hallway. A small room, it had a single window that let in some light but was overall quite dim. His glass and metal desk took up a majority of the space, but there was room enough for one chair for me to sit in.

"Excuse my office. I generally don't get visitors. Take a seat and tell me what you've been up to."

His voice telegraphed loud and clear that he was uncomfortable, which only served to make me more uneasy than I'd been just minutes before out in the waiting area. Taking a deep breath, I said, "I wanted to talk about us."

"Us? Uh, what about us?"

My hands fidgeted in my lap, and I planted my feet on the floor to stop my legs from shaking. "Cal, I was in a car accident a few weeks ago. I can't remember anything from right before my father died four years ago. I know we're not together anymore, but I was hoping you could tell me what happened to break us up."

A look of discomfort settled into his features. "Oh, I don't know, Nina. That was a long time ago."

"It's important to me, Cal. Anything you can tell me would help."

He seemed to study me for a moment and then a slow smile spread across his face, reminding me of that person I'd dated all those years ago. "I think it's about time I apologized, Nina. I was a real ass. To be honest, if it weren't for the fact that you can't remember anything, you'd probably never speak to me again, and I'd deserve it."

"What happened to us? I remember us being happy. I mean, I know we weren't ready to make it forever, but I thought we were happy."

Cal shifted in his office chair. "We were young. I was probably more immature than most guys at that age. I didn't...uh...I didn't realize what I had."

I didn't know what to say to that. Jordan had made him sound like the worst of all men, but the man who sat across the desk from me seemed to regret how we'd ended. If anything, he looked sad.

"I guess I just needed to know it wasn't me, Cal."

Shaking his head, he knitted his brows and frowned. "No. I don't want you to think that. It wasn't you. It was me."

"Oh, the old It's-not-you-it's-me thing," I joked.

He reached over and touched my hand resting on the edge of his desk. His eyes told me he didn't think this was a joking matter. "I hate to think that before your accident you thought it was because of anything you did that we broke up."

I didn't know what I'd thought then, but he was right. Ever since Jordan told me what had happened, I'd been convinced Cal had cheated on me because of some lack in me. That whoever he'd chosen over me was prettier, smarter, or better at whatever else he wanted.

"It's okay, Cal. I can't remember that now. It's just nice to know that what happened wasn't because of some deficiency in me."

He grimaced at the word 'deficiency.' "I'm sorry that you thought that. That's not right. You were lacking nothing, Nina. I was the one lacking in maturity."

We sat there quietly for a long moment before a knock on his office door broke the awkward silence. Calling the person in, he quickly shook off the seriousness of his words and put on his professional face again. As he and his coworker spoke, I stood to leave, having gotten what I'd come for.

His colleague left, and Cal stood from behind his desk. "Would you like to have coffee sometime? It would be nice to be friends, if you think we can."

"That would be nice. I can't promise I won't want to ask more questions, though. Everything's such a blank from around that time. But I don't want you to think I blame you for anything. That was a long time ago, and we've both moved on."

"It's the least I could do, Nina. And don't worry about blaming me. I deserve it. I just hope we can be friends."

I extended my hand to shake his. "It's a deal."

"Good." He wrote something on a piece of paper and handed it to me. "Here's my cell number and email. I'd love it if we could grab a coffee before the holidays."

I took the information with a smile and slipped it into my purse. "Me too. I'll email you and let you know when I'm going to be in the city again."

"You still live in Brooklyn? I heard you and Jordan were sharing an apartment in Sunset Park."

His mention of my place in Brooklyn surprised me. I shook my head and said for the first time to anyone since I left the hospital, "No, I live upstate now in Duchess County."

Cal's expression showed his surprise. "You introduced yourself as Nina Edwards, so I thought you were still single. Did you marry?"

"No. I'm still Nina Edwards, but I live with my boyfriend out there. Tristan. Tristan Stone."

I had the sense that the mere mention of Tristan's name changed everything in the room, and Cal's smile seemed to fade just a little.

"You did well for yourself, Nina. Stone's a big deal."

I nodded, unsure of what exactly Cal meant. Turning to leave, I smiled and said, "We'll do coffee before Christmas. Thanks again, Cal. I appreciate you taking the time to talk to me."

As I opened the door, Cal said quietly, "Take care, Nina. I look forward to seeing you again."

My talk with Cal had buoyed my spirits. I'd been so afraid that he'd left me because of me that I hadn't wanted to give Tristan a chance to do the same thing. Now I felt like I could truly let him in and begin to make those new memories, just as he'd promised.

TEN

TRISTAN

Looking down at my phone as it buzzed against the top of my desk, I saw a message from Jensen. *Driving home now.* After waiting for nearly an hour to hear from him after his first message telling me Nina had left Macy's and gone to an office building four blocks away, my stomach was tied up in angry knots. The bodyguards who followed us at all times were little help too. All they seemed to know was that she'd gone to the fifteenth floor to some insurance company to see someone named Cal Johnson.

Just seeing that name come up on my phone made my blood run cold. Three little letters and I could barely contain the rage that exploded inside me. Cal, the guy she remembered while I was a stranger. Cal, the ex-boyfriend who had broken her heart. What the fuck could she want with him?

Swiping away Jensen's message, I dialed another number I knew would help me find out what Nina had been up to. A few rings and finally I heard the raspy voice of Daryl Knight.

"Daryl, I have another job for you."

"Tristan. Just the man I wanted to talk to. I finally got something on that Edwards business. We should meet."

Daryl Knight was the man I used to investigate private matters associated with Stone Worldwide, such as researching the actresses' backgrounds to make sure there was nothing unsavory in their pasts before I was seen with them in public. A big, burly guy, he looked more like a mountain man than a private investigator with his full reddish-brown beard and wild curly hair. At first glance, he hadn't seemed to be someone who could find out much of anything without getting noticed, but he'd proven me wrong enough times that I knew if I wanted the details about someone, Daryl was the man to call.

"Fine. Let's say two days from now. In the meantime, I need you to find out everything you can about a man named Cal Johnson."

"Is Cal his real name?" Daryl asked with a chuckle.

"I have no idea. I just know I want everything you can find on this guy."

"Okay. I'll have it for when we meet. You looking for this for business or personal use? You know I don't care and it's none of my business, but do you want me to focus on the gorier details?"

"Both. I want to know where he lives, what he eats, how he makes his money, who he's fucking and if she likes it. You understand me?"

"Got it. What time are we meeting?"

"Thursday at noon."

I ended the call, pushed my phone away in disgust, and leaned back in my chair. I had to hold myself back from racing home at a hundred miles an hour to ask Nina why she'd lied and snuck off to some office where her old boyfriend spent his days.

Jealousy coursed through my veins, and my stomach turned at the thought of her with any other man. In my mind, I saw her naked body sprawled across his desk as he fucked her next to his low budget sticky notes and dollar store stapler. He wore a cheap suit and feared being found out, so he didn't even take his shirt off. Muffled grunts came from his mouth as he rammed his cock into her, his middle manager features all twisted into an ugly sex face while he hovered over the woman I loved.

Over and over, the awful scene played in my head until I couldn't take it anymore. I couldn't just sit there in my corner office torturing myself all afternoon. Pressing the intercom on the corner of my desk, I called for my assistant.

Michelle opened the door to my office and stood waiting for my instructions. The last showing of the ugly movie of Nina cheating on me played in my mind, and I heard Michelle say, "Mr. Stone? You wanted me?"

I shook away my thoughts and focused on the woman in front of me. In many ways, Michelle reminded me of Nina. Gentle and sweet, she cared about her job and me, always making sure every detail was taken care of for every assignment I gave her. Slightly older than Nina, she had dark brown hair, brown eyes, and was married to some advertising guy whose main claim to fame was the semi-successful campaign for some Greek yogurt made here in the

States before every yogurt maker in the business began doing the Greek thing. I vaguely remembered her referring to him once as Jeff or Jess and saying they lived in Queens.

"Yes. I'm leaving, so cancel any meetings I have this afternoon. Message me if anything comes up that I need to know about."

"Yes, Mr. Stone. Should I call a car for you?"

Shaking my head, I stood from my desk and slipped back into my suit coat. "No. I'm taking my car."

"What should I say to Mr. Dreger if he calls?" she asked as I walked toward her to leave.

Karl would surely be calling if he got a sense that I'd left the office. The man had basically taken to stalking me since he'd found out about Nina, which had necessitated the two bodyguards who followed Nina and me around whenever we went out, and Nina whenever she was alone.

"Tell him I chose to work from home today. If he presses you for details, tell him you know nothing more and have him call me directly."

Michelle smiled and stood aside as I opened the door. Remembering Karl's penchant for trying to sneak around behind my back to spy on me, I added, "And lock this door when I leave. Do not let anyone in."

She looked at me with surprise in her eyes, but I knew she understood what I was telling her. "You can trust me, Mr. Stone. No one will get in."

"Thank you, Michelle. I'll message you if I'm not coming into the office tomorrow. If I don't, the same thing applies. No one gets in. No one."

"I understand. Have a good night," she said with a sympathetic smile, likely sensing there was something wrong but never asking since we weren't that close. She wished me a good night anytime I left the office, and rarely had I made the effort to say it back to her.

For some reason, the way she was looking up at me at that moment made me want to say it now, though. "Have a good night, Michelle."

My simple effort was rewarded with a broad smile, which made me feel better until I thought of Nina smiling just like that for Cal as she left his office, her light brown hair and her clothes all disheveled from her time with him. Disgusted, I turned and stormed out to get into my car, eager to take my aggression out on the highway between Manhattan and home.

Jensen was outside the garage when I pulled up to the house. I parked the Jag and saw he wasn't there by coincidence. He was waiting for me.

"Mr. Stone, I want to apologize. I neglected my duties and Miss Edwards could have been harmed."

Jensen's mouth turned down in a frown as he stood waiting for me to respond to his confession. While Nina might not remember anything of the recent past, he did and he knew I did. After the attack on her at the apartment by that guy fucked up on whatever drugs he was on, I'd been clear with Jensen that if she was hurt again, it would mean his job.

But she hadn't been hurt, and now that the bodyguards were always around, I didn't expect Jensen, a man in his fifties, to do the work of younger men.

"She wasn't hurt, so we're fine. In truth, the bodyguards I hired are there to protect her more than you are. I still expect you to keep your eyes open for anything suspicious, however, so letting her give you the slip today is a problem."

He hung his head. "I know. I shouldn't have listened to her when she said she was meeting her friend to go shopping. I'm truly sorry, Mr. Stone."

As furious as I was, it wasn't directed at my driver. He was merely someone caught in the middle, and there was no point reaming him out. Reaching out, I patted him on the shoulder. "It's fine, Jensen. No harm, no foul. Just don't let it happen again. I rely on you."

He looked up at me with tired eyes and nodded as relief began to wash over him. "Thank you."

"Where are West and Varo? I want to talk to them too," I asked as I looked around for any sign of them.

"I believe they're around back. They arrived right after we did."

"Okay, relax, Jensen. If Nina and I go out tonight, I'll be driving, so unless something changes, you have the night off."

I followed the brick pathway around the back of the house and across the property to find the bodyguards and hear what they knew about Nina's afternoon adventure. Both men stood near the carriage house where they stayed after my firing of the gardener. Large and bulky, they were exactly what I wanted in the people protecting Nina. They had a bouncer look to them, but as long as they did their job, I didn't care what they looked like.

They stood talking to one another, and a twinge of embarrassment pinched at me as I thought about what I needed to ask them. I suddenly felt like a goddamned fool.

"Gentlemen, I want a report of what happened today."

I spoke with as little emotion as possible, hoping for a matter-of-fact tone to hide the anger and jealousy that continued to churn in my gut. It was bad enough that I knew Nina had gone to see her ex. Having to hear these two tell me the details of it was nothing short of painful.

West was the more talkative one, so he spoke up first. "Miss Edwards left Macy's by a different door than the one she entered through and walked four blocks to an office building on West 39th. She entered the building and rode up to the fifteenth floor to the Peak International offices, an insurance company. She met with a man named Cal Johnson for about twenty minutes and left, returning to the car to ride home."

Talkative for West meant doing the Joe Friday thing—just the facts and little else. He even had that uptight cop look. I was going to have to ask for details.

"Did she look like she'd been harmed? You better hope the answer is no, gentlemen."

Varo, the younger of the two men, shook his head silently, his piercing dark blue eyes staring at me as if he knew what I was getting at, as West continued his report. "She looked the same as when she entered the building, sir. Hair and dress were exactly the same. In addition, she didn't look upset. She looked just as she always does."

"And the person she met with?" I asked with my heart in my throat.

"Average height and athletic build. Brown hair and neither of us noticed the eye color. He seems to be some kind of insurance salesman."

"Did she see you following her?"

Both men shook their heads, and Varo answered for the first time. "She never sees us. She's not looking for us, so we're not seen."

Nothing in what they'd said should have added to my unhappiness with the whole situation, but their answers hadn't helped me feel better either. I waved them away as I walked toward the house to face the final person in this whole affair.

Unfortunately, Rogers was waiting in the foyer, yet another person I had to deal with before I got to Nina. I was definitely not in the mood for his thoughts on my love life at that moment, but his expression looked almost pleasant.

"What do you want, Rogers? I'm in a hurry."

"Just to ask if dinner was to be served at the usual time."

"No. Nina and I are going out."

Rogers nodded slowly. "As you wish."

Behind him on the table in the center of the foyer lay an envelope. It was the same kind I used for her letters and had my name written on the front of it.

"Where is Nina?"

"In her room, I believe."

My hands shook at the thought of what she may have written in the letter. Was this her way of breaking the news to me that she and Cal were back together? Just the idea made me feel empty, like I'd lost everything important to me. Snatching the note from the table, I left Rogers standing there with his semi-smiling face and hurried to my room.

I sat down on the edge of the bed, the note still in my hand. Every time I'd written to her had been to express something I couldn't say to her face— something that was dear to me but I couldn't get out in person. Was it the same for her this time? She'd never shied away from telling me exactly how she felt, so why begin now?

All these questions raced through my mind as I looked down at that white envelope with her handwriting on it.

I wasn't letting her go. It didn't matter what the letter said. I wasn't giving Nina up. Cal couldn't have her back. He didn't deserve her. I didn't even know what he'd done, but I knew he didn't deserve her. Maybe I didn't deserve her either, but at least I loved her. I loved her and I wasn't going to give up on her.

The envelope wasn't sealed and the flap lifted easily, so I slid the letter out and unfolded it. The paper felt heavy in my hands, as if it was a two ton weight I was holding. My eyes focused on the first words, and I began to read.

Dear Tristan,

I didn't think it was fair that you had no letters from me, so I chose this way to say what I have to say. I realized today that even if I knew nothing about you except what I've come to know in the weeks since meeting you in the hospital, I'd know that I'm the luckiest woman in the world. I can't wait to go to our favorite restaurant tonight!

Yours,
Nina

I threw the letter on the bed and raced to Nina's room, overcome with relief from what she'd written. My heart slammed against my chest with excitement as I marched down the hallway to her room, and I stopped short at her door to calm myself before I charged through it like a mad bull. Taking a deep breath, I knocked and pushed the door open to see her sitting on her bed as if she'd been waiting for me.

"Hey, what's up?" she asked sweetly. "Did you get my letter?"

Her smile lit up the room, and I walked to her bedside to pull her into my arms. All the anger and jealousy that had churned inside me for hours disappeared when I held her, as if she was the lone antidote to all my misery.

I kissed her hard on the mouth, not wanting to hold back anything I was feeling for one of the first times since she'd come home. She was my Nina, and I wanted every part of her for mine.

She pulled away and looked up into my eyes. "Tristan, are you okay? I thought you'd be happy with my letter."

Cradling her face in my hands, I kissed her again, softer this time. "I was. Very happy. I liked that you wrote me something."

"Then what's going on? You have this weird look in your eyes. Is something wrong?"

I wanted to hear her tell me where she went that afternoon and what happened. I wanted to believe that she wouldn't keep that from me, but as I stood looking down at her, she said nothing.

"No. I was happy to read your letter and wanted to see you. What made you write it?"

Looking away, she took a deep breath and looked back at me. "I just realized that maybe I am someone you could love."

"Definitely."

"You're home early. Working from home again, Mr. Casual?" she asked as she tugged playfully on my tie.

"Always about my suit and tie. Maybe it's time I changed it up a bit."

"Sweatpants?" She looked me up and down and giggled. "Yeah, I can see it. Grey sweatpants with a mustard stain down the front of them. Maybe a ripped T-shirt?"

Nina's teasing lifted my spirits and I couldn't help but smile. "I'm going to have to work on how you see me. Sweatpants?"

"Well, maybe shorts? You have nice legs. It's something we have in common."

"I think we have other things in common. Did you have a nice shopping trip with Jordan? Are you ready for a great dinner tonight?"

Nina sat down on the bed with a thump and leaned back on her elbows. Eyes wide, she faked an innocent look and ignored my questions. "I swear to God, Tristan Stone, that you're trying to fatten me up. I don't think I've ever eaten this much in my life."

I looked down at her dress as it rode up her thighs, showing just a hint of the top of her stockings. I wanted to hear her answer about her shopping trip, but my need for her overtook my need to hear why she met with another man behind my back. Leaning down over her, I slid my hand up her leg as I balanced on my other forearm. "You look incredible no matter what I feed you." Looking down at my fingers as they slid under her stocking, I said, "I like the way these look."

Nina moaned softly as my fingers traced up her thigh to where it met her body. Arching her back, she groaned, "Oddly enough, I only seem to have these kind of stockings. Would you know anything about that?"

Smiling, I gently pushed my hand between her legs and felt the damp cotton. I slid my middle finger under it to feel her cunt soaked and willing for me. She closed her eyes and licked her lips as I slowly trailed my fingertip from her excited clit to her wet opening.

I loved the feel of her tender skin under my touch. The way her body opened up to take me into her and give me everything she was.

Then, from somewhere deep in my mind, a tiny spike of jealousy tore through me, ripping every gentle feeling from me until all I could think about was Nina with Cal just hours earlier. I pulled away from her and stood up as the knot in my stomach returned and my hands clenched in rage.

Nina opened her eyes and stared up at me in confusion. "Tristan, what's wrong?"

"I have work I have to do. We'll leave at six. No need to dress up. Wear whatever feels comfortable."

Sitting up, she frowned. "Oh. I thought we were going to our favorite restaurant."

Straightening my tie, I nodded. "We are. I'll see you at six."

And with that I left, needing to escape from everything she made me feel. The ecstasy. The pain. And everything in between.

ELEVEN

TRISTAN

I couldn't turn off the feelings just thinking of Nina and Cal created in me, so I did what I always did when I couldn't control my emotions. After an hour run and beating the hell out of the speed bag, I could at least say I'd reined in the worst of the ugliness that had threatened to take me over. I stood in the shower with my head hung as the water streamed down my back until it ran cold, unable to wrestle those final shreds of jealousy and hatred that continued to spin inside my mind. Over and over, I told myself that Nina cared for me. That I wasn't reading her signals wrong.

And over and over the truth that I couldn't shake from my soul raised its ugly head and forced me to admit its existence: she'd snuck away to meet another man and hadn't told me when I'd given her the chance.

My chest felt like a weight was pressing down on it. Every breath I took hurt, as if the simple act of taking air in was all wrong. An emptiness made the pit of my stomach ache as I tortured myself with that same scene of Nina with Cal on his cheap desk.

I knew I couldn't show her this side of me. She'd never love me if she knew my demons. How many times had my shrinks lectured on the need to control my emotions? I'd been more than successful, in my opinion. I kept myself and my heart walled off and life had been good. Well, if not good, at least not painful for me or the rest of the world.

Then Nina came into my life and every emotion she brought out in me seemed magnified. I wanted her. I needed her. She was all I thought about from the moment I found out what Karl and his friends on the Board planned to do. And then I fell in love with her and she became my life.

My brain raced with thoughts about her ex. I hated him, and I didn't even know him. I didn't care. I hated him because he had a place in her mind. She'd let him into her heart once, so why wouldn't she again?

Of all the things I could give her, he had that one priceless thing I couldn't. Her past.

I waited for Nina at the end of her hallway, not knowing what I'd do if she kept her visit to Cal a secret. At six exactly, she opened her door and came toward me in the same dress she'd worn earlier.

When she'd snuck off to meet him.

She stopped dead in front of me and looked me up and down. "You aren't in a suit? I don't think I've ever seen you not in a suit. Well, except when you're not wearing any clothes at all."

A cute blush pinkened her cheeks, making her even more beautiful.

"I don't think jeans and a shirt are anything that different, Nina."

Stepping toward me, she hooked her thumbs in the belt loops near my zipper. "I like this look. Even jeans look incredible on you. You okay now?"

I wasn't okay, but she was too sweet standing there looking up with those beautiful blue eyes for me to shut her out again, so I pushed down my feelings about Cal. "Troubles at work. Nothing to worry about. I'm hungry. I hope you are."

As I turned to walk toward the car, she caught my arm and pulled me back to kiss me. Standing on her toes, she crushed her mouth into mine as she pushed her body against me, exciting me even if I didn't want to want her at that moment. That's what kind of effect she had on me.

When she pulled away for a moment, I asked, "Did you remember something you want to tell me?"

"Yes and no. Let's just say that I'm looking at things between us a little differently now."

I liked this new Nina, but I hoped her change of heart didn't have anything to do with her midday rendezvous. "Really? Anything you want to talk about?"

She kissed me softly and smiled. "First, I want to see our favorite restaurant. After that, who knows?"

I accepted her answer and tried hard to push Cal and all my jealousy away. "Your chariot awaits, my lady."

I'd arranged for Tony's Little Pizza Heaven to be ours exclusively for the night, just in case she remembered something. I didn't want her feeling overwhelmed by a memory and have to deal with the other patrons at the same time.

We walked from the parking lot around to the front of the building, and just as we reached the front door, she took my hand in hers. It was the first time since before the accident, and when I looked down at the sight of her hand so delicate in mine, it seemed so natural, like that's where it belonged.

"I can't wait to see this place!" she said as she looked in the window.

We sat at the same table as the first time we ate there, and I hoped that even that might spur some memory. Nina looked around wide-eyed at the decor as the waitress who'd been there the night I asked her to marry me arrived to take our order. In seconds, I realized I hadn't thought of everything.

Recognizing us, she lowered her order pad and pen, and smiled, her eyes wide with friendly enthusiasm. "I haven't seen you guys in weeks! How are you?"

Nina looked at me, unsure of what to say, and before I could answer, the waitress said to her, "I have to tell you I've told everyone I know about how lucky you are. What he did that night was so sweet. So when's the big day?"

She winced, like she was embarrassed, and I quickly stood from my seat. "Nina, excuse me. I need to speak to the waitress for a moment."

The woman looked even more confused than Nina did as I guided her toward the back room. In a low voice, I whispered, "I'm sorry, but she doesn't know what you're talking about. There was an accident and she suffered a head injury that made her forget a lot of things."

"Oh, sweetie. I'm so sorry. I didn't know. You two were just the nicest couple and what you did that night was so romantic. I just wanted to wish you well."

"It's okay, but she doesn't remember."

The waitress touched my arm in sympathy. "Are you saying she doesn't remember saying yes or she doesn't remember anything at all?"

I looked over at Nina sitting alone and said quietly, "Nothing at all."

"I'm so sorry. I'll get your usual, if that's okay, and leave you two alone. I hope things get better for you real soon."

Taking my seat next to Nina, I saw the sadness in her eyes. Our night out was already a mess.

"I'm sorry about that."

"Tristan, did you make sure we'd be alone here tonight?"

I nodded. "Yeah, but I didn't remember that the waitress who served us before might be here. I'm sorry. I should have thought of that."

She covered my hand with hers and smiled. "That you went to that much trouble is so sweet, but you can't shield me from everyone who may remember more than I do. I appreciate the effort, but you don't have to. I have to accept that people like her remember things I don't."

An uneasy silence settled in between us as Nina slid her hand back to rest in her lap. It felt like we were strangers suddenly, so different from the two people flirting in her hallway just a short while earlier.

The waitress brought our drinks, and we pretended like nothing was wrong, fooling no one. Sitting there drinking semi-flat birch beer, I wondered if we'd ever get past this stage of one step forward and three steps back. Just when I thought we'd turned a corner, we were back to being like strangers again.

"You proposed here?"

"I did. I promise it was more romantic than the time we're having now."

Nina smiled and leaned over toward me to squeeze my forearm. "Don't be so hard on yourself, Tristan. I'm having a great time. I'm here with you and I remember I love pizza, so I'm looking forward to this."

"You're being kind," I said, allowing my disappointment to show.

"Well, you said that was something you liked, right?" she asked with searching eyes.

"I did. Just one of many things."

"Like what? What do you like best about me?"

What I can't give you. Yet.

I brought her hand to my lips and kissed it, looking up at her. "I love your honesty most, Nina. When we grow old and grey and neither one of us looks like we do now, if I have your honesty, that's all I could ask for."

A pained look came over her, and when she turned away, my heart skipped a beat. Something had happened at Cal's office and she just didn't want to tell me. My blood felt like it ran cold in those moments as I waited for her to turn back to face me.

Biting her lip, she looked at me and took a deep breath. "About that. I have something to tell you."

I pasted a smile on my lips as my stomach dropped to the bottom of my body, and I feared that the next words out of her mouth would be to tell me she'd decided that she wanted to be with Cal again. Maybe having a second chance at life had made her want more. Maybe she wanted to rekindle that relationship.

No. I couldn't let her do that.

"You can tell me anything, Nina. Always remember that." Even as the words were leaving my mouth, I silently prayed that she'd never tell me what I feared I'd hear in the next seconds.

"I don't want us to start this relationship again with anything bad between us. I need to tell you about some things."

"Okay."

Nina smiled meekly and began. "I dated a man named Cal long before I met you. When I was with Jordan the other day she told me that he broke my heart by cheating on me the very night I told him I loved him. I guess it sent me into a depression. I didn't know that I ever suffered from depression until she told me."

"Nina, I'd never look down on someone because of that."

"I know. But that's not what I wanted to tell you. I had to know why he could so easily throw me away, Tristan. I had to find out."

I couldn't hold back anymore. "Because he's a fucking idiot. He's not worthy of someone like you, Nina."

Nodding, she continued. "I know. He knows too. I went to meet him at his office today. I didn't tell you because I didn't know how to say I wanted to go see an ex-boyfriend to find out why he didn't love me enough to not cheat on me."

I waited for her to say those next words that would make my world come crashing down around me. That she realized that Cal was the man she wanted, not me. With each second that ticked away, it seemed like an eternity until she finally spoke again.

Her blue eyes filled with tears, and my heart clenched in my chest as she spoke. "Cal was an immature boy back then. He knows that now. It felt so good to hear that, Tristan. All I could think of since Jordan told me what he did was that I was lacking in something that would mean he couldn't love me. But that wasn't the case. It was him, not me. I know that now."

"Nina, it would never be you. You're a beautiful woman with a lot to offer any man," I mumbled as the sound of my heartbeat pounded like a sledgehammer in my ears.

"But I guess I needed to hear Cal say that it wasn't me back then. I needed to hear that so I could believe that someone like you would really ever want me. Do you know what I mean?"

I nodded silently, waiting for her to get to the part where I was supposed to give her up.

"Tristan, you've been so patient with me and I can't thank you enough for that. I know it's been hard on you too. I think it might even be harder on you than on me. Remembering what we were when all I know is what we are now must be so painful. I'm sorry most for that."

Sorry most for that. Her words rang in my ears, like the final shot from a gun right before the bullet slammed into my heart and ripped it to pieces.

Just then, the waitress returned with our pizza, saving me from hearing what else Nina was sorry about. As we ate, I pretended that I was happy to be there and enjoying our time together. Nothing could have been further from the truth. This place that had been the scene of one of the best memories of my life was now just an empty room with us taking up a tiny sad space in it.

Nina enjoyed her return to Tony's, but I barely finished one slice of pizza before I felt too sick to stay. My mind raced with ideas, my demons trying desperately to take over. I could take her away and Cal would never be able to find her. I could make sure Jensen never took her anywhere without me, ensuring she never left. I could work at home from now on so I was always there to make sure she stayed.

"Tristan, you're so quiet. I thought you loved this place, but you only ate one piece of pizza. Are you okay?"

"I'm fine. Let's finish up and get out of here."

She was obviously surprised by my desire to leave what I'd described as our favorite place. Now it was just another place I remembered being in love and she didn't.

I threw a couple twenties on the table and stood to leave, but Nina grabbed my arm and I looked down to see her staring up at me with that look that never failed to make me want to take her in my arms and hold her forever. If this was when she planned to tell me goodbye, I'd let her say it and then deal with her hating me because I had to protect her, even if that meant watching her want another man.

"Tristan, I want to finish what I started to say. I went to see Cal today because I needed to know if there was something wrong with me. Ever since I saw you that first time in the hospital, I've doubted that you could ever feel what you say you do for me. It didn't matter how many times you said you loved me. I still felt like I didn't belong with you—that I wasn't good enough."

"Nina, whatever you thought, I need you to know that I'm not going to just give you up. I love you, and you loved me once. And if you loved me then, you can love me again."

Her eyes lit up with surprise. "Tristan, what are you talking about? I'm telling you that I finally believe everything you said. All this time I'd doubted myself, but now I realize I'm not some defective female no one can love."

Every ounce of stress left my body and I slumped back down into my chair. "Defective female? Baby, you are perfect. I don't know what those assholes you dated in the past were thinking, but you're everything I've ever wanted."

Nina leaned over toward me and kissed me gently. "I hope you aren't mad that I didn't tell you I was going to see Cal."

"I wish you would have told me."

"Would you have been okay with it?"

Shaking my head, I said, "No way. I'm never a fan of the woman I love spending time with another man, especially her ex."

"You couldn't actually think that I'd want anyone but you, could you?"

"I think it's time to go."

I stood and stepped back to let Nina out, and she reached up to put her arms around my neck. Standing on her toes, she slid her tongue over my bottom lip, teasing me. "You thought I was going to say something else, didn't you?"

Chuckling, I shrugged off her question. "No. I had no idea what you wanted to say."

She stared up into my eyes for a moment and a sexy little grin spread across her lips. "You just seem happier now. That's all. Seems suspicious."

I pushed the hair away from her face and pressed my forehead to hers. "Did you have anything else you wanted to say?"

A tiny whimper escaped from her mouth and she closed her eyes. "I think I'll save that for when we get home."

"I wasn't thinking of doing much talking when we get home," I said quietly in her ear.

We walked out to the car as rain began to fall, and my mind flashed back to that night in Venice. Covering Nina's hand with mine, I squeezed it and she looked up at me. "The last time you and I were caught in a rainstorm was in Venice."

She stopped short as the rain began to fall harder. "I've been to Venice?" she asked in a stunned voice.

"Yeah. You loved it." I tucked her hair behind her ears and caressed her damp cheek. "That was where I told you I loved you for the first time."

"We fell in love in Venice? That's so romantic!"

Shaking my head, I smiled down at her. "No, I fell in love with you long before Venice. I just didn't tell you."

Nina wiped the rain from her forehead. "Why?"

"I was afraid to say it because I didn't think I could handle it."

"Did I love you before Venice?"

"I don't know."

Chuckling, she stuck her tongue out. "Now you're just playing dumb. I bet I was crazy in love with you before Venice."

An awkward silence came over us. Even if she had been crazy about me, that was then. Now, she wasn't in love with me. Yet. I had to believe that what we'd had before could be again, though.

"Let's get out of this rain. We can continue this at home," I said as I guided her to the car.

She flashed me a devilish grin. "I thought we weren't going to be doing much talking when we got home."

As I opened her car door, I tilted her chin up and kissed her full on the mouth, loving the feel of her lips on mine. "We aren't."

TWELVE

Nina

After standing in the rain staring into each other's eyes in Tony's parking lot, we were both drenched, but I don't think either of us cared. We made out all the way down my hallway, finally stumbling into my bedroom as he slid his hands under my dress to cup my ass. Lifting me, he held me just above his cock as I wrapped my legs around his waist, desperate to feel him inside me.

Tristan lifted his head from my neck and looked over at my bed where the babydoll he'd bought me was laid out. Turning back toward me, he licked his lips and grinned. "I want to see you in that tonight."

God, he could drive a woman insane! There I was, my body ready and waiting for him, and all he could think of was window dressing.

"Really? You want to stop?" I said with a pout.

"I love that on you. I want to see you in it when I fuck your brains out," he groaned against my neck.

"If I put it on, what do I get?" I teased as I rubbed my achy clit against the front of his pants.

"Other than me fucking you like a man on a quest to make you come more times than you ever have?"

I loved it when he talked like this. His voice was so deep and so filled with need, and something in it traveled straight to my core.

"I do like that, but what else? I should get something for putting up with you stopping right in the middle to make me put on a babydoll."

His eyes flashed his desire—or was it something else? With a firm grasp, he cupped my ass and pulled me to him so I could feel the full length of his stiff cock. "You tell me what you want and it's yours."

I couldn't think of a thing I wanted at that moment more than to feel him inside me. I slid my tongue across his bottom lip. "Surprise me."

Tristan lowered me to the floor and as I turned to grab the lingerie from the bed, yanked me back until I was pressed hard against him. In my ear, he whispered heavily, "Don't make me wait long."

I raced to the bathroom and changed, wanting to make a real entrance for him. I wanted so much to make him happy, to be the woman who drove him mad with desire. He had such power over me that with just a word or a glance, he could make me forget all my fears to be what would please him.

As I dressed, I glanced at the mirror, not entirely happy with what I saw. I pushed up my breasts to look more like the woman who'd served us at his club, but the effect wasn't the same. No matter. I was the woman he lived with, the woman he said he loved, I told myself.

When I came out of the bathroom, he was sitting on the edge of the bed, still fully dressed. Confused, I walked toward him. "Is something wrong? You're still dressed."

His brown eyes seemed to dance as he looked at me. "Not a thing. Turn around for me, Nina."

I did as he commanded, twirling the babydoll so the panties beneath showed. When I faced him again, he was staring at me, his eyes focused on mine. He sat there silently while I waited for him to speak, each moment that ticked by making me uncomfortable as his gaze never wavered.

"Tristan?"

He shook his head. "Shhh. Come here."

Taking my hand, he pulled me onto his lap so I straddled him. I pressed my hands to his chest as he slid his finger under the strap on my right shoulder, teasing my skin with his touch. He leaned in to lightly pepper kisses across my collarbone, and I shivered from a chill that ran down my spine.

I wanted him so badly. How he could be so calm and controlled when I could barely contain my need to have him touch every inch of me drove me wild. It was enthralling, sexy, and maddening all at the same time.

My body ached for him to do anything, yet he seemed content to simply watch me as he lightly traced the outline of my babydoll across the top of my breasts. Breathing became next to impossible as I waited for him to do something to ease my need for him.

His cock pressed hard against my excited pussy, and I began grinding slowly against him, wanting so much to feel a sense of release from everything building up inside me. Leaning forward, I tried to kiss him, but he backed away, leaving me lost and frustrated.

Staring up at me, his brown eyes heavy with desire, he pushed down on my hips until our bodies met. Holding me there, he whispered, "I want nothing to come between us, Nina. When I think of you, you're mine. Every inch of you, mine. I want every man who sees you to know you belong to me."

As he spoke, he lifted his hips ever so slightly off the bed to slide his hard cock over my needy clit. His words created a desperation to have him inside me that I found hard to control.

"Yes," I whispered. "I'm yours. Please..."

"Patience, baby. You'll get what you want soon."

I didn't want to be patient. I wanted him to fuck me hard as I rode him until he made my body shake from my release and my limbs felt boneless.

Tugging his shirt, I tried to pull it over his head, but he stopped me and took my hands in his. Holding them above my head with his right hand, he trailed the fingers of his other hand over my breast, lingering on my excited nipple until he squeezed it hard between his thumb and forefinger. I cried out in a mixture of pain and pleasure, unsure of which I felt more.

"Tell me what you want and it's yours. Jewelry, clothes, trips—name it and it's yours," he said with a sexy smile. "I'll give you anything you want."

I didn't care about any of that. For the first time in my life, things I could buy with money didn't matter. I could have anything my heart desired, and none of it meant a damn thing. All that mattered was him. I loved him. I needed him. I couldn't deny him. In just weeks, he'd become everything to me and I wanted to make him see that.

"I want you. I want to feel you inside me as we make love. I want to taste your lips and feel your tongue in my mouth when you kiss me like you can't live without me. I want to hear you moan when I make you come. I don't care about things. It's you I want."

He closed his eyes and spoke in a voice that sounded strained. "I'd give you anything to make you happy. Just the thought of you visiting your ex-boyfriend makes me crazy, Nina. You live here in my house, just feet away from me each night as I lay in bed alone and wanting you so bad it hurts."

When he stopped talking, he opened his eyes and I saw all the need he hid so often. He yearned for the Nina who'd loved him and I could finally give him that. I loved him. I adored him. His happiness was in my hands, and I wanted to be what he loved.

"No more waiting. I want to be yours. Heart and soul. I love you. You're everything to me, Tristan."

For a moment, he sat there perfectly still, like he was frozen in time, but then those gorgeous brown eyes that had haunted me from the first time I saw him gazing down at me as I lay in that hospital bed softened and in them I saw all the emotion he kept hidden inside. I leaned in and kissed him deeply, wanting him to give me those feelings he so rarely showed.

Releasing his hold on my wrists, he slid his hands over my back and pulled me to him. His voice was ragged as he whispered hoarsely, "I love you, Nina. No more distance between us."

"No more," I promised as he let me slide his shirt over his head.

I filled my eyes with the view of his muscular body as he lifted me off him to take off his jeans. Every inch of his body looked hard, like he was in total control of every muscle's movement. My gaze slipped from his broad shoulders, down over his chest with that unusual double snake tattoo, to his rock hard abs. He stepped out of his clothes and as I stood there enthralled with how beautiful he looked, he knelt before me.

"I want to see you," he rasped as he slid his hands up underneath my babydoll. He made quick work of my panties and then moved to pull the straps of the lingerie down as the entire silk and lace top dropped to the floor around my feet.

Tristan licked his lips and looked up at me as I stood naked before him. His hands caressed my hips, and he placed a tiny kiss just below my navel, making my legs go weak from desire. So good at drawing out our lovemaking, he was always in control while I craved him so much I would have raced to the part where he was deep inside me. He was pure seduction, and he drove me wild.

He knew it too.

He drew his fingertip down through my wet slit until he reached my opening. Quickly, he thrust two fingers inside me, and I almost fell to the floor at how incredible my pussy felt filled with any part of him, even if fingers weren't what I wanted.

"So tight," he groaned. "I love how your cunt feels. So wet for me. Do you hear how wet you are?"

"Yessss..." I mewed as he fucked me with his fingers and the pad of his thumb drew delicious circles on my clit.

"Do you know how sexy you look right now?" he asked while his eyes searched my face for how good he made me feel.

It was all too raw, and I closed my eyes to save some part of me from those eyes staring up at me. But he wouldn't let me escape.

"Keep your eyes open, Nina. I want to see every sensation through them. I want to see your soul through them."

I opened them and looked down his body to see his cock standing thick against his stomach. It touched the bottom of his navel, and I yearned to be filled with it instead of his fingers. To feel him push deep into me and retreat, leaving me empty and wanting more, before he filled me again, taking my breath away in the most sublime way.

"Tristan, don't make me wait," I whimpered as he continued thrusting two fingers in and out of me.

"What does my Nina want?" he asked in a voice laced with sex and just a touch of sharpness.

"You. More than just fingers. All of you."

In one swift movement, he slid them out of me and stood to his full height. "I promised you slow and easy the other night."

I palmed his thick cock, wrapping my fingers around it as far as I could, and looked up at him. "Give me slow and easy the second time. Now I want to feel you inside me fucking my brains out, like you promised."

"That I can do," he said in that deep voice I loved as he took me in his arms and pushed me onto the bed.

He held his body over mine and ran his cock through my wet folds, skimming its full length over the tiny bundle of nerves at the top. The feeling was exquisite, a mixture of aching desire and pure pleasure like nothing else in the world.

I reached up to wrap my arms around his neck as he rammed deep into me, nearly taking my breath away. His cock stretched me, forcing me to accept him, as he fucked me just as I'd asked. I wanted to see him stripped of the control that ruled him. I wanted to see the real Tristan Stone.

He groaned next to my ear as his hips flexed back and forth, pistoning his cock into me as I grasped at him to hold on. Our sex was animalistic, but I loved watching him shed the veneer of civility he wore around everyone, including me.

My body was his to do with as he pleased with no fight from me. Even if I wanted to resist, I couldn't. I craved his touch, the feel of his body invading mine as he made me his completely.

"God, you feel so fucking good," he moaned into my ear as he buried his head in the pillow next to me.

"Don't stop," I cried out when he slid out of me and didn't return. "Please, Tristan."

"Roll over, baby. I want to watch your face as I fuck you this way."

I flipped over onto my stomach and raised myself onto my hands and knees. Looking up, I saw the image of us in the mirror above the dresser—him kneeling behind me in control of our pleasure and me smaller in front of him and his to take as he chose.

He pressed his body against my back and tenderly wrapped his hand around my throat, his lips grazing my earlobe as he spoke. "Don't take your eyes off the mirror, Nina. Watch me as I fuck you."

I waited to feel him enter me again, anticipating how it would feel in this position and wondering if we'd made love like this before. His cock nudged into me slowly, like sweet torture, until he was fully seated inside my body. With his hand still around my neck, he began stabbing into me, creating the most incredible sensations with each thrust in and each pull out.

In the mirror, he watched me watch him, his gaze never wavering as he stroked in and out of me. He was power and desire personified, and I couldn't get enough of him. I pushed against his cock, eager for him to move faster, and he met my silent desire for more, fucking me faster and harder.

His body crashed hard against my ass, pushing me forward on the sheets, but I leaned back, guided by his hand around my neck. The sensual sounds of our lovemaking filled the room—his moans and mine, the slapping of skin as our bodies met each time he entered me. He snaked his arm around my waist and pulled me upright, changing the angle of his cock and sending my body into overdrive as he continued to fuck me.

I watched in the mirror as he slid his finger over my clit, making my thighs quiver as my orgasm began deep inside me. I was so close and only needed just a little more. One more thrust of his cock inside me. One more touch of his finger on my clit. One more delicious moan of my name in my ear.

"Come for me, Nina. Let me feel you surrender to me."

His hand tightened around my throat, and I came so hard I was afraid I might collapse if he wasn't holding me to him. I heard him groan and just as I was sure I couldn't take anymore, he thrust his cock into me one last time and came, sending jets of hot liquid deep inside me.

He held me close until our bodies finally calmed and kissed me softly on the cheek. "I love you, Nina. Thank you."

He slid out of me and eased me down onto the bed, taking me in his arms. I looked down our bodies to see our legs entwined as if we were one. With my head on his chest, I heard his heartbeat slowly return to a normal rhythm. I'd never felt so relaxed and safe in my life.

"Tell me your favorite memory," I whispered against his skin.

"Right now," he said. "I've never been happier than right now."

"Even when we were together before?"

Tristan sweetly pressed a kiss on the top of my head. "Every day is better than the last one. No matter how happy I was then, I'm even happier now."

I lifted my head from his chest and looked up at him. "Why?"

"Because we've been given a second chance. Not everyone gets that in life. I've gotten it twice now."

"What was the first time?"

A look of sadness settled into his face. "When I didn't die and the rest of my family did."

"I'm sorry. I didn't know. Well, you know what I mean."

He nodded and forced a smile. "It's okay. I understand."

I looked down at the tattoo on his chest and traced the outline of the two snakes that formed an inverted heart over his left pec, lingering on the place where they joined at a point. "What's this tattoo mean?"

"I got it after the accident. A metal rod pierced me just above the heart there where the scar is and continued to run through my brother's heart, killing him. It symbolizes our twin hearts joined even in death."

"I'm so sorry, Tristan. Were you identical twins?" I asked, hoping to lighten the mood slightly.

"Yes. We looked the same. Many people couldn't tell us apart, unless they knew us. But we were like night and day otherwise."

I heard something in his voice—a change in tone or a hitch that told me their differences weren't as simple as that. "Who was older?" I asked with a smile, knowing how silly the question was.

Tristan returned my smile with a tiny one of his own. "Taylor was by seven minutes. He never let me forget that he was my older brother either."

"I've always wondered what it would be like to have a sister my same age. Kim is six years older and we've never really been close. Those six years were always between us."

"It's like having any other sibling, just that you look exactly like another person."

His voice trailed off as his sentence ended, and I got the surest sense talking about his brother was painful for him. I didn't want to ruin our time together, so I hastily changed the subject. "Did you get the tattoo on your arm after that one on your chest?"

He looked down at his left arm and shook his head. "No, that one is from those days before I became the man I am now I told you about. My wilder days."

That was a topic I wanted to hear more about. "And about this wilder days guy, was he really different from the Tristan of now?"

He hesitated a moment before he answered. "Yeah, a lot."

I was nothing if not inquisitive, and this sounded like a mystery. "Tell me about him. I can't imagine you were that different than you are now."

"I can barely remember him anymore. He wasn't anyone you'd want."

"I can't believe that, Tristan," I said and kissed him.

His face told me he was uncomfortable. "You should. That man wasn't someone who would deserve someone like you."

"I probably would have been crazy about that man and he wouldn't even have known I existed is more likely."

Turning toward me, he lifted my chin with his forefinger. "Then he'd have been an ass not worthy of your time."

"Tell me about those wilder days, Tristan. I want to imagine you as the type of guy you were then."

Instead of telling me anything about his bad boy days, he rolled me onto my back and pinned my hands above my head. He loomed over me, his deep brown eyes staring down into mine, and said in a low voice, "I've got something far better in mind."

By the time I woke in the morning, Tristan was gone and I saw through the window that snow was falling, covering the grass and making it finally look like winter. My room was still warm, though, and my thought of venturing outside to go to visit Jordan suddenly seemed like something for another day.

Thoughts of the Atlanta suite filled my head, so after lying around enjoying memories of my time with Tristan just hours before, I finally crawled out of bed to face the day. Throwing my robe around me, I knew he'd be long gone at work, but I walked to the kitchen for my morning coffee with the hope that he'd be there to join me for breakfast.

Disappointment washed over me as I rounded the corner and saw no one there. I understood a man like him had to be a slave to his work, but always waking up alone in bed made me feel as I was something extra in his life, like an addition he didn't need.

I was being silly. I knew Tristan loved me, and the wonderful life he offered didn't come easily for him. Being CEO of Stone Worldwide was a twenty-four hour a day job, if the phone calls and emails he received at all hours of the day and night were any indication. That we got to spend any time alone at all was something I should appreciate instead of whining to myself about waking up alone.

The French Vanilla roast in my mug began to work almost immediately, and I was wide awake in no time. Grabbing a sesame bagel Rogers had brought home from the local bakery, I headed back to my room to get ready for my day of research for Atlanta.

THIRTEEN
TRISTAN

"Mr. Stone, Mr. Dreger is here."

Ten o'clock. Karl was getting a late start to his daily stalking today. I looked over at the speaker on the edge of my desk and groaned. No day was a good day to deal with him, but after the night I'd just spent with Nina, I didn't want him to ruin how good I felt.

The man himself opened my office door and without even being asked in made himself at home on the leather couch on the side wall. A big man, his scalp showed more of his large bulbous head every day, and he seemed to be gaining weight in exchange for the loss of his hair. The seams of his suit pulled, as if at any moment it was going to give way and cease to hold back the girth it was containing.

I crossed my arms and leaned back in my chair. "Karl, what can I do for you today?"

"You know what I'm here about. It's the same thing every day. Your time is running out. We've been patient, son."

"Don't call me son, Karl. My name is Tristan Stone. My father was Victor Stone, not you. So remember who the fuck you're talking to."

"Fine. And you remember who the fuck you're talking to, Tristan. You aren't all-powerful at Stone Worldwide. The Board has power too."

I knew he was baiting me, but I took it all the same. "Power to do what? This company has never seen better days. Everyone's making money, Karl. Are you saying the Board isn't happy about that?"

"You know what we're unhappy with. If you don't want all this to come to a screeching halt, you have to take care of the loose ends. She can't continue to be a risk to this business."

Ten o'clock in the fucking morning and I already had a splitting headache, thanks to this asshole. Pinching the bridge of my nose, I repeated to him what I'd said so many times it was like the words were tattooed on my tongue. "Karl, she has nothing. She knows nothing. She would never do anything to hurt me, and that includes anything that would hurt this company."

"And what happens when she finds out the truth? What happens if she finds out that her father died because he couldn't keep his damn nose out of other people's business?"

"She knows her father's dead. Why would she find out anything about how he died? That was years ago. There's no reason for her to go digging about it. It will remain as it always has—an unsolved murder. So you and the Board can rest easy. Nina cares nothing about that."

Karl lurched off the couch and moved to stand in front of my desk. "You don't have any silly romantic plans to tell her yourself, do you? You can't imagine that would be a good idea."

I nonchalantly pushed a pen back and forth across the top of my desk, praying to God my plans to confess everything to Nina weren't written all over my face. After her show of honesty about Cal the night before, I didn't want to go on lying to her anymore. I could make her understand that no matter what my father had done to hers, we could be happy together. I knew I could.

"If you're done with your daily visit, feel free to let yourself out, Karl. And don't feel the need to come back tomorrow. Nothing is going to change. Nina is the woman I love—the woman I intend on marrying—so she's going to stay a part of my life."

"Son, you're not going to win this. We helped your father build this company into the gem you now get to claim as yours, so we won't be cut out."

"Nobody's trying to cut you out, Karl. You and the Board members are safe."

He sneered at my comment, and in a flash, my patience was all used up. Standing from behind my desk, I approached him until we stood toe-to-toe. "I'm going to warn you just once, Karl. If I get the sense that you or any of your friends in this even think about going through with your plans to hurt Nina, I'll kill you myself. I'm not like you old men who won't get their hands dirty. So remember that when you go back to them today. Let what happened with Victor Stone and Joseph Edwards end with their deaths."

Karl chuckled, but I heard the nervousness in his voice when he spoke. "Your father always said you were the one not to cross. Everybody thought Taylor was the piranha, but your father believed otherwise. I guess he wasn't wrong. Fine. You should know, though, that this isn't over."

I turned away from him and waved him off. "Yes, it is."

He stormed out, barking something at Michelle as he passed her desk, while I thought about his comment about my father. Never close to me, my father had always favored Taylor. They'd sit for hours talking about business, sharing his favorite brandy and smoking cigars in his study as they plotted their takeover of some helpless company one of them had spied in distress that day.

That world had never appealed to me. Even now, I remembered the stink of their cigars as I passed that room on my way out at night, never asked to join them and happy for it. They were like strangers I was oddly related to but had nothing in common with. I couldn't imagine sitting around in leather high backed chairs playing like some captain of industry in their private, real life game of Monopoly.

I wasn't a saint, but I wasn't the kind of men they were. Maybe it was because I'd never wanted this. I was happy living a life of excess and good times, hurting no one but myself. Well, that wasn't exactly true, but I certainly wasn't guilty of the things my father and brother were.

"Mr. Stone, Mr. Knight is here to see you," Michelle announced over the speaker, tearing me from my daydreams about the past.

What was Daryl doing here today, a day early? "Send him in, Michelle."

I prepared myself for Daryl's report on Nina's ex and more importantly, what had happened with her father. Daryl came in with a bounce in his step he always had, like the world's biggest leprechaun, and took a seat in one of the chairs in front of my desk.

"Tristan, I know I'm a day early, but I thought you'd want this information ASAP."

My heart pounded against my chest at the thought that Daryl was about to tell me something about Cal and Nina. I took a swig out of my water bottle and sat back in my chair as I worked to calm my nerves. "What did you find out?"

"Which do you want first, loverboy or the father?"

"Give me the information on Cal Johnson first," I answered with a lump in my throat.

Daryl reached into his suit coat and pulled out a notepad. Looking up at me, he smiled. "Loverboy it is. Let's just say your guy has gotten around. I don't know how he does it, but on what amounts to a clerk's salary, this guy has seen more ass than a toilet seat."

Fucking fantastic. This day was just getting better and better. Forcing a smile onto my face, I said, "Love the way you describe things, Daryl. What are we talking about this for?"

"I thought you wanted to know who he was fucking."

Leave it to Daryl to make this amusing. I had said I wanted to know that, but only because I was afraid the answer would be Nina. Chuckling, I said, "Okay, is he fucking anyone interesting?"

"Not in your league, but he does like women who have money. He's piss poor, but the women he sleeps with aren't."

"What is he, some kind of Casanova, Daryl?" I asked, sure my jealousy was obvious.

"Not as far as I can tell. Used to be some kind of college athlete. Rugby or something like that. Now he's just some guy who runs numbers at an insurance company."

"Then I doubt he's piss poor. Actuaries make good money. I think your detective skills are getting rusty, Knight."

Daryl raised his eyebrows at the joking insult. "You didn't let me finish. He used to make good money at the firm he worked at before this one, but he was fired under a cloud of suspicion that he'd stolen from the company. As far as I can tell, he didn't steal money but was sleeping with the boss's wife. He hasn't been able to get a decent job since. This one at Peak International appears to be a favor from one of his college profs."

So Cal was a philandering dick. I wasn't surprised. From what Nina had told me about him, I hadn't expected much better.

"Does he have a girlfriend now?"

"None that I can find, but he's left a long line of girls behind him. Did you know one of them is the daughter of the man whose murder you have me investigating, Nina Edwards?"

"Yes," I answered, adding, "Nina is my fiancée."

"Ah, I get it. Well, from what I can tell, she's not with him now. I can watch him to see if they still speak, assuming you don't think they do."

"I know they've met once recently. I don't think they'll be meeting again."

Daryl grinned and shrugged his shoulders. "Okay, but it's not a big deal to watch him for a little while."

I thought about it and even though I knew I shouldn't, I nodded my silent agreement to watching Cal Johnson.

"Okay, onto bigger fish than our boy Cal. This Edwards thing is going to get ugly, Tristan. I just want to warn you. The daughter's your intended and what I'm finding out is bad. I don't know if you're ready for this."

I leaned forward and planted my elbows on the desktop. "If you're going to tell me you know who murdered Nina's father, let me save you the effort. My father had Joseph Edwards killed. I just don't know why."

Daryl twisted his face into a scowl. "You could've told me that when you set me on this. Christ, I thought I was going to have to tell you that your own father was responsible for the guy's death."

"I know all too well what Victor Stone was capable of, Daryl. Joseph Edwards wasn't the first person he had disposed of, and he might not even have been the last. My father was every bit the monster you're going to tell me he was."

Shaking his head, he frowned. "I don't have all the details yet. All I know is that he was behind it. I haven't found out exactly why yet, but I do have one piece of information I'm planning on acting on."

"And that is?"

"There's a storage facility in Plymouth Meeting, Pennsylvania that Joseph Edwards stored things in a week before his death. It's in his wife's name, though. Seems she's been dead for years and he had her belongings stored there, but it's interesting that he'd visit it right before he died. I think there might be something useful there."

"Has anyone opened the storage unit since then?"

"No," Daryl said, shaking his head. "The guy at the storage facility said that their records show it wasn't opened for years and then one day Edwards came and opened it just once. That was a week before he was murdered. Since then, it hasn't been opened even one time. My guess is that your fiancée doesn't know it's there."

Or she didn't remember it was there, even if she had known about it. I doubted she had since it was simply a place her father had kept her mother's things after her death. There would be no reason to tell her about it since she was so young when she died. But did her sister know about it, I wondered.

"When are you planning to go out there? I want to know what you find."

"I can go anytime you want. I was planning to wait until after the holidays, but if you like, I can go sooner."

"I don't want to wait, Daryl. Get out there tomorrow and find out what's in there."

"Okay, tomorrow I can do. I'll take a nice drive out of the city and do my best Storage Wars impression. Christ, I have to admit I'm never a fan of digging around these storage units. I think it's ever since that scene in Silence of the Lambs. I'm always afraid I'm going to find some head in a jar. Remember that scene?"

"Yeah," I answered absentmindedly as I thought about what he might find in Joseph Edwards' storage unit. Daryl continued to ramble on about dismembered bodies and other grotesque oddities he'd heard about being found in storage facilities, but I wasn't paying attention. He had a tendency to go off on tangents like that, so I'd learned to just wait until he was finished. Ordinarily, I wouldn't give someone that much leeway, but Daryl was a decent guy, even if he was a little weird.

I stood from my desk and held out my hand to shake his, a not-so-subtle sign I was ready for him to leave. Daryl took the hint and stood to go, still mumbling about the things he could imagine uncovering the next day.

"Call me as soon as you get in. I want to know everything you find," I said as I escorted him out toward Michelle.

"You got it. Talk to you then."

Dinner was ready at five when I got home, but Nina was nowhere to be found. I quickly hunted down Jensen, but he hadn't driven her anywhere all day. West reported that she hadn't left, but he did think he'd seen her on the grounds within the hour. The snow that had been falling all day had tapered off, but it was getting colder now that the sun had gone down. I called her cell phone three times, but it went directly to voicemail. Frustrated, I stuffed my phone back in my pocket and set off to find her without even grabbing my coat, scared something might have happened to her.

The doctors had warned me that she may act abnormally at times because of her head injury, so immediately I was concerned about her walking the grounds since she'd never spent any time outside, as far as I knew. I hurriedly walked around the house and then headed out toward the gardens, finally catching a glimpse of her as I rounded the first stand of hedges.

"Nina! Wait up!"

She turned and waved at me, giving me the sense that she wasn't out there for any dangerous reason. I jogged over to her and saw she was dressed for the cold weather, so at least she wasn't wandering around half-clothed unsure of where she was or what her name was.

"It's freezing out here, Tristan. Where's your coat?" she asked in a worried voice.

"I'm looking for you. Why are you out here?"

"I was feeling cabin fever inside after working all day. I was going to go into the city to see Jordan, but I decided not to. When it stopped snowing, I figured I'd take a stroll around and see what the rest of the place looks like. It's nice out here."

She seemed okay and was making sense, so I guessed she wasn't having some episode from her injury like the doctors had described. "It's cold out here. Let's go inside."

Nina held out her hand to take mine, and we walked back to the house together as she described her day researching pieces for the Atlanta property. It was moments like these that erased all the bad of my days—everything with Karl, the job I had Daryl doing for me—and made me feel as if things were going to be okay between Nina and me, no matter what came our way.

I took her coat as we entered the house and felt for her cell. Sitting in her pocket, it showed no calls at all. One of the disadvantages to living out in the country.

"How was your day at work? I was so busy talking about my day I didn't even ask how yours went," she said as we sat down to dinner.

"Same as always. Just another day at work," I answered, knowing it was a half-truth but preferring her to believe that my days were like hers instead of the nightmare that they were.

We ate and then laid in each other's arms after as we watched one of her chick flicks I hadn't wanted to deprive her of again. As if the universe had chosen to give me a sign, Nina picked a film about some woman dealing with the death of her mother. I watched and patiently waited until it was over to ask her about her own mother's death, my conversation with Daryl weighing heavily on my mind.

"Does watching something like this make you think of your mother?"

Shaking her head, she said it didn't, but I saw it did. The woman in the film had died of cancer. Had hers?

"What happened to your mother, Nina?"

Cuddling up next to me, she quietly said, "She died of leukemia. It was fast, I think. I was so young I don't really remember, but my father told me she didn't suffer. They diagnosed her and a few weeks later she was gone."

The sadness in her voice made my breath catch in my throat. I'd always thought that losing my mother the way I did was better than watching her fade away for months or years, but I could tell by what Nina said that it wasn't that way for her. Maybe because she'd had so little time with her mother. At least I'd gotten most of my life with mine.

I kissed the top of her head and hugged her tight. "I'm sorry. I know it hurts."

"Even after all this time, it still does. I sometimes think of what it would be like if she was still here."

"I know. I think the same thing about my mother. What would she think of me now?" I wondered out loud.

Nina lifted her head and smiled. "She'd think you're an incredible success with a great girlfriend."

"At least the second part," I said, unsure if anything I'd done could be considered a success.

"You would have liked my mother. She was sweet and kind. My father used to say I was just like her. Were you more like your mother or your father?"

"My mother, I guess. Taylor was always closer to my father, so I naturally gravitated toward her."

As she curled up closer to me, Nina whispered, "Then I would have liked her."

We laid there silently thinking about the people we'd lost, good and bad, and for the first time in a long time, I missed my mother. I rarely thought of her, something that my shrinks always considered to be a serious problem. They'd always talked about the need for me to mourn her, but I had mourned her. Just not the way they wanted me to.

Nina fell asleep on my chest as I remembered the last time my mother and I talked alone just days before the plane crash. She'd been upset about my unwillingness to do anything but party and sleep around, not that she knew the full extent of either activity in my life. I'd pushed her off with my usual ability to charm her as I always had as her favorite. I saw in her face the worry that I'd never grow up and be the man she believed I could be or find someone to spend my life with.

My mother sat alone at the dining room table with three empty place settings. I had no idea where my father and Taylor were instead of sitting with her for our traditional Sunday afternoon dinner, but I'd just rolled out of bed a half hour before and wanted nothing more than something to bring me back to life after a night of partying till dawn. One thing was for sure. Sunday dinner around the family dining table wasn't it.

She looked up at me as I entered the room, her big brown eyes telegraphing she wanted to talk to me. I knew what she wanted to say. It was always the same.

"Tristan, come sit with me. I want to talk."

"I'm just grabbing a roll and heading out, Mom. Maybe when I get back."

"Tristan Ryder Stone, I want to speak to you."

Anytime my mother used my middle name and said anything in that choppy tone, I knew there was no escaping whatever she wanted. Sighing, I hung my head and pulled out a chair at one of the empty places.

"I'm concerned about you, sweetheart. You're twenty-four now. I realize you're not like your brother, but you can't stay a boy forever."

If she knew what I did with my nights, she wouldn't call me a boy. With a charming smile, I said, "Okay, Mom."

"Tristan, it's time you grew up. Again, I'm not saying you have to be just like Taylor, but your father and I are concerned that you don't seem to have any direction, other than toward parties and girls. I want to see you settled and happy."

"My father's concerned?"

I knew by the look that crossed her face that it was only she who was worried about me and my nightly behavior. I wasn't even sure my father knew I existed most of the time, even though we lived in the same house.

My mother reached out to touch my hand. I looked down at her long manicured nails that screamed opulence and then up at her face to see those big brown eyes once again fixed on me.

Two could play at that game.

"I'll settle down when I meet the perfect woman. You wouldn't want me to settle for anything less, would you?"

Now it was her turn to sigh. My usual answer never satisfied her. "Tristan, I want to believe that you mean that and you aren't just playing on my emotions."

"Who, me? Your favorite son? I wouldn't do that," I said, oozing the charm that never failed to work on her.

I rose from the table and leaned over to kiss her cheek. "Don't wait up. I might spend the night in the city."

She said nothing but simply smiled at me as I turned to leave. I felt her stare on my back as I walked out, but I didn't turn around. There was no point. We both knew that.

I watched as Nina snored lightly on my chest and stroked her soft hair. For whatever it was worth, I'd finally figured out that my mother was right. I just hoped she could see that at least she'd been wrong about me finding someone to love.

FOURTEEN
TRISTAN

I chose a tie and closed my bedroom closet door. "Jensen, I want you at my office at quarter after nine exactly," I instructed him as I fixed my tie. "Michelle will have a package for you. I want you to bring it back here and give it to Rogers. He'll know what to do with it."

"Yes, Mr. Stone."

"Tell Rogers to come here. I need to talk to him."

As Jensen left, I dialed Daryl's number, hoping to catch him before he took off for Pennsylvania. I'd thought about that storage unit all night and didn't want him rummaging around in it, an unfeeling stranger rifling through Nina's mother's things.

"Tristan? How are you this morning?"

"Plans have changed. I want you to keep an eye on Cal instead of heading out to Plymouth Meeting. Text me address of the storage facility."

"You sure you want to do that? You usually have me do the dirty work."

At that moment, Rogers appeared in my bedroom doorway. "Daryl, you stay in the city. And call me if you see anything I might want to know about."

"You got it. Enjoy your day trip."

I put away my phone and turned my attention to Rogers. "Jensen will have a package for Nina. Make sure she gets it as soon as she gets up. I want you to give her this note also."

"Will you be going out of town, Tristan?"

Looking up from my letter, I shot Rogers a glare. "Taking to eavesdropping now?"

"Not in the least. I just happened to hear part of your conversation, sir."

I wasn't in the mood for his attitude this morning, so I ignored his use of sir again and read over my letter to Nina.

Dear Nina,

You looked so cute lying there all curled up in bed that I didn't have the heart to wake you up, but I had to leave on an emergency business trip. I hope you like your new phone. Text me when you get this letter, and I'll call you this afternoon.

Think about me. I'll be thinking about you. Miss you already.

Love,
Tristan

Folding the note in half, I slipped it into an envelope and handed it to Rogers. "Make sure she gets this."

"Are there any other instructions?"

I put on my suit coat and adjusted my tie in the mirror. "I don't know if I'll be home in time for dinner, so make sure Nina gets whatever she wants. I expect to hear that she was happy. Are we clear?"

Rogers' expression showed his hurt at my comment. "I would never do anything to foster Nina's unhappiness, Tristan."

I didn't entirely believe that, but I wasn't going to stand there and debate the issue with him. "Just make sure, Rogers. I'll call you to let you know if I'll be home for dinner."

As I walked past him to leave, he asked, "Is she allowed to leave the grounds?"

Sighing in frustration, I stopped and turned toward him to see that same hurt expression still on his face. "She's not a prisoner here, Rogers. I've had enough of this. I'm doing my best to make things right. Just give me a break."

I didn't give him a chance to respond. I didn't care what he thought. I didn't care what anyone thought but Nina. She was the only one I owed any explanation to.

Daryl had texted me the address of the storage place right before I left, and less than two hours later I pulled up in front of U-Store on Chemical Road in Plymouth Meeting. The clerk behind the counter was barely out of his teens and still working through an acne phase, so he was easy to get by. He also didn't seem to have any knowledge of the law whatsoever, so all I had to do was tell him I was Joseph Edwards' son and I'd lost my key to my mother's unit and he was happy to oblige.

We walked past a dozen green garage doors until we reached the last one in Row 8. The clerk unlocked the door and turned to me with a smile. "If you need anything else, Mr. Edwards, just let me know."

I looked in and saw the 10 x 10 unit wasn't packed to the ceiling, thankfully. Stacks of boxes four high lined the three walls, but it was organized so someone could walk easily through the middle around a few chests and belongings that weren't in boxes.

Now that I was standing in the middle of Nina's mother's things, I suddenly realized I didn't even know her name. All I knew was that she was the woman who'd given birth to the one person I loved in the world and she'd died when Nina was young. Her life was now only memories and her things stored in a dark storage unit.

A feeling of guilt came over me as I looked at her entire life around me. I was an intruder, a stranger about to search her things for something that had never had anything to do with her. It was like I was ransacking a grave for my own benefit.

I had to remind myself that I wasn't there just for me. If I didn't find the evidence of my father's actions that Karl and his friends were sure Joseph Edwards had hidden somewhere, they'd never leave Nina and me alone.

The first box I chose solved the mystery of what Nina's mother's name was. Written on the box were the words *Diana's Clothes*. That one had nothing but clothes in it, so I moved to a second box filled with pictures. I stood there as the photographs I looked at told the story of her life. Her in a 1960s bikini at the beach. When she was pregnant with Nina's sister and sitting at a picnic table on a beautiful sunny day. Diana at an art show standing next to a sculpture with a blue ribbon on it. Nina's parents kissing under the mistletoe at a Christmas party.

I stared for a long time at the picture of Joseph and Diana Edwards, wondering how they'd met and if they were happy. They looked like two people in love. Her hair was long, much longer than Nina's, and darker brown. She was beautiful like her daughter, and Joseph Edwards was a good looking man. A good six inches taller than his wife, he had dirty blond hair. I noticed these things randomly as my eyes remained riveted to that picture.

My phone vibrated in my coat, and I pulled it out to see a text from Nina. *I love my new phone! I'll finally be able to call out here. Wish you were here to thank. :) Love you. Come back soon.*

Her text made me smile, but as I looked around at where I was, I wondered if she'd still love me if she knew what I was doing. I couldn't think about that, though. If this was what I had to do to keep her safe so we could have a life together like those two people in the picture had, then I'd do it.

I texted back *Miss you. Wish I was there with you right now. I'll try to get back tonight. I love you* and put my phone away to get back to work, wanting more than ever to get back to her.

Within two hours, I'd rummaged through the three walls of boxes and found nothing that appeared to be related to Joseph Edwards' work or his investigation into anything concerning my father or Stone Worldwide. Turning to the middle of the storage unit, I began to look through more boxes, but these were filled with art materials like paintbrushes and sculptor's tools, along with paints, clays, and stone. Diana Edwards had been an artist like her daughter, but I suspected she wasn't a painter but a sculptor. Stainless steel tools and finished clay and stone sculptures of animals, mythological creatures, and people filled a chest that sat next to an artist's easel.

I wondered if Nina knew her mother had been an artist. That she was very much her mother's daughter. Hopefully, someday I'd get to tell her what I knew without sounding like some crazy stalker guy.

Even though I was sure I wasn't going to find anything I was looking for amongst everything in the sculpture boxes and chest, I inspected each tool and piece of sculpture the best I could without harming Diana Edwards' art. Finally, after I'd looked at every item, I saw at the bottom of the chest sat a wooden box with the initials DE carved into the top. Kneeling on the cold ground, I opened the box and found a set of stone carving chisels. Just as with the other tools, they had no identifying marks or symbols on them, other than the name of the company that made them.

I'd looked through every inch of that storage unit and found nothing. Disappointed, I sat down on the ground next to the chest and hung my head. I'd hoped that I'd be able to find some shred of evidence to give to Karl so Nina would finally be safe, but there'd been nothing. I'd failed.

Diana Edwards' chisel set box was still in my hands, and I traced the outline of her initials as I sat there feeling lost as to what I was supposed to do next. Maybe Daryl had another lead. Maybe there really was nothing to show what Nina's father had found out. I sighed from the weight of this entire thing with Karl and his insistence that there was evidence out there that could do them all in. What had begun as disgust at my father's actions had snowballed into a problem that I thought of day and night and still hadn't figured out how to solve.

As I slowly traced her initials over and over, my finger moved the lid of the box to reveal an inset that could be removed. Tipping the box over, I tapped the lid and the center came out, leaving a small compartment open where a key and a slip of paper sat. The key had no name or clue as to what it opened, but the paper had written on it one word: Fidelity.

Quickly, I typed into my phone the words fidelity and Plymouth Meeting, getting two results that might be useful. There was a First Fidelity Bank and a Fidelity Securities in that very town. Looking down at the key, I saw it had no grooves like an ordinary house key or basic lock key. It was a safe deposit box key.

Had Joseph Edwards left a key for his daughters to find something important in a safe deposit box at a nearby bank in the event of his death? I could only hope that was the answer, but since Nina and her sister were his only children, there was no way I was going to convince a bank to allow me access to the box, even if I had the key. A young kid working part time at a storage unit facility was one thing, but a bank manager was going to be harder to fool.

I stuffed the key and the paper into my pocket and called Daryl. If I could find out more information about Kim's husband, I might be able to get the bank to let me see what was in that box.

"Hey, Tristan, how was your trip to Pennsylvania?"

"Daryl, I need the name of Joseph Edwards' son-in-law. He's married to Nina's sister Kim."

"Hang on. I think I have that somewhere. Give me a minute."

As I waited for Daryl to flip through the notebook he carried with him at all times, I walked out into the sunlight, shocking my eyes after all that time in that small room full of the remnants of Diana Edwards' life. Pulling the door down, I turned to walk toward my car and prepared to drive to the closest of the two banks.

"Sorry, I knew I had it written down, but I couldn't find it. His name is Jeff Hopkins."

"Okay, thanks Daryl."

"What's up, Tristan? What are you doing?"

"I'm going to pretend to be Jeff Hopkins. I found a safe deposit key I think might help give me the answers I'm looking for."

"Whoa, before you go off and do whatever the hell you're planning to do, maybe you should know something else about him other than his wife's name.

They have two kids—two girls—named Emily and Sarah. You know the guy's a lawyer, right? So if you're planning to say you're him, you need to keep this stuff in mind."

"Right. Kim's the wife, Emily and Sarah are the daughters, and he's a lawyer. How old are the kids?"

Daryl was silent for a moment. "Six and eight, I think."

"You think?" I asked as I got into the car.

"Sorry. I didn't spend a lot of time on anyone but Edwards' daughters."

"Okay, Daryl. I have a hunch I found something here. I'll let you know."

"You sure you want to do this, Tristan? I can be out there in no time and handle things. That's what you pay me for."

"No, I'm here already and I can do it. How hard can it be to pull off being a lawyer?"

Daryl laughed at my attempt at humor. "You might have to convince them not because you don't look like you could be a lawyer but because you're wearing a suit no small town lawyer could afford."

"Point taken. I'll keep it mind, just in case."

"Just remember this. People are more willing to do things for people who sweet talk them. Use some of that charm I know you have and hope you get a woman at the bank to help you. Also, pray you aren't going to a bank where they'd actually know this Jeff guy. If they do, you're probably shit out of luck."

"Thanks for the pep talk," I said sarcastically.

"All you have to remember is charm. Let me know if you need help."

I ended the call and started the car, programming the GPS to give me directions to both locations. Fidelity Securities was closest, so I put the car in gear and drove there first. I was lucky enough to have a female employee in her first month on the job wait on me, but when she saw the key she knew it wasn't from her institution. That left First Fidelity.

I could only hope I'd be lucky enough to run into another young woman like the first one.

First Fidelity Bank was just what I'd hoped it wouldn't be. A small building on the corner of Main Street and Park Avenue, it looked like a bank I had for my miniature train set when I was a boy. I parked across the street and prayed to God there would be more than two tellers and a branch manager who knew everyone in town by their first names and what teachers they'd had in high school.

Two steps into the building and I knew I was going to have to work for this one. Three tellers stood at their stations, each one in their fifties or older. One had teased up hair the color of pewter and smiled when she saw me, so she was my go-to girl. Hopefully, the smile meant she was at least friendly.

In my best schoolboy voice, I said, "Hi, I need to get into a safe deposit box." I looked down next to her stack of envelopes and saw her name. Roberta. As my mother always said, "There's nothing as magical as hearing one's name," so I flashed her a smile and added, "Roberta, I'd so appreciate it if you could help me. It would mean a lot to me."

She looked up at me with faded blue eyes and smiled a grandmotherly smile. "Oh, that's easy. All I need is your name and the key."

I let out a sigh of relief and then she added, "And your identification, of course."

Fuck.

Holding the key up for her to see, I said, "My name is Jeff Hopkins and here's my key, but there's a problem. I don't have my ID. I had my wallet stolen the other day when I had to take my daughter to the specialist in Philadelphia, and that's why I need to get into the safe deposit box. That's where my birth certificate is, and I can't get my ID again without it."

"Oh, well, we can't let you into the box without some form of ID, Mr. Hopkins. You don't have any form of identification?"

I was going to have to lay it on thick if this was going to work. Leaning forward, I settled my gaze on Roberta's pale blue eyes and stared deeply into them as I softened my voice. "I can certainly understand, Roberta, but that man who stole my wallet has made that impossible. Is there no way we can get around this? Without that birth certificate, I can't get my driver's license. I've already gotten one ticket after getting pulled over for driving without a license and I can't afford another one, but I need to drive my little girl to the doctors."

This kind of wheedling had never been my strong suit, and I was sure by the look on her face that she wasn't convinced as she sat there staring silently at me. Breaking the connection, I looked down at a picture on her desk of a little blond girl I guessed was her granddaughter and then back up at Roberta with the best pleading look I had. Just when I was sure our silent standoff would end in my defeat, her shoulders sagged and she said with a sigh, "Oh, one time can't hurt."

"Bless you, Roberta. You've just made my day."

As I suspected, she was a God fearing woman and my words only served to convince her she'd done the right thing for a decent soul in need. As I explained that the box was, in fact, my father-in-law's and told her about Joseph Edwards' wish to keep all his family's most important documents safe, she checked his information and located the box. She escorted me to a back room full of metal filing cabinets and I sat down at a conference table in the center of the room.

Roberta returned with the box and placed it in front of me. "I remember Joseph Edwards coming in with his little girl. She was a cute little thing. Nina I think was her name. How is she?"

I smiled at the mention of Nina's name. How was she? I had to keep up the facade of being not Nina's fiancé but her brother-in-law, so I simply said, "She's doing well. She lives in New York now and works as a curator."

Roberta nodded her happiness. "That's so good to hear. Please let me know if you need any additional help, Jeff."

As she walked out to help other bank customers, I quickly turned my attention to the safe deposit box. I would have loved to spend my time thinking about Nina, but I needed to find what Joseph Edwards may have hidden here and then get the hell out of that bank before someone figured out I wasn't who I said I was.

I lifted the metal lid and saw only a notebook sitting there in the bottom of the box. As much as I wanted to read what Nina's father had written about what my father had done, I simply stuffed the tablet inside my coat and left, thanking Roberta as I made my way outside. I hurried to my car with my heart racing at the knowledge that in minutes I might finally know what had started the chain of events that had led to the death of Joseph Edwards and ultimately, my finding the love of my life.

FIFTEEN

Nina

At three o'clock, I looked down at my new phone as it buzzed with a new text. I swiped the screen and saw it was from Tristan. *Probably won't be home for dinner. Make sure Rogers has the cook make you anything you want. Can't wait to see you. Love you.*

Disappointed, I texted back that I missed him and loved him too before I fell back onto the bed in frustration. While I'd loved this house in the good weather, now that winter had finally arrived, I was feeling cabin fever more and more. Being stuck out in the hinterlands in the snow without Tristan was definitely not how I wanted to spend the next few hours.

Well, if I couldn't spend time with the man I loved, then I could spend time with Jordan. We hadn't had a girls' night out since I left the hospital, and one was long overdue. A minute later, her phone was ringing and I was thinking of the perfect place to grab some dinner and drinks.

"Hello?"

"Jordan, it's Nina. This is my new number. Let's get something to eat."

"Are you nearby or out at the house?"

"I'm still at the house, but I can be there in an hour. Sooner, if Jensen is in the mood to drive fast," I joked. "I'd love it if we could get dinner tonight."

Jordan hesitated. "Well, Justin and I were supposed to hang out and watch wrestling tonight, but he won't miss me if I beg off. We better have a good time, though, since I'm missing hot guys beating the hell out of each other."

"Well, I'm not sure I can do better than that. I was just thinking of some good food and drinking these chocolate martinis Tristan introduced me to. They're delicious! You have to try one."

"I'll do dinner, but I'm not a martini girl."

"No matter. It's the company that's important. Can you be ready in two hours? Maybe we can go shopping too."

"I'm just getting out of school now, so two hours will work. Are we being driven around tonight, or is it like old times?"

No matter how much I may have wanted it to be like old times, I'd accepted the fact that Tristan wasn't about to have me driving or taking the subway. All the better, actually, since it was cold and snowy.

"We're going in style, girl. I'll have Jensen honk when we get there," I joked.

"Some date you are," Jordan said with a chuckle. "Okay, I'll be ready in two. See you then!"

I reread Tristan's text to me, focusing on the words *Can't wait to see you. Love you* and wishing he was there next to me as I lay on my bed. I understood now how I'd fallen in love with him the first time. He was like an addiction I never wanted to quit. My spare moments were filled with thoughts of him—how my heart raced when he kissed me, how my stomach did somersaults at the merest touch of his fingers on my body, how his beautiful brown eyes said so much even when he said nothing.

In just this short time, he'd become my everything. I couldn't imagine life without him.

I rolled over to run my hand across where he'd laid the night before, fantasizing about the way we'd made love, his hands so powerful as he held me in place while he thrust into me, so completely in control of every moment of our fucking.

Even now, with him miles away, just the thought our lovemaking caused a need in the pit of my abdomen, and I squeezed my legs together to feel the sweet ache the desire for him created in me.

I grabbed my phone again and texted once more before I got up to get dressed. *Just the thought of you makes me wish you were here in bed with me. When you get home I'm going to show you how much I missed you.*

He didn't text back immediately, so I got into the shower. By the time I finished and had touched up my makeup, he had texted back but only a brief message. *Miss you. You have no idea how much.*

Something in those words sounded so lonely as I read them, so I called him but got no answer. I tried again as I dressed, but still no answer. Hopefully, he'd be home when I got back, but just in case he'd had a terrible day, I wrote him a letter and slipped it under his bedroom door.

I found Rogers in the dining room looking as surly as ever. "I'd like to go to Jordan's. Can you tell Jensen?"

He looked at me as if he were looking through me, and I repeated my question, which only seemed to irritate him. "As you wish, miss," he said sharply as he walked past me out the dining room door.

I stood in that spot unsure of whether I should wait or follow him and wishing Tristan was there to deal with his butler. Maybe there was a good reason he was always so short with him. As I wondered what Rogers had against me, he returned with Jensen, who was always much nicer.

"Miss, I'm ready to go as soon as you are," he said with a nod and a hint of a smile.

Shooting Rogers a nasty look, I thanked Jensen and followed him to the Town Car. "We need to pick up Jordan at her place and then we're going to go out for dinner. We're not going to make it a late night, though, so you won't have to be out too late."

Jensen closed the car door behind me and slid into the driver's seat. "It's fine, miss. I'm available for as long as you need."

"Thank you, Jensen. I appreciate you driving me and Jordan around."

As Jensen pulled through the gate at the bottom of the driveway, he looked back at me in the rearview mirror. "It's my job, miss. Mr. Stone expects me to drive you wherever you need to go."

The mood between us was suddenly awkward, and after I told him what restaurant I'd chosen and we stopped at the ATM, I leaned back against the leather seat to wait silently until we reached Brooklyn. Jensen got us there in no time and as I'd promised, I had him blow the horn, over his polite protests that he'd be happy to escort me to the building's front door to get her.

Jordan popped her head in the back driver's side door and scrunched up her face. "Honking? What am I? Some cheap high school girl?"

"Get in! We're on a mission for great food and chocolate martinis!" I squealed.

She sat down in the seat and as we drove off, she looked at me and smiled. "I never get tired of seeing you this happy. Do you know that?"

"I guess what you always say is right. Good things do happen to good people."

I never got tired of being that happy, to be honest. Everything in my life had changed so much, and at the center of it was the reason for all that happiness. Tristan. I slipped my phone out of my bag and checked for new messages. Nothing.

Jordan leaned against me and stared over my shoulder. "Didn't you just leave Mr. Tall, Dark, and Gorgeous?"

I elbowed her gently in the arm. "He's out of town. I was just hoping he'd text me again."

"So, while the cat's away the mice will play, huh?" she joked singsong. "Where are we mice heading to tonight?"

Putting my phone away, I turned toward her in my seat. "I thought we could try The Channel. I heard it was great, and it's supposed to be a great club too."

She looked down at her black dress and back up at me. "I'm not sure I'm dressed for that place, Nina. I feel like your poor country cousin."

"That's ridiculous! You look incredible, as always. You've always had much better style than I have, no matter how much you spend or don't spend."

"I just don't want you to look bad," she said quietly. "I mean, now that you're with Tristan..."

I stopped her with my hand on her arm. "Jordan, my being with Tristan has nothing to do with what clothes we should wear. Well, it does for me since he bought most of mine, but we're still the same two girls we've been since we met that day in college."

She laughed at my admission that my clothes were all bought and paid for. "So you're a happily kept woman now? Whatever that's like, it looks good on you."

"How did Justin take you bowing out of this week's wrestling matches?" I asked, eager to change the subject.

Rolling her eyes, she said, "He said he was fine with it, but something in his voice said he wasn't, so I promised him I'd stop by his place before I go home."

"And you tease me about checking for texts? Sounds like someone else is crazy about a guy too."

She jabbed me in the arm with her fingers, tickling me until I giggled. "No more of that. This is a girl's night out, so let's get this party started!"

Jordan and I were like two peas in a pod, as we'd always been, and dinner was a great time. We laughed ourselves to tears as she told me about her third grade students and their very demanding letters to their parents about what gifts they wanted for Christmas.

I took a sip of my chocolate martini as Jordan's laughter ebbed away. She looked at me intently, as if she was studying me. "What? What is it?"

"You look so different tonight drinking that martini and wearing that dress I know cost a fortune, but even though the outside seems to have changed, you're still the same old Nina. I like that even with all the changes you've been through that you're still you."

"Of course I'm still me. Who else would I be?" I asked, unsure of what she meant.

She took a gulp of her beer and shrugged. "Well, you're basically Mrs. Tristan Stone, aren't you? That might change someone." Looking down at my left hand, she got a confused look on her face. "Why aren't you wearing the engagement ring he gave you? Aren't you still planning to marry him?"

I didn't know what to say to that. I wasn't wearing the ring because I wasn't sure he still wanted to marry me. I believed with all my heart that he loved me just as much as he said he did before the accident, but he hadn't mentioned our engagement or any plans to marry me since we'd rekindled our relationship, and I didn't want to pressure him. I was happy with the way things were going between us and didn't want to ruin it.

Instead of telling her this, though, I fibbed and hoped she wouldn't see right through me. "Of course, but since the accident I've lost a little weight so it doesn't fit right."

"Good. I don't want to hear you two are breaking up or anything stupid like that. I know things must be pretty strange since you don't remember him from before yet, but if any two people are supposed to be together, it's you and Tristan."

"No need to worry about us. I promise. What about you and Justin?"

Jordan sighed deeply and smirked. "We're doing fine, but it's not like you two. We're just average people in a regular relationship. No bells and whistles. Just comfortable."

Quickly, she stood from the table and looked around. "I need to find the ladies' room. Be right back."

I knew Jordan well enough to know she was uncomfortable about me asking about Justin. Her tone said boring instead of comfortable, but I didn't think I should press the issue. In my eyes, Jordan was anything but regular and average. She deserved a man who set her heart racing and turned her world upside down in the best ways. My heart was sad at the news that she didn't believe he was that only a few months into the relationship.

She returned in just a few minutes wearing a smile from ear to ear. Grabbing my arm, she squealed, "Oh my God! Nina, I just saw the most gorgeous man, and I swear he was checking me out too. Brown hair, the darkest blue eyes I've ever seen, and a body to die for!"

I looked around for this perfect specimen of man but didn't see anyone. She sat down and while she gushed about her sexy mystery man, I joked, "Um, weren't you just saying you have a boyfriend? I think his name is Justin or something like that."

"I know. I know. Justin is nice and everything, but this guy was stunning. And I think he was into me too. Well, enough of my mystery man. I can't wait to hang out with you and Tristan on New Year's Eve. We're going to have such a good time, especially compared to last year. You don't remember what we did last New Year's Eve, do you?" she asked with a giggle.

I shook my head. "Still nothing. Why? Tell me. What did we do?"

Putting her hands up to cover her face, she groaned. "I'm still trying to forget Paul. He's teaching fifth grade this year. His classroom is right down the hall from mine."

"What happened? Don't keep me in suspense! I'm a woman with a head injury, for God's sake!"

"He tried to have sex with me in the coatroom of the hotel just as it turned midnight. As if I was going to just hike up my dress and bang him right then and there!"

"No way! You have to tell me what my date was like."

"You got off slightly better with his friend, a short accountant who spent the night unsure if he wanted to kiss you or bore you with details about his job.

Thankfully, he only tried to maul you once and you didn't have to fend him off like I had to with Creepy Paul. You know, that's what I silently refer to him as every time I see him at school."

"You're terrible! The poor guy was probably in love with you from a distance and just jumped the gun a little that night," I joked.

"I think the best part of that New Year's was laughing ourselves to sleep that night," she said with a smile. "We began the year pretty badly, but we've come pretty far since then, don't you think?"

Her phone buzzed on the table and I saw that it was Justin. As she took the call, I accepted with disappointment that our night out was over. It was okay, though. All the better that I got home early just in case Tristan was there. The sadness of his message stayed in my mind still, and I wanted to be there for him in case his trip had gone badly.

"I have to go, Nina. I have work tomorrow. A few more and I'll never be able to handle the little angels."

She was lying, but it was okay. "I'll have Jensen come around and pick us up," I said as I moved to get up.

"No, that's okay. I'll take a cab. Finish your drink."

"Are you sure? Jensen can take you to Justin's. It's no problem."

Jordan gave me a definite shake of her head. "No need. It's out of your way to take me back to Brooklyn." Opening her arms, she smiled. "Come here and give me a hug before I go."

"I'll see you in a few days, so tell Justin I'm looking forward to spending time with both of you," I said as she hugged me. I released her and stepped away. "I know we usually give our gifts on Christmas morning, but yours won't be in until after that, so get ready to be blown away when it comes in January."

Jordan waved me off. "You don't have to get me anything, Nina. I know you've been dealing with a lot just before the holidays."

"Forget that. I have just the perfect gift for you, so get ready. I know you'll love it!"

Her phone rang again, putting an end to our goodbyes, and as I watched her walk out, I saw my phone light up on the table. Excited to finally talk to Tristan, I swiped the face to see it wasn't a call but an email notification. I tapped the little envelope and saw a message from Cal asking if we could meet. Since I was in the city, I figured it was perfect timing and emailed back for him to stop by The Channel if he was free and able to make it. A minute later, he replied he was nearby, so I ordered another of those candy sweet martinis and sat back to wait for him.

Checking my phone, I saw Tristan hadn't texted again. Disappointed, I quickly texted him the words *I love you* and hoped that would make him reply. Within fifteen minutes Cal had arrived but still no text from Tristan.

"I'm so glad you emailed me, Nina," Cal said as he sat down across the table from me. He settled into his chair and smiled. "You look incredible. Life certainly has treated you well."

"Well, except for that whole car accident and amnesia thing," I joked.

He looked at me as if he were sizing me up and shook his head. "I don't know. Maybe forgetting the past is something we all should do because you look great."

"Happiness does that for a person. You look pretty good after all these years, so you must be doing something right too."

In truth, Cal looked a little haggard. His grey wool coat was old and worn, and I'd noticed when he took off his gloves that the leather was ripped between his right thumb and forefinger. He still had those boyish good looks that had attracted me years ago, but now they were tinged with worry or weariness. I couldn't decide which.

"I have to tell you, Nina, that I was surprised at first that you came to see me, but now I'm so happy we're getting a chance to get reacquainted."

"I am too, Cal. I think bygones should be left as bygones."

I finished my drink and a waiter arrived almost instantly to ask me if I'd like another. I probably shouldn't have, but they tasted so good, so even though I was already feeling a little lightheaded and giddy, I ordered another martini.

"And you, sir?"

Cal shook his head and forced his lips into a thin line. "No, thanks." The waiter moved away from us, and Cal turned to face me. "This is a fancy place. I don't remember you liking places like this."

I couldn't tell if the tone in his voice was condemnation or insecurity. Either way, it made me uneasy to see Cal like this. As if I had to come up with an excuse why I'd want to eat in a nice restaurant, I said, "This place has gotten great reviews. I just thought I'd try it and see if it lives up to all the hype."

The truth was that I enjoyed restaurants like this now. I could afford them and I'd learned quickly from Tristan that I deserved to enjoy myself. I wasn't hurting anyone, so why shouldn't I have a nice meal in a trendy restaurant? As I sat there silently defending myself and my desire to eat good food, no matter how expensive it seemed to Cal, he shifted in his chair and seemed to not know where to put his hands as he moved them from the table to his lap and back again.

"Cal, you seem uncomfortable. Is something wrong? Is there something you didn't tell me the other day that I should know?"

He hung his head and quietly answered, "No, there's nothing more to tell. I was an ass and deserve anything you say to me."

Reaching over, I gently touched his sleeve. "It's okay, Cal. Things happen when you're young. That's why they say people are young and stupid. Nobody ever says someone's young and wise."

He frowned at my attempt to make him feel better. "It's just that I have no right to ask you for anything."

His voice strained as he spoke the words, and I could have sworn I saw him tear up. This wasn't the person I remembered at all. He was suffering right there in front of me, and I couldn't just let that happen.

"What's wrong, Cal? What's happened to you?"

He blew the air out of his cheeks and shook his head. "I've had a bad run of things, Nina. My mother was sick for a long time and passed away just a few months ago. She always liked you, I think because you were a lot like her."

"Oh, Cal. I'm so sorry. Your mother was a terrific lady. I had no idea."

"It's just been one thing after another, and tonight I found out that my girlfriend has been seeing someone else and is moving in with him. I just don't know how I'm going to afford our apartment since I signed the lease thinking we'd both be paying toward the rent."

My heart broke at the sight of this sad man sitting in front of me. The boy who'd broken my heart was now feeling what I'd felt, but it didn't give me any pleasure. I'd been blessed with a great man in Tristan, and I wanted everyone I knew to have the same wonderful luck I'd had. I couldn't help Cal out in the girlfriend department, but I could give him some money to help with his rent. I had it, and it would be a crime not to pay it forward.

I reached into my purse and pulled out all the money I had left after paying for dinner, leaving just enough to pay for my last martinis. Handing him the cash, I pressed it into his palm. "Take this."

"No, I couldn't," he weakly protested.

I understood. He didn't want to be emasculated by an ex-girlfriend he'd recently asked forgiveness from. "Then consider it a loan. You were right when you said life has treated me well. It has, but it means nothing if you can't help out a friend in need. I know it's only a few hundred, but I can give you more tomorrow."

"Nina, no. It's okay. This is more than enough. Thank you."

I squeezed his hand before he moved to pocket the money. "You know how to contact me if you need more."

He began to say thank you again, but we were interrupted by Jensen, who suddenly appeared behind Cal. "Miss, I'm sorry I'm late. The car is waiting just outside."

For a moment, Jensen's words confused me, but I realized as he stood there looking down at my purse as it sat on the table in front of me that he believed he was safeguarding me. Before I could set his mind at ease, Cal stood and thanked me again as he quickly headed toward the door.

Tristan's driver nodded silently at me, and I slipped into my coat to return to the house. I considered asking him if he planned to mention any of this to Tristan, but I knew the answer already. Jensen worked for Tristan Stone, not Nina Edwards, and his employer likely knew all about my friendly loan to my ex.

I followed Jensen to the car and got into the back, half expecting Tristan to be sitting there waiting for me. A stab of disappointment hit me when I saw the car was empty, and as it pulled away from The Channel, I knew I'd have to explain what I'd just done, but I wasn't worried.

I hadn't done anything wrong, and once Tristan heard about the hard times that had befallen Cal, I knew he'd understand. No matter what the rest of the world saw, in my heart I knew Tristan was a kind soul like me.

SIXTEEN

TRISTAN

I'd driven halfway back to the house, but I couldn't wait any longer to read Joseph Edwards' notes. Pulling over at a diner on the side of the road, I bought a cup of coffee and opened up Nina's father's notebook on the table in front of me. I took a sip of the drink that tasted like a cross between dishwater and mud and pushed the cup and saucer away from me. Pressing my phone on again, I brought up Nina's message telling me she loved me and stared at it, silently promising to show her how much she meant to me when I returned home.

As I'd driven here, the need to see what was written in the notebook had been overwhelming, but now that it sat there in front of me with nothing stopping me, I hesitated, unsure I could see the truth he'd uncovered about my father that had gotten him killed. My hand hovered over the tablet, shaking at the thought of what could be contained in those pages.

I was no fool. There was no way I'd be able to read the proof of my father's crime and not tell Nina the entire truth of her father's death, but the memory of how she'd reacted the last time was like a fresh wound still nearly splitting my heart in two. I couldn't lose her again, this time possibly forever.

But I couldn't live in ignorance not knowing what had happened between Victor Stone and Joseph Edwards.

Taking a deep breath in, I swallowed hard and opened the notebook. My eyes flowed over the page, taking in each word and its meaning.

Stone Worldwide—Victor Stone—Taylor Stone

I was surprised to see my brother's name mentioned so prominently at the top of the first page. Taylor had worked closely with my father in Stone Worldwide's business, being groomed to take over when he retired, but he was more an office mate than anything else. At least it had seemed that way.

Atlanta—October 2008

-civil suit—sexual harassment/judge?? Why a problem? Name of judge?

Joseph Edwards' notes made no sense. A sexual harassment case wasn't particularly noteworthy in Stone Worldwide. Thousands of employees across the globe meant at any time someone may feel they had a case, especially considering my father's proclivity for young women who happened to work for him. Sexual harassment cases had become commonplace by the time I was old enough to understand much of anything my father did at work each day.

Had Taylor been involved in one of those cases? I had a hard time believing that. If anything, he was the good son, never getting into trouble with drugs, women, or anything else. He'd graduated with honors from college and gone on to earn an M.B.A. He was the one who rose everyday before dawn to be ready to leave for work at six and stayed until late at night, often putting in fifteen hour workdays.

I'd been the one who'd been arrested twice for drugs, only getting off when the Stone family money had conveniently found its way to that local police chief in northern Jersey. It had been me who'd been carted out of apartments and clubs by Rogers more times than either he or I wanted to remember, usually costing my father money to keep the press quiet and women I liked to call girlfriends pacified so they wouldn't talk about the sex and my all-day coke binges.

As I remembered those days of my past, I shook my head in disbelief that it could be Taylor who had some part in anything unsavory. That was my role in the family—I was the black sheep. He'd always been the golden child, at least as far as my father was concerned.

October 2008. Taylor and I had been twenty-four then. He was still in graduate school being the exemplary student he'd always been.

Edwards' note indicated that something about the judge in the case had been a problem. What had he meant by that? I continued to read down the page, hoping to understand any of this.

-Amanda Cashen—July 1992-May 2008

My mind raced as I tried to find a memory of anyone with that name, but it didn't ring a bell. I'd never heard that name. 1992? Had my father had a child with another woman then and Amanda was the name of the baby? There had always been rumors that my father had other children. More than once I'd walked in on my parents fighting and heard my mother accuse him of fathering children with other women. His response was always the same—a sneer thrown in her direction as he belittled her claims as the rantings of a pathetic woman who didn't understand the way of the world for men like him. He never outright denied her accusations, which I was sure hurt even more than the painful doubts she had about her husband's love for her.

If a child named Amanda did exist and Edwards had found out, perhaps making that public would be reason enough for my father to want him out of the picture. As I sat there staring down at this mystery female's name, I couldn't imagine that could be the case, though. The note about a sexual harassment case made an illegitimate child a non-issue, unless the child was the product of my father doing something illegal.

I turned the page after unsuccessfully trying to read a number of notes that appeared to be simply scribblings and illegible symbols and saw a sentence that stopped me cold.

Atlanta 2008—gas explosion cafe—end of Stone's problems

-sexual harassment case ruled in his favor November 2008

What did some gas explosion have to do with a sexual harassment case that ended up going in Stone Worldwide's favor shortly after? Edwards' notes were too vague for me to understand what he was referring to. I flipped to the next page and saw one word over and over and in all caps at the top of the page.

TAYLOR

What had Joseph Edwards meant by writing my brother's name all over the page? None of this made any sense. I kept going, baffled by what the connection was between my father's illegitimate child, a sexual harassment case against him, and some explosion at an Atlanta cafe.

Folded in half between the next two pages was a newspaper article from the front page of the Atlanta Journal-Constitution dated October 23, 2008. I laid the paper out flat on the table. In the center of the article was a picture of a cafe that looked like it was in the middle of a war zone. The front of the coffee shop was blown out, leaving a gaping hole in the building. Chunks of concrete lay everywhere, exposed wires hung low, and remnants of the store that had once served people their morning coffee lay in pieces inside the building.

Under the picture read the caption *50 Dead In Rush Hour Explosion*.

My hands began to shake as I leaned forward to read the report of the bombing. The words swam in front of my eyes as I struggled to comprehend the horror of what had happened.

50 men, women and children killed at coffee shop blast. Gas explosion thought to be the reason.

Investigators still looking for clues.

Witnesses report the scene was "pure carnage."

7:38 am the explosion rocked the Corner Cafe one block from the courthouse.

Children on their way to school killed. Hundreds injured.

Reports of people smelling gas just before the blast.

Judge Albert Cashen one of the victims.

I flipped back through the pages to where the illegitimate child's name was written. *Amanda Cashen.*

There was no way it was a coincidence that a judge with the same last name as a child who could be my father's was killed in a gas explosion at a coffee shop near where he worked. And that he was a judge was likely no coincidence either.

My mouth tasted like bile as my insides churned at the idea that would explain this all. My father had the judge in a civil suit murdered. My father had been a monster, no doubt. Victor Stone was a man who got what he wanted, and if that required the sacrifice of someone, he wasn't above that. There was a long line of damage trailing behind him for most of his adult life. I didn't want to believe any of this, but it was all too easy. My father was like many powerful men. Any obstacle in his way to what he wanted was overcome or eliminated. If he hadn't been able to overcome Judge Cashen, then he would have eliminated him.

I leaned back against the booth and closed my eyes. The room felt like it was spinning around me. Taking a deep breath, I tried to push out the images of all those people lying dead and maimed because of my own father's actions. Children suffering, their parents devastated, all so Victor Stone could once again slip out of being held responsible for his behavior.

"Are you okay? Can I get you more coffee?" I heard someone ask and I opened my eyes to see the middle-aged waitress standing over me with a look of concern on her plain face.

I shook my head and mumbled, "Just a water, please."

She left me sitting there, my stomach sick as I turned the idea of my father's crime over and over in my mind. I didn't want to know any more. Not only had he killed the judge and Nina's father, but he'd killed innocent men, women, and children who'd never heard of him just going about their daily lives on their way to work and school.

My phone vibrated in my coat pocket, and I reached in to see a text from Daryl. I read it, feeling like the Universe had suddenly decided it was time to pile on. *Need to meet. Got some interesting pics of loverboy you want to see.*

A hollow feeling took over my insides as my mind raced with thoughts of Nina with her ex again. I didn't want to think about that now. *Meet tomorrow at noon in my office.*

The waitress returned with my water, placing it down and patting my shoulder as she walked away. I had to continue reading Joseph Edwards' notes, no matter how sick what he'd found out made me. After downing a big gulp of water that tasted faintly of chlorine, I flipped to the next page of his tablet.

Jessica Cashen—3:30 pm 1/6/09   832 Sturges Way Alpharetta

The rest of that page was filled with my father's and Taylor's names, along with Albert and Amanda Cashen's names linked with arrows showing how Edwards had attempted to figure out the connection between these four people. In the center of this drawing was one word followed by a question mark.

Child?

Was it a simple case of an illegitimate child that had led to the death of so many?

I read over the note about Jessica Cashen again and guessed Edwards had arranged to meet with her. Those were the details that would tell me what I needed to know.

Two empty pages later, I found his notes from his meeting with Jessica. I read the words, but they didn't sink in. I couldn't comprehend them, my mind unwilling to accept the truth of them.

Doubts it was a coincidence

Taylor and Amanda—together for months, according to Jessica

Found out she was pregnant March 2008—told Taylor soon after

Refused to see her or answer her calls—begged to see him but nothing—devastated became depressed

I knew what was coming next. Even so, when I turned the page, the words hit me like I'd crashed into a brick wall at a hundred miles an hour.

Hanged herself May 12, 2008 — 3 months pregnant
  -father found her in the basement

Jessica Cashen's story of how her sister died and how her father blamed Taylor for her suicide went on and on for lines down the page, but I couldn't read anymore. I pushed the tablet away in disgust, my heart sick from what I'd read.

The person described in these pages wasn't someone I knew. Taylor had always been the good son. He'd never even really dated many women, sticking with one shy, rather nondescript girl he met freshman year in college. My mother had always said he'd marry her, have children, and live happily ever after, unlike me, who had no stability in his life and refused to even consider any kind of happily ever after that didn't involve late nights and a different female for each one.

Taylor and I had never been as close as twins were supposed to be, but I thought I had known him, at least. Never in my wildest nightmares could I have imagined he was this person. Amanda Cashen had been a girl — fifteen years old. What the fuck had he been doing with her?

For the first time a horrifying thought settled into my mind. Had Taylor raped her? Jesus Christ! Even if she had agreed to sleeping with him, she was just a child, a minor he had no business touching.

I had to get out of there. The dingy yellow diner walls felt like they were closing in on me, suffocating me. Scooping up the notebook and newspaper article, I threw a twenty on the table and got the hell out. By the time I reached my car, it was all I could do to toss it all onto the front passenger seat before I bent over behind the rear bumper and puked up coffee, water, and whatever the fuck I'd had for lunch. I stood there hunched over in the cold night air until there was nothing left in my stomach and all I had left was dry heaves that made my ribs ache in pain.

Finally, I stood up and wiped my mouth, thankful for the bracing December air against my face. Swallowing hard, I tried to push every terrible word I'd read from my thoughts, but I couldn't. All I saw over and over was the image of my brother on top of some helpless girl and my father standing behind them coldly ordering the death of Albert Cashen.

I floored it, hitting over a hundred and twenty at times as I raced home. I wanted to be as far away from that storage unit and that diner, but it was no use. Everything I'd found out stayed with me, and I feared it would never leave me.

As I drove up to the house I shared with Nina, the realization of what I'd learned hit me. How could I face her after everything I now knew about why her father had died? It was worse than I'd ever imagined. Joseph Edwards hadn't just uncovered some shady land deal or my father's philandering ways. He'd pulled back the protective cover shielding my father and my brother and their unspeakable actions. Nina's father had been murdered to protect Taylor's despicable acts with a teenage girl and my father's callous desire to have the world bend to his orders, no matter how terrible or depraved they were.

I shut off the car and sat back in the seat, drained from my trip. I'd flown halfway around the world at times and not felt this exhausted. I didn't know how I'd face Nina now. She had no idea of the kind of people I came from. How would she ever forgive me for what my family had done to hers?

I sat there staring into the darkness until I knew I couldn't avoid facing her any longer. As I walked through the door, Rogers met me, almost as if he'd been waiting for me. His expression was stony, instantly making my blood run cold. Had something happened and Nina was already gone?

"Tristan, Jensen needs to speak to you. He's waiting in my part of the house."

"What's this about? I'm tired, Rogers. I'll deal with him tomorrow," I said as I brushed past him to see if Nina was still there.

"She's in her room, Tristan. That's what Jensen needs to talk to you about. He's worried you're going to fire him this time."

I spun around to face Rogers, my heart racing wildly in fear. "Did something happen? Is she hurt?"

He slowly shook his head. "No. She's fine. I think it would be better to hear what Jensen has to say before you speak to her."

"Rogers, what the fuck is wrong? If Nina isn't hurt, then what could Jensen be worried about?"

I turned to leave and he caught my arm. Surprised, I turned my head and looked at him and saw a look of concern I hadn't seen on his face since those days when he was rescuing me from my self-destructive behavior.

"You need to speak to him. Take a few minutes before you go to her to hear what Jensen has to tell you."

Something in his voice convinced me and I followed him to his part of the house. I found Jensen a worried wreck pacing the floor of Roger's personal study.

His usually calm expression twisted into one full of fear. "You told me to make sure she was safe, and I know the bodyguards are always there, but I thought I should step in. I meant no harm, Mr. Stone."

"Stop. Tell me what happened."

Jensen took a deep breath as he quit his pacing. Hanging his head, he said, "I took Miss Edwards to pick up her friend Jordan and then took them to a restaurant. When West and Varo told me her friend had left, I pulled the car around to pick her up, but instead another person joined her. A man she obviously knew. I didn't want to intrude, but as I watched, she gave him money. I finally did interrupt them to tell her the car was ready because I was afraid he was going to take even more money. I'm sorry if I was out of line. I was concerned she was giving this strange man so much money."

So this was what Daryl was talking about when he texted that he had interesting pictures of Cal. Nina had met him again, and now he was busy trying to con her out of money, as he had with other women, and doing it quite successfully, it seemed. On top of everything else I'd felt that night, jealousy and rage now burned in my gut.

Struggling to hide my feelings, I patted Jensen on the shoulder, thankful for his attempt to keep Nina safe. He'd done the right thing.

If only Nina had.

SEVENTEEN
TRISTAN

Instead of going to see Nina after hearing Jensen's report, I went to my room alone, thankful in some ways for having a reason to avoid seeing her. On the floor just inside the room lay an envelope with my name written in her handwriting and a tiny smiley face drawn on the front. As with her other letter, fear flared inside my mind at the thought of what she might have written. Maybe she'd confessed to giving her ex-boyfriend money while they sat at a restaurant earlier that night. Or maybe she'd remembered something and this was the letter in which she finally told me she couldn't forgive me for what my father had done.

Fuck. Not knowing was like torture. If only I could dismiss her as easily as I'd always been able to dismiss the rest of the world, but I couldn't. I loved her to distraction, and even the unknown words she'd written on a sheet of paper inside that envelope could tie me up in knots.

I slid my finger under the flap of the envelope and tore it open, unable to wait any more. Unfolding her letter, I silently prayed for some release from all of this soon.

Dear Tristan,

I like our letter writing back and forth. It feels like we're romantic pen pals separated by some huge distance and someday someone will find our letters and see that no matter what separated us, we ended up together because we loved one another. What can I say? I'm an incurable romantic. ♥ You didn't answer your phone, so I'll tell you what I wanted to say here. I hope your day was good. I missed having you near me. Come find me when you get home. I'll be waiting up for you.

I love you.
Nina

I didn't go see her right away. I needed to be able to look at her without feeling guilty, but that wasn't going to happen without at least taking a shower. Maybe if I did that I'd find some way to wash off some of the ugliness and be able to deserve someone like Nina.

Half an hour later I'd stood in the shower until my fingertips wrinkled but it hadn't worked. The reality of what I was—the son of the man who'd done so much to hurt so many—couldn't be washed away, no matter how much I tried.

The story Jensen had told me rattled around in my head as I walked over to her room. I didn't want to be jealous, believing the whole thing had been just another example of Nina's goodness in helping that manipulative fuck of an ex. I couldn't help it, though.

Anything that made me feel like it would take her away I hated instinctively.

She was already asleep when I reached her room, but I quietly slipped in and stood beside her bed watching her as she softly breathed in and out, her mouth in that beautiful pout she hated and I loved. I wanted to kiss that mouth and wake her up, my Sleeping Beauty who I could whisk away to another kingdom and take care of forever.

Nothing was stopping us. I had enough money to last for this lifetime and the next. We could run away and never be found again, just the two of us living for love. No more of Karl and the Board. No more Cal. No more anyone but us.

That wasn't right, though. There would always be something we couldn't run away from. Someday she'd remember who I was and what part my family had played in taking her father from her, and then there would be nowhere in the world I could go for forgiveness.

I had to tell her what I knew. I had to tell her why her father had been taken from her. I had to tell her everything.

As I stood there watching her, she stirred awake and smiled up at me. She had no idea the man she was happy to see could very well be the one person she'd never want to lay eyes on again.

"Hey, what are you doing there staring at me as I sleep?" she jokingly asked. Stretching her arms above her head, she pushed away her drowsiness. "I missed you."

"I missed you too. I got your letter."

Nina sat up and rubbed her eyes. "Did you like it?" Looking up at me, she held out her hand. "Sit down. Tell me about your day."

I sat down beside her and ran my fingers through her hair. "I'd rather hear about yours. Jensen tells me you and Jordan had a girl's night out."

"I'm guessing he told you about me seeing Cal too."

"He did," I said flatly, hoping to hide how jealous it made me.

She squeezed my hand. "Don't be angry, Tristan. He's down on his luck and I did him a little favor. That's all."

"I don't think you know your friend Cal very well, Nina. What you call down on his luck is actually his con. He does this to women all the time."

"No, you're wrong. Remember, he didn't come looking for me. I found him after all these years. He's just going through some bad stuff now. You'd help someone like him too. I know you would."

I lifted her chin with my forefinger so her gaze met mine. "You're too nice. I know all about him and I'm telling you he's playing you."

"I don't believe it. No girlfriend cheating on him and leaving him with an expensive apartment to pay for? He told me his mother died too. Was that a lie?"

Shrugging my shoulders, I admitted I knew nothing about either of these things. "But I can find out. Whatever he's claimed, I'm guessing it's a lie. He does this all the time, Nina. You're going to have to be careful now that you have money."

"About that. Why do I have all that money? You can't be paying me that much to be your private art curator."

"I can pay you whatever I want."

Nina pulled me by my T-shirt until my mouth was next to hers. With a smile, she said, "Well, I guess that answers that, now doesn't it?"

I kissed her lips and whispered against them, "Now promise me no more money to Cal."

"If what you say is really true, I won't give him any more."

"You doubt me?" I asked, half-teasing and half bothered that she might not trust me on this.

"You know I like to question everything. I thought you liked that about me."

"I like you questioning other people, not me."

"Cro-magnon much?" she said with a giggle. "Somebody has to keep you on your toes, Mr. Stone."

"On my toes?"

Nina playfully ran her tongue over the seam of my lips. "And all those other fine body parts."

My cock stiffened as she teased me, and for at least a little while I wanted to believe I could forget all the bad I needed to confess and get lost in her. Fisting my hand in her hair, I tugged her head back and covered her mouth with mine, thrusting my tongue into her mouth to find hers. I wanted to escape inside her body.

"I want to be inside you so bad," I groaned as I trailed kisses down her neck.

She arched her back, rubbing her breasts against my chest and cooing as she wrapped her legs around my waist. Looking down at the silk pajamas I wore, she licked her lips and slid her forefinger just under the waistband. "Then get these off."

Not waiting for my answer, she tugged them down over my hips while I pulled her shorts and panties off. I threw them away from me and watched as she did the same with my pants.

"Didn't we buy you something nicer to wear to bed?" I asked as she stripped off my T-shirt.

Nina skimmed her hands over my stomach and looked up at me, her eyes sparkling with desire. "Uh huh, but what's the purpose of wearing them if it's just me?"

I tore her shirt from her and pulled her to me. "It's never just you. I'm always nearby, even if I'm not right next to you."

Her teeth nipped at my collarbone as she mumbled against my skin, "I like it better when you're right next to me."

I loved the feel of her mouth on me, exciting me as she showed how much she wanted me inside her. Slipping my hand down over her stomach, I probed between her legs, loving when I found her dripping wet.

"Tell me what you want, baby," I whispered as I pushed a single finger inside her eager cunt.

She wriggled against my hand, desperate for the pleasure I wanted to give her, and whimpered, "I want you. Inside me. Fucking me until I come and then until I come again."

I loved when she talked like that. There wasn't a man on Earth who didn't want exactly this kind of woman—a lady in public any man could be proud to show off and a whore in the bedroom who knew what she wanted and wasn't afraid to let her man know. That Nina could be both thrilled me and made me love her even more.

Her hand stroked my cock from base to tip, making my control ebb away. Struggling to hold back, I had to give in and pushed her back onto the bed. I wanted to feel her warm and wet cunt surrounding my cock as I thrust into her to reach that place where I could give her what she wanted and find some peace from everything that plagued my mind.

Taking a nipple into my mouth, I sucked it hard and bit down gently until she cried out more in pleasure than pain. Her heels pushed against my lower back, urging me to enter her and leave the foreplay for another time.

"Don't tease, Tristan. You always tease," she whispered in a needy voice as she clawed at my back to pull me close.

"Not teasing, princess. Control," I said low in her ear as I slowly eased my cock inch by inch into her eager body.

She thrust her hips upward to welcome me into her and pressed her fingertips into my back. "I don't want controlled Tristan. Let me see what's inside your heart instead of always being so in control."

"You don't want that, Nina," I said in a strangled voice as I began to slowly make love to her.

Cradling my face, she stared deep into my eyes as I continued to push my cock into her. "I do. Show me that man," she moaned.

I slowed to a languid pace in and out of her body. I wished I could show her that man—the one who didn't need to be in control of everything in fear that if he didn't, his life would spiral down to nothing. Burying my head in the pillow next to hers, I said quietly, "I am who I am, Nina."

She stopped my motion with her heels against my back, keeping me inside her as she threatened to tear away the walls I made sure to protect myself with at all times.

"I love who you are, Tristan, but I know there's someone else inside there. Someone who has nothing to do with control or money. That Tristan wants to say things to me. I wish you'd let him."

"I love you, Nina. I love you with an need that scares me sometimes. I've never loved anyone like this. I spend my days dreading that you're going to wake up one day, realize who I am, and tell me you can't do this anymore. That you can't live with someone who's as fucked up as I am."

She kissed me softly on the lips as tears welled in her eyes. "I don't know what you're talking about. You're not fucked up. Why would you say that?"

Closing my eyes, I took a deep breath. "There's so much about me no one would want."

"That's not true, Tristan. No matter what you think, you're wonderful."

I stayed silent for a long time until I finally admitted the truth at the heart of us. Opening my eyes, I whispered, "One word of rejection from you would kill me, Nina. Please tell me that even if you ever think that you can't take who I am anymore, you won't leave. Give me a chance to show you I love you."

No matter how much I asked for her to make that promise, I knew there was the real risk that she would leave again when she found out what my father had done and how much I'd known about it all this time. This time I'd make sure things turned out different, though. I had to.

"Tristan, I'm not going anywhere. I promise no matter what. I love you. That means no leaving."

We made love sweeter than it had ever been before between us or between me and any other woman. Deep inside, I hoped that Nina would want to live up to the promise she'd made. The time was coming that I'd have to finally confess everything. Each day that passed meant the risk that she'd remember everything grew, but until I knew the whole ugly story, I had to wait.

I just hoped that when the time came, it wouldn't be too late.

As always, I slipped out of Nina's room after she fell asleep and returned to my room. I'd grown used to my nightmares since the plane crash, but I knew tonight would be filled with more than usual. Over and over, I was haunted by the image of Taylor and my father standing over two dead bodies. I got less than an hour's sleep total, tossing and turning until I woke up in a cold sweat twice before I just gave up and got ready for work.

I stood in the kitchen hoping coffee would undo what my lack of sleep was working hard to accomplish, but even the caffeine in the special blend Rogers bought for me wasn't able to do the job. My eyelids drooped heavily as I leaned against the center island, my day ahead and all that I'd learned in Pennsylvania weighing on my mind.

My eyes closed, but I felt a hand touch my arm and I looked around to see Nina standing in front of me, her expression full of concern.

"Hey, are you okay?"

I shook the grogginess from my head and forced a smile. "I'm fine. Good morning." Bending down, I kissed her softly on the lips. "Sleep well?"

She stroked her fingertips down my tie. "Better than you, I'm guessing since I'm not sleeping standing up. I thought only horses did that."

"I'm fine. Long day ahead of me."

Nina wrapped her arms around me and pulled me into her. "I'm worried about you. Why don't you ever stay with me all night?"

I couldn't tell her the truth—that I wasn't sure she was ready to see the real me, the man who suffered through each night with nightmares, sometimes just one but other times dozens. Would she even want me if she knew I was so fucked up?

"I'm one of those workaholic types. My brain never shuts off, so a lot of times I get up and do work when you're sleeping. I don't like to bother you, so I go back to my own room."

She squeezed me in her arms and looked up at me with a smile. "It wouldn't bother me and it would be nice to see you there when I wake up."

I couldn't say no when she looked at me like that, with those blue eyes so sweet. "Okay." I didn't mean it. There was no way I could stay with her all night feeling like I did now.

Nina turned to pour herself a cup of coffee. "I'm going to do some work on the Atlanta suite today. I have some good ideas, I think. How's your day look?"

Atlanta.

"I need to move up our trip there. Be ready to leave this afternoon," I said before I took my last sip of coffee.

Spinning around, she splashed coffee down the front of her shirt and rushed to pat it dry with a towel from the counter. "What? I'm not ready. I need more time."

"I have things I have to take care of there, and they can't wait. I'm sure whatever you choose will be great," I said calmly. "Be ready to go by three. I'll be back in a few."

I left Nina stunned in the kitchen and quickly got away from the house before she could ask any questions. I wasn't ready to explain everything yet.

Michelle was waiting for me when I got to my office, along with Daryl and Karl. While I would have liked to make both of them disappear, I had to deal with them. As I breezed past them on my way in, I decided Karl and his threats would be the first hurdle of the day.

"Karl, how nice to see you. Join me in my office."

He barely let me sit down before he began. "Is there anything you want to tell me, Tristan?"

I looked up and saw him standing in front of my desk. He held his chin high, as if he was looking down on me or had something over me.

"Other than what I told you last time, Karl, no. So if you're here with some bullshit bluster, I'm not in the mood. Go bother someone else."

He stepped forward and placed his palms on the edge of my desk, pushing the platinum nameplate aside. The symbolism wasn't lost on me. His meaty, rough hands with their thick knuckles shoving me out of the way.

Leaning forward, he jutted his face toward me. "Made any trips lately, Tristan?"

I'd been foolish in thinking he hadn't had someone watching me. Faking nonchalance, I leaned back in my chair and laced my fingers behind my head. "None recently, but I'm planning to head to Atlanta right after New Year's. Would you like me to bring you back some peaches, Karl?"

His expression changed as he mentally filed away the nugget of information I'd just given him, and then he grinned. "Speaking of peaches, how is your young lady? Feeling well?"

I bristled at his reference to Nina. "Have you taken to caring about Nina's welfare now, Karl?"

"I'm just here to remind you that if there is anything incriminating, she would be in grave danger."

I couldn't help but chuckle at him. "You been watching A Few Good Men recently? Your threat might work better if you sounded like Nicholson."

Karl didn't seem to understand my joke and continued, "This is almost at its end, son. Remember that."

He turned to leave as the triumphant victor of our lame battle of wits, mumbling something as he flung open the door and stalked past Michelle. This was a hell of a way to start the day. And now I had to deal with Daryl and his pictures, which would require more playacting on my part to avoid looking like a boyfriend who was in the dark as to what his woman was doing.

"Tristan, I have so much I want you to see," he announced as he entered my office and closed the door behind him.

"Take a seat, Daryl. Let's see what you have."

He sat down in front of my desk and pointed toward the door. "Before I begin, I should let you know that I saw him watching your lady while I was watching loverboy."

I couldn't hide my surprise at hearing that Karl himself was watching Nina. Thank God I had two bodyguards on her. But he was beginning to be a real problem. Stalking me was one thing. Stalking Nina was an entirely different thing and one I didn't like.

"I'm guessing by the look on your face that you didn't know. He didn't get close to her, but he was there and watching her."

"Thanks, Daryl. Did you see anyone else there?"

"Just the two giants who are always around her. I'd keep them with her at all times. That guy is no good, Tristan."

"So what do you have for me, Daryl?"

He handed me the pictures he'd taken as he watched Cal. "Pics of him with a handful of women. That boy gets around. Pics of your lady with loverboy. He's a real player and unless I'm reading her entirely wrong, she's way out of her league with him. You need to make her realize he's playing her. Got a decent amount from her the other night."

I sifted through the pictures of Cal Johnson and his catalog of women, stopping when I reached the few of Nina and him at the restaurant she'd told me about. I couldn't help but stare at her expression as she sat listening to the lies he spewed about a girlfriend breaking his heart and whatever other bullshit he told her. She looked so innocent sitting there next to him, her blue eyes intense as she sympathetically listened to his tale of woe, her mouth turning down slightly as the pictures went on and she heard how awful his life was. Did she look like that next to me, I wondered? In many ways, Cal resembled someone like me. I'd been accused of being manipulative many times by women. Had they seen me like I saw him now?

"I'm happy to report that nothing happened between them, you know, sexually. If you ask me, he doesn't seem interested in that from her at all. And she gives off no vibe that she wants him. I think it's a case of she's too nice and he knows it."

I handed the pictures back to Daryl, my gaze still fixed on the last one of Nina smiling warmly at Cal as she gave him money. "I'm wondering if it's time I paid our friend Cal a visit."

"If you're asking me, I say no. Don't bother yourself with this. Deal with your lady. I really don't think she's planning some kind of rendezvous. I think she's just naive and wants to help out an old friend who's down on his luck. She doesn't know this is his game. Let her know what's going on and I guarantee you I won't have any more pics of them together."

I thought about Daryl's suggestion and nodded my agreement. I didn't expect to see anything more from him about Nina and Cal, but it was best to keep an eye on loverboy for a while longer. Standing from my chair, I walked around to lead him out. "Keep on him for a little while. I want to be able to show without a doubt that he's scamming women."

"No problem, Tristan. Want to schedule a time to meet after Christmas? Say, the Friday after?"

Patting him on the back, I escorted him to Michelle's desk so she could mark the date on my calendar. "That's fine. If I don't see you before, have a merry Christmas, Daryl."

"You too, Tristan. Enjoy your holiday with your lady."

When he was out of earshot, I turned to Michelle. "I'm going to be out of the office until after the holidays. The same order as before applies. Do not let Karl in, but I want you to tell him I'll be in Dallas for Christmas when he asks."

"Okay. I will, Mr. Stone," she said quietly, as if her agreement was to be a secret too. "Is everything okay?"

I ignored her question as I spied the gift box at the back of her desk, evidence that Angelo had gotten her the Christmas gift I'd wanted. I'd told him to choose a necklace, something classic but nice, leaving him as much room to choose as he liked.

She blushed and looked back at the box. "You didn't have to go to such trouble, Mr. Stone. It's lovely."

Michelle knew as well as I did that I hadn't gone to any trouble since Angelo had done all the leg work. Smiling, I said, "It's the least I can do to make up for years of not doing enough. I hope he picked something you like."

She turned back toward me with the necklace laid across her palm. A white gold necklace with a diamond and pearl pendant, it was very much her style—classic and understated. Thank God for Angelo because if I had to pick out gifts like that, I'd likely be standing dumbfounded for hours in front of the counter at Saks.

"I love it. Thank you."

"I hope you have a nice holiday, Michelle. Make sure security locks the suite as you're leaving on Monday. I'll see you when I get back."

"Monday? You don't want me here on Christmas Eve, like every other year?"

Suddenly, I felt like Ebenezer Scrooge. I had made her work every other Christmas Eve since I'd started at Stone Worldwide. I was there, so it had never occurred to me that she shouldn't be there working too.

Shaking my head, I smiled at her. "No. Enjoy your holiday, Michelle."

"You too, Mr. Stone. I hope it's a happy one."

I didn't continue the conversation, silently praying that Nina and I would have a happy Christmas. It was our first, and I wanted it to be perfect for her. But first, I needed to find out the rest of the story from Amanda Cashen's sister. After making arrangements to fly out that afternoon, I took care of some business and headed back to the house to find Nina, my stomach in knots about what I'd find in Atlanta.

EIGHTEEN

TRISTAN

The flight was thankfully uneventful, even though the smoothest plane ride was still terrifying for me. I spent the entire time sitting like a statue in my seat while Nina talked about what she planned to do for the Atlanta suite, intentionally trying to take my mind off the trip. I hadn't exaggerated about wanting to join the Mile High Club with her when I'd teased her about it, but the minute I stepped onto the plane, it was like every other time I'd flown since the crash. My heart raced and I didn't feel like I was getting enough air in my lungs, as if someone had their hands wrapped around my neck and their fingers were pressing against my throat, slowly strangling me. None of the tricks the doctors had given me worked, but I couldn't help but smile at Nina's attempt to make the flight bearable.

The Atlanta Richmont was all decked out for the Christmas holiday with a twenty-five foot evergreen tree decorated with gold and red ornaments as the focal point in the lobby. It resembled the kind of tree my mother used to love for the holidays.

"Tristan, this hotel is gorgeous! Do all of them look like this?" Nina asked as she swiveled her head left and right to take in all the view.

"Pretty much. Some are better than others. This is my first time here too, but I must say it's not bad."

She jabbed me in the ribs with her finger and grimaced. "Always so understated. This place is great!"

I leaned down to kiss her and whispered, "I'm glad you like it. Let's hope you think the same way when you see the suite."

Located on the top floor of the hotel, the Peachtree Suite was one of two suites that took up the space a penthouse in other hotels would. I'd originally chosen this suite instead of the other Dogwood Suite because I'd hoped it would be a good way to ease Nina back into work. Unlike in Dallas, with its ugly gold everywhere, the designers my father had hired for Atlanta were top notch, so all she'd have to do was choose a piece or two she loved and she'd have succeeded.

Nina followed me into the suite and whistled behind me. "This is even nicer in person than it was online. I'm still not sure what artwork I could pick to improve on it, though."

I poured myself a drink to calm my nerves from the plane and what I was about to do. "I'm sure whatever you pick will be great, Nina."

Wrapping her arms around me, she pressed her cheek to my back. "Is there something wrong? I know you said you hate flying, but all of a sudden, you seem different."

I put my glass down on the bar and placed my hands over hers on my chest. "Nothing wrong. I'm always like this after a flight."

"You sure? Anything I can do?" she asked sweetly, making me wish I could just tell her what was making my stomach twist in knots. I couldn't. Not yet, anyway. I had to do this alone, but I hoped that once I met with Jessica Cashen that all the secrets I'd kept from Nina could finally come out.

I turned in her hold and cupped her chin. "I need to take care of some business this afternoon, but I hope we can have dinner when I get back. I shouldn't be long."

Nina smiled up at me, blissfully unaware of where I was going. "Okay. I'm going to get working on the artwork for this nearly perfect suite, Mr. Stone. Don't worry. I'm on the job."

I couldn't help but smile. She did that to me. "I'm happy to hear it, Ms. Edwards. I'll expect a full report when I return then."

"Of course." She faked a bow and stood on her toes to kiss me. "Don't work too hard, okay? Tell whoever you're meeting that I'm going to have something to say to them if you come back here all grouchy because of work."

Kissing the tip of her nose, I promised not to work too hard. I couldn't promise I wouldn't be a miserable fuck when I returned, though. I hadn't been able to get all those terrible things Joseph Edwards had detailed in his notes out of my mind and what Judge Cashen's daughter had to say likely wouldn't make things better. But at least I'd know the full truth.

The concierge had a car service take me to Jessica Cashen's home in Alpharetta, and nearly an hour later I was standing on the front porch of her home with my heart in my throat. A cool breeze chilled me as it began to lightly rain. I rang the doorbell and balled up my shaking hands, bracing myself for what was to come.

The door opened and in front of me stood a woman I guessed wasn't even Nina's age. Maybe twenty-two, she had short blond hair and brown eyes that grew larger by the second as she stared at me. She was petite, but quickly I found out that small package was full of power.

"Who are you? How can you be here?" she asked in a voice seeped in rage.

I raised my hands in front of me in surrender, hoping to put her at ease. "I'm sorry. I didn't mean to upset you. My name is Tristan and I was hoping to speak to you about your father."

"There's no way you can be standing here in front of me. Is this some kind of cruel joke? If so, I don't think it's funny."

She tried to slam the door on me, but I quickly stuffed my right foot next to the doorjamb and said quietly, "Please. I don't know what you're talking about, but it's very important I speak to you."

"Who are you?"

I looked in through the opening and saw a look of horror on her face. "Don't be scared. My name is Tristan Stone. I just want to talk. Please."

The look in her eyes told me she recognized my name. Slowly, she opened the door and her gaze scanned me up and down. Finally, she stopped on my face and narrowed her eyes to angry slits.

"You look just like him."

I didn't have to ask who she meant. Nodding, I said, "He was my twin."

"I heard he died. Is that true?" she asked with venom in her words.

"Yes."

"Good. I hope he suffered." She looked away and then faced me again. "I'm sorry. I just can't feel bad that he's gone."

"May we talk? I need some answers, and I'm hoping you can help me understand some things."

Silently, she welcomed me in and we sat in a small living room off the entryway with a small, unlit Christmas tree in the corner. I studied her for a moment as she did the same with me, and then I said what I guessed no one in my family had ever said to her. "I'm sorry about the deaths of your father and sister."

"I'm having a hard time believing you knew nothing about that, Mr. Stone. Your brother sure did."

"My brother and I were two very different people. I swear to you I knew nothing about what happened to your family. That's what I'm here for tonight."

Jessica Cashen sighed heavily and her mouth turned down into a frown. "You don't understand how hard it was to accept what your brother did. Even today, if I hear the name Taylor, I have a hard time not lashing out. My husband has been through so many nights of me being miserable over this I had to promise him I'd let it go."

"I understand, Jessica, but I need to know things only you can tell me. There's another person hurt by all this, and she'll be helped by what you tell me."

"Are you saying your brother did this to another girl too?"

I shook my head. "No, but there was another person hurt by my brother and father. What you can tell me about what happened may help her deal with the loss of her father."

"I'm sorry to hear someone else went through what my family had to endure. My mother died last year right in this house, never fully recovered from the shock of losing my sister and father just months apart. She just shriveled up."

"I'm so sorry."

She wiped a tear away and took a deep breath. "I'll tell you what I know. You'll have to fill in the blanks."

"Thank you." I sat back on the couch and listened as she began her story.

"My sister was only fifteen when she met your brother, Tristan. Even now as I look at you, I can see him. Those same brown eyes and look of money you both have. How old are you?"

"Twenty-nine."

"Did you like teenage girls when you were twenty-four? Your brother did. I never found out how he met her. I can't imagine why a fifteen year old girl, a freshman in high school, would be anywhere near where a grown man would be. Amanda was sweet and innocent, not in the way people say someone is but in reality they're out every night sleeping with anyone. She was still a virgin when she met him."

My stomach turned at the idea of being with a teenage girl when I was twenty-four.

"Wherever they met, she was crazy about him from the first night. I remember she came up to my room and told me she'd met someone. I thought she meant some boy at the mall. She told me his name was Taylor and he was gorgeous with big brown eyes she was sure were the most beautiful eyes she'd ever seen. I bet you've heard that a lot too."

Jessica stopped for a moment and stared at me. "It's amazing how much you look like him. When I first saw you standing in my doorway, I wanted to lunge at you I was so angry. You're identical down to the shape of your face and even your teeth."

For the first time in my life, I hated the way I looked as she described Taylor through my features. "You met Taylor, I assume?"

"Once. It was then that I realized my sister had gotten into something that was going to be bad for her. I just didn't realize how bad."

"What happened to make things go bad?" I asked, knowing the basic outline of the story. My brother had gotten a teenage girl pregnant and like a coward, had turned his back on her and the baby. What I didn't know was why.

"She found out she was going to have his baby. I tried to convince her to have an abortion. She was only fifteen, for God's sake. I was nearly nineteen at the time and I couldn't have handled a baby. She was too young, but she wouldn't listen to me. She was in love with him and thought they'd get married and live happily after. I tried to explain things to her, but she just said over and over that he could take care of her. I guess she thought since he was wealthy that he'd do just that."

"Did she tell your parents who the father was?"

Jessica shook her head sadly. "Not at first. She told him, but then the calls from him stopped. He wouldn't talk to her. She became depressed and stayed in her room all the time. My mother began to ask questions and finally Amanda told her she was pregnant. But even then, she wouldn't give up his name. She was sure he would come around. She thought he might be scared because of who our father was. Amanda wasn't stupid, even if she was naive. She knew a twenty-four year old man with a fifteen year old girl was considered statutory rape, even if she was madly in love. My father was a judge, and she was worried that Taylor might be afraid to live up to his responsibilities because of the difference in their ages."

I tried to imagine this person Jessica was describing, but I didn't know him. My brother had always been so on the straight and narrow. I couldn't imagine how he'd think sleeping with a teenage girl was okay.

Knowing what I was about to say may upset Jessica, I lowered my voice and quietly said, "Was your sister a willing participant?" I couldn't bring myself to ask if my twin brother had raped a child.

"If you're asking did he force himself on her, the answer is no. He wasn't a rapist, Tristan. He was a son-of-a-bitch who discarded my little sister when things got too real for him. He was fine with her when she was a simple thing to play with, but when real life crashed in on them, he abandoned her, leaving her to deal with a baby on her own."

"Why?" I wondered aloud. "He'd have to pay for the child whether he admitted it or not."

"Because he never cared for her like she cared for him. She was a toy he liked playing with. She adored him and hung on his every word. She'd tell me about meeting him and I never heard her say they talked about her. It was all him. He was a narcissist and she was his adoring fan. As long as she stayed in that role, everything was fine, but once she began to make demands on him, he wanted nothing more to do with her."

"I'm sorry, Jessica. I had no idea. I wasn't part of Taylor's world then. I was busy making my own bad choices. Nothing like he did, but..."

I let my sentence trail off. This wasn't about me and my stupid decisions.

"Something tells me you're not as alike as I would have thought. Do you have children, Tristan?"

Shaking my head, I forced a smile. "No. None yet."

"Your brother's child would have been going to kindergarten this year. I think about that sometimes. A little boy or girl ready to begin school. That never came to be, though."

"What happened?" I asked, my heart heavy at the thought of her sister dealing with having a child at such a young age herself.

"Amanda tried to get him to talk to her, but he wouldn't even answer her phone calls. She didn't know where to find him and when he changed his number, she became depressed. It broke my heart to see her like that. She cried all the time, wouldn't eat, and stopped going out. Finally, she gave up and took her life when she was three months pregnant."

Jessica could no longer hold back her tears, and as they streamed down her cheeks, all I could do was sit there feeling like I was in the middle of a horror story. Taylor's neglect had been the direct cause of Amanda's death, and nothing had ever been said about it by my father or mother. Had they known about it? My father had, if the dots Joseph Edwards had connected were true. My father had known what Taylor did and then made it worse.

I wanted to reach out to touch her hand, but how could I, the identical image of the man whose monstrous behavior had taken her sister away?

She wiped under her eyes and sat quietly for a moment. "She made me promise not to tell our parents who the father was, but when she died, I couldn't lie to my father and mother anymore. I told them about Taylor and who he was. They deserved to know who had done this."

"Do you remember talking to a man named Joseph Edwards after your father's death?"

Shaking her head, she suddenly got a look of recognition in her eyes. "I do, actually. He came to see me because of the bombing. He wanted to know about your father, though, not Taylor. I told him I didn't know anything about him, but then I explained everything that had happened with Amanda and your brother. He seemed to think that they were connected, I think."

"The bombing and what had happened to your sister."

"Yeah. The police never thought that, though. They still believe it was a gas explosion. I don't. I find it too coincidental that after my father tracked down your brother and told him what had happened to my sister and then your father's company is part of a case my father is judging that he suddenly is killed in a gas explosion."

"Do you remember anything about the case?"

"Not much. It was just a basic sexual harassment case, a civil suit. Your father's company was being sued by some woman and my father was the judge in the case."

I thought back to what Joseph Edwards had written in his notes about Stone Worldwide winning the case once Jessica's father wasn't the judge anymore. As much as I wanted to believe my father hadn't been responsible for Albert Cashen's death, there was too much to show me otherwise.

"That man, Joseph Edwards, told me he'd want to talk more with me, but he never returned. How did you find out about him?"

I swallowed hard before I began to tell the events that had brought me to Nina and ultimately, to Jessica and the truth of my family. "Joseph Edwards was murdered shortly after he spoke to you. His daughter is the person I believe may be helped by what you've told me."

Jessica covered her face with her hands. "Oh, my God! He was murdered? They killed him, didn't they? Your father and brother killed him like they killed my father."

Unable to hide from the overwhelming facts anymore, all I could do was nod in agreement. A young girl was dead because my brother had been a manipulative bastard and coward, and my father had had two men killed to protect Taylor and his own despicable actions.

"I don't know anything else, Tristan. That's all I have. I heard your family was killed in a plane crash a few months after my father and sister died."

"They were," I said quietly.

"I'm sorry. I guess you're the CEO of Stone Worldwide now. You know, I fantasized at least a thousand times about what I wanted to do to ruin your family like your brother and father ruined mine. I used to think about exposing everything they did and taking all that money your family has. I wanted to hurt you like they hurt me."

Jessica's voice caught in her throat and she looked away. When she turned back to face me, her expression wasn't one of hate or anger as it had been seconds earlier but sadness. "I think I feel sorry for you, Tristan. We've both lost everyone in our families, but I get to remember my sister and father as good people who never intentionally hurt anyone. You can't do that. Now that I've met you, I'm sorry you have to go through life knowing that."

I felt like I'd just been slammed in the chest with a cinder block. The truth of her statement was almost too much to handle. Here I was in a common suburban home I could buy twenty of with someone who had lost everything in her life, and I was the one being pitied. I, Tristan Stone, was worthy of pity for my family's guilty behavior.

"Please tell Joseph Edwards' daughter that my sympathies are with her. I know what she's going through."

I stood to leave, needing to get out of there as quickly as possible. She followed me to the door as we said our generic goodbyes, and as I left, she grabbed my arm to force me to turn around. I stopped dead and looked at her, not wanting to hear any more.

"I believe you're trying to do the right thing, Tristan. I can't imagine how hard this must be for you. I hope after what I've said you can find some kind peace with all this."

The car waited for me at the end of the sidewalk, and while I watched Jessica's house grow smaller as I drove away, I also hoped someday I'd be able to find some kind of peace after everything I'd learned.

NINETEEN

Nina

I had basically fallen in love with the Peachtree Suite within an hour of being there. This was my first trip to one of Tristan's hotels since my accident, not counting his incredible penthouse, and I loved the idea that I could add my artistic touch to such beautiful places. The colors of the suite were muted neutrals, but the designer had included a splash of color with deep burgundy draperies. I wanted to highlight that accent and really make it pop.

That's not to say I was even sure I could do the job. I hadn't told anyone, not even Jordan, but just thinking about picking out art made my palms sweat. Hours and hours of studying artistic styles and techniques in my room each day since I'd been released from the hospital had given me a small sense of confidence, but the real litmus test would be when I had to choose pieces for my first assignment.

I had a feeling Tristan had picked this suite as a simple job so I could ease myself back into things. As I scanned the over one thousand square foot area surrounding me, I tried not to feel intimidated. How couldn't I, though? The rooms rivaled the country house in beauty. The walls were painted to look like aged cream colored plaster, heavy white crown moldings typical of southern architecture framed the rooms, and the showstopper of the living room was a white cararra marble fireplace flanked by two French doors draped in that stunning burgundy color.

What could I add to all that?

All the ideas I'd had when I was searching at home felt wrong now that I was standing in the middle of this stunning suite. I wondered if maybe I should focus on something that would resonate with the local area instead of choosing something based on a certain style or color palette. I'd always loved the art at the Philly museums in part because it showcased the flavor of the local art scene. If I could find a piece or grouping that was not only beautiful but meaningful to Atlanta area instead of focusing on improving what the decorator had chosen, the room might actually be better because of the art.

At least that's what I tried to convince myself of as I stood there in the center of all that beauty.

I set off to the first bedroom to do some searching. Sitting legs folded on the bed, I tapped away on my laptop for information on artists right there in Atlanta. As I looked through page after page of artwork, none of them seemed right. They were all beautiful, but I was looking for something else—something that spoke to me—even if I wasn't sure what it was.

And then I saw that something. A local artist, Everett Shean, painted scenes of Cumberland Island, a barrier island off the coast of Georgia, and as I studied his oil paintings, I saw a turtle he'd created a series of paintings around. A few clicks to get to the series' page on his website and I found out the turtle was a loggerhead sea turtle that was an endangered species on Cumberland Island.

Déjà vu struck as I stared at that turtle and all of a sudden I realized I was having a memory from the past four years! The turtle looked like the turtle character from Finding Nemo, the one that sounded like a surfer and called everyone "Dude." The memory of watching that movie with one of my nieces hit me and out of the blue I had remembered that entire evening I'd babysat for Kim and Jeff!

I needed to tell someone, and since Tristan wasn't back from his meeting yet, I grabbed my cell phone and called my sister. She'd be so happy to hear my memory was finally coming back.

She answered, and I blurted out, "Kim, I remember that night I babysat and we watched Finding Nemo! Do you remember? You and Jeff went to dinner, and I babysat. Isn't it great?"

"Whoa! Slow down. What are you talking about, Nina? Are you okay? Where are you?"

I jumped off the bed and began to pace, my free arm flailing as I spoke. "I'm great! I'm in Atlanta with Tristan and as I was researching the art I wanted to show him for the suite, I saw this turtle that's endangered on one of the barrier islands off of Georgia. The turtle is the focus of a series by a local artist. He paints in oil, which is always so rich. You should see these paintings, Kim. They're gorgeous!"

"Baby, what turtle are you talking about? You're talking so fast I can't understand what you're saying."

"The one who calls everyone Dude, like he's a surfer."

"What?"

"In the movie," I explained in frustration. "What's the Finding Nemo turtle's name?"

"Nina, I have no idea what you're talking about. Who's Nero?" she asked, sounding almost as frustrated as I was.

"Nemo! You know. The fish. He's lost and his father has to find him. Oh, forget it! The point is that I remembered something from the past four years. My memory is coming back! Isn't that great?"

"It is, but I'm still not comfortable with you staying out at that house with someone you barely know, Nina."

Her voice had that condescending tone it got when she was chastising me for something. I hated that tone of voice. "Kim, Tristan isn't a stranger or someone I barely know. I was engaged to him before the accident. He's a good man, and I love him. Don't ruin this for me. I was so happy when I called you."

"I don't want to ruin anything for you. I just think you're too naive and get yourself into things you don't understand."

My chest tightened as tears welled in my eyes. I couldn't help get emotional. All I'd wanted to do was share my wonderful news and now I had to defend myself once again to my sister, whose opinion of my life I didn't give a damn about.

"Why? Because I don't keep myself all closed off and guarded? Because I give people a chance? I know that people like you think that makes me stupid or idiotic, but it's who I am. I can't change that, and I don't want to. I like being open to new things, and that includes new people. If I was like you, I would have never gotten to know Tristan."

"How would you know, Nina? You can't even remember. For all you know, he manipulated you into this whole thing. You don't know everything about him."

"Thanks, Kim."

I jammed my fingertip onto the screen of my phone and hung up on her. Throwing the phone on the bed, I let the tears come as I stood there with my shoulders hunched from the weight of her negativity.

I should have known better. Why didn't I call Jordan?

A noise behind me made me turn around and I saw Tristan standing there looking as beaten down as I felt. His tie was loosened, his suit looking like it hung from a body exhausted from dealing with the world all day. I wiped the tears from my cheeks and forced a smile.

"Hey, you look as bad as I feel."

"What happened? Did someone come by the room?" he asked in a voice filled with worry.

Shaking my head, I tried not to think of Kim's words, but I couldn't help it. I'd been so happy just minutes earlier and now sadness that my only family member left couldn't find any joy in my news made my heart heavy. "No. I was just on the phone with my sister."

Just as he had in the hospital, Tristan grew stiff at the mere mention of Kim. "What did she say? I hope you aren't listening to her, Nina."

"I'm not. I just called her with good news and she was so negative. All I wanted was to share something that had made me really happy, and she didn't care."

Tristan walked toward me and stopped just inches away. Leaning down, he kissed me and stroked the pad of his thumb over my damp cheek. "I'm here now, so you can tell me."

I leaned into his hand, loving the strength of it beneath my head. Looking up at the concern etched into his features, I smiled, hoping to ease some of his worry. "I remembered something. It's not much, but it's something."

His expression changed to one of surprise, but I sensed his concern wasn't abated. Brown eyes that said so much about how he was feeling looked intently into mine as he spoke. "What did you remember?"

"Babysitting my nieces one night. It's nothing important."

Pulling me close, he held me tight as he kissed the top of my head, whispering low, "Don't say that. It's very important. You're beginning to remember things."

I loved the feel of his arms around me, protecting me from even the unkind words of my sister. I wished I could do the same for him. As strong as he was, I knew whatever he'd been dealing with had worn him down.

"Thank you. That's all I wanted to hear when I called her, but instead she just harped on how stupid she thinks I am. She thinks you're manipulating me into doing things I shouldn't be doing." I looked up at him and smiled. "As if falling in love is something I shouldn't do."

He cradled my face and shook his head. "Don't listen to her. Falling in love with me was exactly what you should do. I should know. I fell in love with you first."

I tapped his chin with my finger. "This time. I'm still convinced when I remember everything that I'm going to find out that I was crazy about you long before you loved me."

A shadow crossed his face and then it was gone and he was smirking at me like I was acting silly. From anyone else in the world, that kind of smirk would have irritated the hell out of me, but from Tristan, it was just too cute.

"So would you like to see the art I think would work here?"

"Sure."

"Righteous, dude," I joked as I headed over to the bed.

"Righteous, dude?" he asked as he raised his eyebrows in disbelief.

I motioned to him to come sit next to me as I browsed through Everett Shean's website. When I finally found the turtle pictures, I turned my laptop toward him. "These are loggerhead sea turtles and they're an endangered species on a barrier island off of

Georgia's coast. I know they aren't fancy or the kind of art you would normally see in a hotel suite like this, but I think they'd work. He blends vivid colors on the turtle backs that I think might look nice here against the effect your designer created on the neutral color walls."

"And these are, what did you call them? Righteous?" he asked as he leaned in to examine the paintings.

I couldn't help but giggle. Sometimes he was so serious. "No. I was making a reference to the turtle in Finding Nemo. You know? The one who talks like a surfer?"

"Finding who?"

"Finding Tristan Stone's sense of humor. It was a huge hit," I teased. "I can't believe you never watched that movie."

Before I could explain any more about the cartoon or the turtle paintings, his phone vibrated inside his jacket and all traces of any happiness slid from his face as he rose from the bed. "I have to take this."

Like always, I wanted to ask who it was who could make him instantly miserable every time they called. I didn't, though, silently swearing that one of these days I would find out who the bastard on the phone was who ruined so many nice moments between us. He walked out of the room and I heard the door to the suite close behind him, but something inside told me to follow him this time. I wanted to know now who was haunting him.

I flung open the door to find him standing in the hallway with a man who looked to be about fifty or so. He was thick and reminded me of a police detective from a TV show. He stood too close to Tristan, like he was trying to intimidate him, and although I couldn't hear clearly what he was saying, it sounded ominous.

"Tristan, is everything okay?"

He spun around, his eyes flashing angrily, and for a second I recoiled back into the room, afraid of what I'd interrupted. Stepping toward me, he took my hand and squeezed it tightly. The other man followed him into our suite, and we stood awkwardly for a moment before Tristan finally spoke.

"Nina, this is the Vice President of Operations for Stone Worldwide, Karl Dreger. Karl, I'd like to introduce you to my fiancée, Nina Edwards."

Karl extended his meaty hand and shook mine. "How very nice to finally meet you, Nina. I've heard a lot about you."

Smiling, I pulled my hand away as soon as I could. "It's nice to meet you too."

"I'm so sorry to interrupt your little getaway. I just needed to remind Tristan of a deadline. Now that I have, I'll leave you to your evening. I hope you have a wonderful holiday, Nina."

His voice made my skin crawl. It was smarmy and threatening at the same time. Tristan's hand continued to clutch mine tightly, as if he was afraid to let go. I was glad for the feel of him holding me, protecting me from this person. This man he worked with was only in the room for a few moments, but I was left with the surest sense that he held something dark or evil inside him.

As the door closed, Tristan pulled me close to him, wrapping his arms around me. "Nina, you are never to be alone with him. Please don't ask me to explain. Just promise me that if you ever see him again without me, you'll get away."

My ear pressed against his chest, and I heard his heart race wildly. "Tristan, is he the person who calls and ruins your mood every time? I won't ask you to explain, but tell me if that's him."

He was silent for so long I wondered if he'd heard me over the pounding of his heart, but finally, he said, "Yes. I'm sorry."

I squeezed him tighter. "You don't have to be sorry. I just wish you felt like you could tell me what's wrong."

Tristan stroked my hair and back as his heartbeat settled into its normal, slower rhythm. Kissing the top of my head, he said sadly, "Someday when you have your memories back, I'll tell you."

"Okay." Hoping to change the subject to lighten our mood, I looked up at this face etched with a frown and said, "I liked the way you introduced me. Fiancée. I don't know if you said that for some other reason than wanting me to be that again, but I'd like it to be true."

His eyes sparkled as he smiled broadly, looking more gorgeous than I thought I'd ever seen him look. "I'd like nothing more in this world, Nina, than for you to agree to marry me again."

Even as he smiled and told me he wanted more than anything to hear me say I wanted to marry him, his voice was still weighted down with a sadness that made me wish he would tell me whatever was eating him up inside. I so wished I could make him as happy as he made me.

"I'd like to wear the ring again too."

"You don't remember this, but we were supposed to get married on December 14."

"Are you asking me to run off and elope, Mr. Stone?" I said in a playful voice.

"Yes. Marry me. We can leave tomorrow from here and go wherever we want."

I leaned back away from him, shocked that he was serious. "You're not kidding? Can you do that? Don't you have to run a huge company?"

"Nina, I can do what I want. Part of being the CEO. Marry me."

I couldn't say no. Looking down at me, he was so cute I didn't want to say no. "Okay, let's do it! I need to go back to the house, though. I only need a few things and we can leave right after that."

"I can get you whatever you need so we don't have to go back. We'll leave from here tomorrow morning."

"Tristan, it will only take me a few minutes at the house and then we can go wherever we want. I promise I won't be long."

"Okay, but we'll go back and leave tonight."

I stood on my toes and kissed the tip of his nose. "You drive a hard bargain, sir. You have a deal."

"Good. Pack your things and I'll let the pilot know we're leaving."

Tristan headed into the other room to get things ready for us to fly back to New York, and even though things felt like they were moving a hundred miles a minute, I was ready to do it.

I was ready to marry Tristan and begin our life together.

TWENTY

Nina

My hands shook as I gathered up my makeup and dumped it all into my suitcase. I grabbed a few dresses from my closet, folding them hastily, and stopped to take a deep breath. Tristan and I were eloping in the middle of the night like two kids in love. This was really happening.

It's not that I didn't want to marry him or that I wasn't in love with him. I was crazy about him and nothing had ever felt as right as when I said yes to becoming his wife. But my sister's scolding echoed in my mind, sowing the seeds of doubt like they always had. I didn't want to think like that, though. She wasn't me. She'd never fall for someone like Tristan and elope in the middle of the night. It was far too risky for her.

But I wasn't her.

I wanted to take a chance and be daring. I'd never really done anything wild or crazy. I'd been the good daughter, always getting good grades and doing just as my father told me to. Even that hadn't been enough for Kim, though. My artistic side had always made me "flighty," according to her. She didn't understand viewing the world through eyes that wanted to see beauty. All she wanted to see was the bad—bad people, bad situations, and mostly, bad men.

Whatever she thought she knew about Tristan, I knew in my heart he wasn't a bad man. Did I know everything about him? No. But who knew everything about the man or woman they loved? I accepted the reality of his life, and that meant I might never know more than I did now about him. That was okay.

What I knew, I loved. What I didn't know, I'd have to deal with if and when the time came. That was part of what you did when you loved someone.

Zipping my bag, I took one last look at my single girl face in the mirror. Oh my God! I hadn't told Jordan. I grabbed my cell phone and quickly called her, not caring that it was ridiculously late to be calling anyone with a job.

She answered in a groggy voice. "Hello?"

"Jordan, it's Nina. I'm sorry for calling so late, but I wanted to tell you that Tristan and I are eloping. We're leaving in a few minutes for an island in the Caribbean."

I heard her make a noise like she was sitting up in bed. "What? Who calls someone and says something like that? I thought you were still planning on a big ta-do on the island like before your accident."

"He asked me tonight if I'd elope with him, and I said yes. I didn't call anyone else but you. Please don't tell me not to do this. I already know Kim would say that."

"I would never do that, Nina. Tristan is crazy about you, and you're crazy about him. I'm just bummed that I won't get to do the whole island thing."

"Thanks, Jordan. We'll do the island thing another time, I promise. I'm just glad you aren't trying to talk me out of it."

"Oh, honey, I wouldn't do that, and don't let Kim do that to you anymore. You live your life and know that I'm here in good times and bad. Now go get married, you crazy kids, and call me when the honeymoon haze wears off."

I choked up at Jordan's words and swallowed hard. "I love you, Jordan. I wish you were my sister instead of Kim."

"I am in every way that's important. A sister from another mother, like we always said. Now go enjoy yourself and don't give Kim another thought. Got it?"

"Got it. I'll call you soon."

"I love you, Nina. Tell Tristan I said congratulations."

I hung up and told myself Jordan was right. No more thinking of Kim and all her negativity. This was my life, and I was going to live it the way I wanted to.

Dropping my bag off in the entryway, I looked for Tristan in his office and his room but didn't find him. I'd taken longer than I'd promised, but I'd expected he'd be waiting patiently for me at the end of my hallway. When I didn't find him in the kitchen, I began to wonder where he was and why no one else seemed to be around either. Where was Rogers and his popping up out of thin air trick?

A noise that sounded like angry voices hit me as I turned to make my way down to the pool area. Rogers' area of the house was directly to the left of the stairs to the lower level, and I stopped to listen, straining to hear if the voices were someone in the house or on TV. I couldn't decide which, so I slowly walked down Rogers' hallway, uneasy since I'd never felt welcome enough by Tristan's butler to visit him in his private quarters.

"There's only one way Karl would have known I was in Atlanta. You told him, didn't you?"

The rage in Tristan's voice was unmistakable as he accused someone of betraying him. But was it possible he was talking to Rogers, the man who'd been with him since he was a small child?

I listened outside Rogers' door as he denied telling anyone where we'd gone, but I knew guilt when I heard it. He had told that awful man where Tristan and I were. But why? Why would he betray Tristan?

"I've told you that I don't care what you think of Nina. I don't care if you think we should be together or not. I've tolerated your sideways looks when we're together and your opinion on how I should handle my life. I won't tolerate you getting into bed with the man who wants to ruin my happiness. When you put Nina in danger, then I fucking care what you're doing."

"I would never do anything to cause hurt to come to you, Tristan. You know that," Rogers said in his stiff, official style.

"What I know is that I have a traitor in my house. Are you going to tell me why? I deserve to know at least that."

"I've never done anything but protect you."

"By putting the woman I love in danger? How does that protect me? How does that show your loyalty to me?"

What did he mean by danger? Karl had made me uneasy, but was I truly in danger from him? My mind raced as I jumped to conclusions. Had my car accident been something else and were Karl and Rogers to blame? Bursting into the room, I pointed at Rogers. "He's never liked me, Tristan. Did you cause my accident, Rogers?"

"Nina, wait outside. I don't want you around this," Tristan ordered.

"No. I want to hear from him why he hates me — why he wants me out of your life. And I want to know if he tried to hurt me already."

We stood there staring at each other in Rogers' plain white room, and I saw Tristan consider what I'd just accused his butler of. His expression morphed from one full of rage to one of hurt as he looked over at Rogers.

"Answer her. Was her accident something else?"

"Karl is only looking out for your welfare, Tristan, as I am."

His lack of denial sent a chill up my spine. Was he saying he'd intentionally set out to hurt me or worse, kill me?

"You've been like a father to me. How could you do this to someone I love? I trusted you!"

Rogers tilted his chin up in a gesture of defiance. "I'm proud to say that as much as you're a Stone, Tristan, you've been like a son to me. I've watched over you, protecting you for years. When your father chose Taylor over you, as he always did, I was there to watch your football games and hockey matches. It was I who was there with your mother to cheer you on, to take pictures of you with your trophies. Never your father. When you got into trouble, I cleaned it up for you. I cared for you. I'm doing that now. This is no different."

His mention of Tristan's trophies hit me like a slap to the face. Suddenly, I had a memory of me looking at pictures of him as a child. Everything around me faded away as I struggled to place where and when I'd seen the pictures. I could see in my mind Tristan as a young boy holding a trophy high above his head, smiling as his mother stood nearby gazing at him in adoration for his accomplishment. But none of the pictures in the house were of him as a child, so where had I seen this image?

I was torn from my memories as Tristan's voice grew increasingly louder at Rogers' continued denials of doing anything wrong. "Answer the question Nina asked you. Did you have any part in her accident?"

"I would never physically hurt her, Tristan."

"Did Karl do something to the car with your help?" he barked at the older man. "Tell me!"

"Her accident was not due to anything I had any part in. What Karl did is something you need to ask him."

Tristan lunged at Rogers, grabbing him around the neck as he yelled, "I trusted you! You know how much she means to me! You know!"

Rogers clawed at his forearms to pull him off him, but he was no match for Tristan, who was much younger and stronger. The strangled cries of the butler filled the room as he was slowly being choked to death. As much as I hated Rogers for what he'd done to me and Tristan, I couldn't let the man I love kill someone.

Pulling on his arm, I struggled to tear Tristan away, but I was no match for him either. The more I tore at his arms to make him release him, the more he fought to hurt him. I watched in horror as Rogers' face began to turn blue.

"Tristan, don't! Let him go! Don't do this!"

He stilled, and I was sure that the old man was next to death. Tristan slowly raised his hands up and backed away, his face covered in revulsion at what he'd almost done to the man who'd been closer to him than anyone else in his life.

Rogers fell to the floor clutching his throat and coughing. He sat there with tears streaming down his cheeks as the blood began to flow back to his face. Slowly, the bluish tint faded and he looked like himself again. Unable to talk, he simply looked up in shock at the man he thought of like a son.

"Get out! Take whatever you think you need and get out," Tristan growled down at him.

A gurgling sound came out of Rogers' mouth as he tried to protest the order, but Tristan merely repeated himself with even more viciousness. He was cold and distant, scaring me when he spoke.

"Leave and never come back. You're dead to me now."

Rogers' eyes grew wide at the sound of those words. He stood on shaky legs and slowly walked past us into his bathroom, still hunched over from the attack. I remained there stunned at what I'd just witnessed, unsure what to say. Gently, I touched Tristan's arm, but even that slightest contact made him spin around to face me, his dark eyes flashing the fury that hadn't subsided inside him yet.

"Tristan, it's okay. It's me. Everything's going to be okay."

He seemed to stare right through me for a moment and then his expression calmed as he pulled me tightly to him. No words came, but I felt the tension and rage begin to fade away as he held me in his arms.

"I'm sorry, Nina. I had no idea. I should have known. I would have sent him away if I'd known."

I looked up into his troubled eyes and cradled his face in my hands. "Are you okay? What's going on? Why would he want to hurt me or want me out of your life?"

Tristan looked back toward the bathroom where Rogers still remained. "I want you to go to my room and stay there. Don't come out until I come get you. Do you understand?"

"Why?"

He bent down and kissed me softly on the lips, whispering, "I promise someday I'll be able to tell you everything, Nina, but for now, please, no more questions. All I can say is that I would never let anyone hurt you. I need you to believe me."

Nodding, I hugged him. "I do. Just promise me you won't get hurt."

Above me, he said, "I'll be fine." He pushed me back from him and cupped my chin. "Now go stay in my room and lock the door. Don't come out until I come get you."

I wanted nothing less than to leave him there to deal with the devastating reality of being betrayed by the person he'd known and trusted longer than anyone else in this world, but I was frightened enough not to fight him on this. Quickly, I ran to his room and locked the door behind me, my hands shaking in fear at everything I'd seen and heard.

Looking around, I remembered the first night I'd come over from my side of the house to pronounce my anger at being held against my will. That Nina had been so ignorant of who Tristan really was. Never a jailer, he was my protector. I trusted him, and now more than ever, I needed to rely on him, even though I didn't know what danger surrounded us.

At that moment, my memory was what could help me the most, but all I had was the recollection of watching a cartoon with my nieces and the fleeting images of looking at pictures of Tristan as a child. I sat on the edge of his bed and closed my eyes, trying to piece together the memory Rogers' mention of sports trophies had caused to become so real in my mind.

No matter how hard I tried, I couldn't remember where I'd seen those pictures. Had Tristan shown me them before my accident, maybe as we began to learn things about one another when we were first dating?

Something about the images in my mind gave me a sense that I hadn't seen them with him, but then how would I have seen pictures of his childhood?

I opened my eyes and scanned the room around me. Maybe I had seen them in this room. He had said we'd shared this room before my accident, so that would make sense. I knew it might be an invasion of his privacy, but I wanted to know more about why this memory seemed so important, so I began to look through his dresser drawers.

Running my hands over pair after pair of black dress socks and cotton boxer briefs, I found nothing that felt like it would be pictures. I moved through all the drawers and there was nothing but what belonged in them. His desk sat across the room, so I tried there found nothing that made me think I had seen them in this room.

But if not here, where in this house would pictures of Tristan as a child be?

A noise outside in the hallway jarred me out of my thoughts, and I stood frozen in place staring at the bedroom door. I listened for it again, but nothing happened. My fear at a strange noise was replaced with concern for Tristan, so I took a deep breath and opened the door to find him standing there.

"Why did you open the door?"

"I was worried about you. What happened? Are you okay?" I asked as I pulled him into the room.

"I'm fine."

His answer screamed that he was putting up walls to hide how hurt he was. I hated seeing him like this. I wanted to make him smile like he had all those times for me when I laid in that hospital bed all those weeks.

I followed him to the bed and sat down next to him. Taking his hand, I brought it to my mouth and kissed it. "I'm sorry, Tristan. I'm sorry all of this happened because of me."

He shook his head but said nothing.

"I don't know what's going on, but don't shut me out. I don't need to know everything right now, but I need to know we're okay."

Turning to face me, he looked at me with soulful brown eyes full of pain. "Everything I've trusted all my life has been a lie. You're all I have that's honest and true. I need to know we're okay as much as you do, Nina."

I cradled his face in my hands. "I'm here with you. I'm not going anywhere, Tristan. I promise."

"Baby, things are going to get bad. You're going to find out things about me that you're not going to like. I need you to remember when all of it comes out that I love you and never meant any harm."

"You'd never hurt me, Tristan. I'd never believe you could."

He hung his head and said quietly, "I'm sorry we're not going to get to elope. Seems we never can take that last step and finally get married."

Stroking his back, I leaned against him. "Next time we will."

He jumped at the sound of a knock on the door and opened it to find Jensen standing there looking pale. I stood up and hurried to stand behind Tristan as his driver told him the police were at the door and wanted to speak to him.

Tristan grabbed my hand, and we walked out to speak to the police. My heart was racing as I wondered what they could want. Had Rogers reported Tristan's attack on him and the cops were there to arrest him? I couldn't let that happen. I'd tell them everything if that's what they were here for.

I squeezed his hand in mine to let him know I was right there with him as we walked up to meet the two men in uniform standing just inside the entryway. Both were chubby and looked like they'd spent too many breaks at the local donut shop, but they didn't look threatening. In fact, they looked more concerned than anything else.

"Mr. Stone? Tristan Stone?"

Nodding, he answered, "Yes. What can I do for you tonight, officer?"

"Do you have a Jonathan Rogers in your employ?" the policeman on the right asked as the other one waited with a pen and notepad for the answer.

"Yes. Rogers is my butler."

"Sir, when was the last time you saw him?"

"About an hour ago."

Tristan's answers were short, and I watched the officers carefully to see if they found them suspicious. Neither man seemed to, thankfully.

"Mr. Stone, a man with identification showing he was Jonathan Rogers was hit by a car just outside the gate to your property. I'm sorry, but he's dead."

I felt Tristan's body deflate next to me, and I quickly wrapped my arm around his waist to support him. The air left his body in a whoosh as he exhaled heavily.

"What? That...that's impossible. He was just here."

"I'm sorry, sir. Do you know how we can contact his next of kin?"

"He doesn't have any family. He's worked for my family for over twenty years and was never married and never had any children." He stopped for a moment and then said quietly, "We were his family."

Tristan's voice sounded faraway, like in a dream. The officer taking notes began to explain about Rogers' body and burial, but his words all flowed together until they didn't make sense anymore. I watched Tristan nod as if he understood everything, but I saw in his eyes it was all a jumble like it was for me.

After they left, I followed him to Rogers' room. He leaned against the doorframe and stared at the spot where just a short while earlier the last thing he'd said was that the soul he'd known for longer than any other was dead to him. My heart broke as I watched what I knew was guilt wash over him. He had nothing to feel guilty for, but that didn't matter.

For someone who said so little, to have his words come back to haunt him was likely more painful than I could ever imagine. I wanted to make it all go away, to bring a smile to his face like he'd done so many times for me, but the pain he was feeling was too deep for me to reach.

TWENTY-ONE

Nina

Christmas came, but it had a pall over it that neither of us could deny. Rogers' funeral couldn't take place until after the holiday, so there was no closure to give Tristan any peace. He pretended to be happy for my sake, but I sensed him slipping into a dark place that scared me.

I wanted to call off the New Year's celebration with Jordan and Justin at the penthouse, but Tristan insisted, saying life had to go on. He didn't seem to be going on, though. He spoke even less than usual, and at times he seemed to be lost in his thoughts, staring off in the distance. Still there beside me, he seemed empty and hollow. The gentle smile that made me so happy was almost entirely absent, and his eyes were always full of sadness.

Just as we'd planned, we all met at the penthouse at ten on New Year's Eve. Jordan and Justin didn't know about what had happened to Rogers, but even they could tell something was wrong with Tristan. It wasn't just that he was so quiet. That was nothing new. It was a feeling of sadness that covered him even as he pretended to be interested in celebrating.

Justin and he sat watching some New Year's Eve special after an incredible dinner of filet mignon that

Tristan barely touched while Jordan joined me in the kitchen, our first time alone since I'd told her the news that we hadn't gotten married.

Whispering near my ear, she said, "Nina, what's going on? Did you two break up and you didn't want to blow us off for tonight? Tristan looks devastated about something."

I shook my head and let my body sag against the counter, finally able to talk about the whole thing with Rogers with somebody. "No. We couldn't elope because Rogers died. Tristan's not handling it well."

Jordan's eyes grew wide. "Oh, my God! What happened? He wasn't that old."

"He was hit by a car right outside the gate at the house. But that's not all. They had a terrible fight before and Tristan threw him out."

"Why? What's going on?"

I lowered my voice even more and leaned in next to her. "I don't know. Rogers was helping someone in Tristan's company who I think wants to hurt me. When Tristan found out, he went into a rage and nearly strangled him. The last thing he said was that Rogers was dead to him, and then less than an hour later he was dead. I don't think Tristan can forgive himself."

"Oh, honey, I'm so sorry for him, but now I'm worried. Who is this person Rogers was helping? Why would he want to hurt you?"

"I don't know. His name is Karl, and I've only met him once. I can only guess it has something to do with Stone Worldwide, but I don't know why anyone

FALL INTO ME

would want to hurt me because of that," I admitted, hoping Jordan could see something I couldn't.

"Does he have security to make sure this Karl creep doesn't get around you?" she asked as she looked out toward the living room.

I thought about her question. "I don't think so. Maybe. I'm not sure. I think he has cameras here at the hotel, so maybe he has them everywhere. He wouldn't let anyone hurt me, Jordan."

"I know. I know," she said as she took my hands in hers and stared into my eyes. "I'm his biggest fan. Trust me, Nina. What did I tell you in the hospital? It doesn't matter what you remember. Just watch how he acts toward you. The man loves you. Of that, I'm certain. I just worry because he's obviously in a funk. I don't want to see either of you hurt."

I nodded, looking out at Tristan as he sat there staring at the TV. I could tell he wasn't even paying attention to what was on the screen. "I'm worried about him, Jordan. He's slipping away right in front of my eyes. He loved Rogers like a father, and now he's really got no family at all."

"He's got you, sweetie."

I squeezed her hand tightly in mine. "I don't know if I'm enough. He keeps telling me he's fucked up. I don't know what he means. What if I'm not enough?"

Jordan lifted my chin with her hand and looked at me with an expression more serious than she had since that first moment I opened my eyes and saw her sitting there in my hospital room. "Nina Edwards, don't you doubt yourself. You're much stronger than your sister

282

or even your father ever thought you were. You love him, so don't you let him fall into something that he may never come out of."

"He doesn't want to talk. He goes out for hours at a time, and I don't know where he goes. I text him to ask and he just texts back that he's clearing his head. Then he comes back home and he smells like he's been drinking. He sleeps in his room, but I swear I hear noises like he's up all night watching horror movies or something. I hear what sounds like someone in pain."

"Maybe if you two got away. I know it's not the time to get married now, but maybe just a vacation to one of his hotels. Get out of town and start fresh?"

"I could try. I don't know what else to do," I admitted sadly. I didn't. I felt helpless to do much of anything. Tristan's walls were so thick, and it seemed like they were getting worse every day.

"Don't give up on him. You were like this after your father died. I didn't know what to do either, but I just stuck with you, telling you that you weren't alone. You came out of it eventually. So will he."

Justin walked toward us and gave Jordan the look boyfriends give when they want to leave. I couldn't blame him. We weren't exactly the host and hostess with the mostess. Ringing in the New Year in such somber surroundings wasn't fun, so after hugs and promises we'd all get together soon, they left.

Tristan sat quietly as the city below exploded in celebration, people toasting a new year and another chance. I curled up next to him, but he didn't move. My heart broke to see him so sad.

"Happy new year."

He said nothing, as if he was thinking about what I'd said, and finally turned his head toward me. "I love you, Nina. Don't ever think I don't."

"I know you do. I can't stand to see you like this. I want to make you feel better like you did for me when I was laid up in that hospital bed, but you keep pushing me away. I'm afraid you're going to push me right out of your life."

Looking away toward the fireworks exploding in the distance, he shook his head. "I'd never willingly let you go."

"Tell me what I can do. Every day, I feel like I'm losing another piece of you."

"You know what my shrinks said after the crash? They kept saying I was supposed to emote. Emote. That's it. As if that was going to make it all go away. Emote. But I didn't have anything to let out."

"Tristan, you can talk to me. Don't forget that. I know what it's like to lose someone. It may have happened four years ago, but it's like I just lost my father."

A look of pain settled into his features, and that hurt I knew he was feeling was right under the surface. If only he could let it out.

By the end of that week, I felt like everyone I knew was in misery. Jordan and Justin broke up on New Year's Day, and even though she claimed she'd seen it coming, I still knew by the sound of her voice that she was hurting. Tristan seemed to spend all his time at work after Rogers' funeral, texting me each afternoon to beg off having dinner together with vague excuses I knew were lies to hide the fact that he was unraveling. Even when he was in bed next to me at night, he was a million miles away.

Each day the distance between us grew, and I didn't know how to stop it.

Then on top of everything, Cal emailed with more of his sad tale. As I read it, something inside me snapped. How dare he play on people's feelings with his phony story about a cheating girlfriend and his dead mother when good people were dealing with real problems. I played the innocent friend, emailing him that I'd be happy to meet him for lunch that afternoon.

He spun the same web of lies he'd done before, but this time, I called him out. I don't think I ever felt better. I couldn't wait to tell Tristan that night, hoping that maybe my triumph in unveiling Cal's fraud right to his face would take his mind off his problems, even if for just a few minutes.

When he finally got home at eight o'clock, I heard him pass by my hallway on the way to his room. I quickly put away my laptop and headed over to his room to share my news. Pushing the door open, I found him standing at his desk with a manila envelope in his hand.

"Hey, you, I have a story to tell you," I said as I peeked my head in.

He turned around with an odd look in his eyes that frightened me. Standing there staring at me, he said, "Did you have a nice day, Nina?"

Even though everything in his body language and voice made me uneasy, I stepped into the room and sat down on the bed. "I did. That's what I wanted to talk to you about."

"Let me help you." He slid something out of the envelope in his hand and held it out toward me. "Is this what you wanted to tell me about?"

I strained to see what he held in his hand. When I didn't answer his question, he walked toward me and threw it on the bed next to me. I looked down and saw a stack of pictures of Cal and me at lunch just a few hours before.

"What are these? Do you have someone spying on me?"

Tristan's eyes flashed with anger. "I told you what he was doing and you still snuck around behind my back to see him. What am I supposed to think, Nina?"

"I'm trying to understand what you're going through Tristan, but I can't believe you'd have someone follow me and take pictures of me."

"And I can't believe you would sneak around and betrayed me with your ex, who is only trying to play you."

His words came out in a hiss. I'd never seen Tristan like this with me. The way he looked reminded me of what he'd been like that night with Rogers.

"So I leave the house once to go to meet Cal and let him know I'm onto his whole scam, and I'm not to be trusted, but you stay away from here day after day and I'm supposed to be fine with that? I'm not the one who's acting like they're doing something sneaky."

Tristan stared down at me with a confused look. "I'm not the one who needed to visit my ex to find out if I could love you."

His words cut like knives across my skin. I'd told him about my insecurities believing he'd understand, and now he was using them against me to indict me on some crime I'd never committed. I threw the pictures at him without saying a word and stormed toward the door before I burst into tears. I didn't want him to think I was sad. I was furious!

He grabbed my arm and spun me around to face him. "Where are you going?"

"I'm not going to stand here taking this!"

"Don't walk away, Nina."

I yanked my arm from his hold. "Why? No matter what I do, you stay away all day and half the night. You're probably cheating on me with whoever you spend all your time with. I bet that's why you're so convinced I'm doing something. Guilty conscience."

"You're being ridiculous. I'm not seeing anyone," he said coldly.

"Nice. Maybe you should practice that a little more in front of the mirror. A little more emotion and I might believe you."

That anger I'd seen just a minute before flashed in his eyes again at the mention of emotion. I hadn't meant to use what he'd told me on New Year's Eve. It just came out. I wanted to reach out and take his hand to show him we could work this out, but something held me back.

"You don't want that, Nina. You don't want me to show that emotion."

"Yes, I do! Finally, show me how you feel instead of pulling away. Let me hear that you still really care instead of making me guess and hope that you do," I cried.

He loosened his tie and walked past me to sit on the bed, avoiding looking at me. Even with me nearly begging him, he couldn't do it. Suddenly, I wanted a fight. After weeks of anger and sadness, there was so much pressure between us I needed to release it.

"So you're going to ignore me? I'm not even worth a few nice words? Everyone in your world wants me out of it. Do you?"

He still said nothing, preferring to close his eyes to block me out. I felt like I was nothing to him.

"You can't even say you want me in your life!" Now my tears couldn't be stopped, and I let them come. I stood there waiting for him to say anything, for him to even look at me as I pleaded for any sign that he still loved me, as everything became blurry from the mixture of tears and makeup clouding my eyes. My mouth was dry at the real fear that he'd never say anything to make me feel like he cared.

Tristan hung his head. "Nina, this isn't going work. I'll have my lawyers draw up a new document saying you're no longer obligated by our contract. I promise you'll never want for anything. I'll make sure that's in there too. I'll make sure you're safe."

His words stunned me. He was breaking up with me over my having lunch of with another man? What was going on?

"Why are you doing this? I don't want anyone else. I just went to lunch with him to tell him I knew what he was doing. I felt so good about it that I couldn't wait to tell you. Now you're sending me away? Don't do this, Tristan. I love you."

"This is best. Just let it happen."

I walked over to where he sat and fell to my knees. I had to see his eyes when he said he didn't want me or us anymore. Looking up, I waited for him to open his eyes so I could see what he was really feeling. No matter what his words said, I knew the truth would be in his eyes.

"At least look at me when you tell me you don't love me. I deserve at least that, Tristan."

He sat silently, his eyes still shut. I laid my head against his thigh and quietly said, "Please tell me what's going on. Maybe I can help. I can't believe you don't love me. I won't believe it. Not unless I see your eyes when you say those words."

I felt his hand gently cradle the top of my head and looked up to see those beautiful brown eyes so full of pain looking down at me. My heart skipped a beat as I waited for him to speak, and I prayed to God that I wouldn't hear him say he didn't love me anymore.

"I'm sorry, Nina. I don't know why I'm like this. I don't know why I make such a mess out of everything. I didn't mean to."

I pulled myself up to my knees and took his face in my hands. "You didn't do anything wrong. It's okay. I get that you're jealous. I felt that way when I saw all those pictures of you and those women at those parties. It's just that I'd never want Cal instead of you. You need to believe that."

"Just the thought of you with him makes me crazy. I'm sorry I'm so fucked up, Nina. I never meant for things to end up this way. I thought I could handle things."

The sadness and pain in his eyes broke my heart. "Things are fine between us. It's everyone else outside of us that aren't okay. We're fine. I love you and you love me. What else is there? I don't know what you mean about handling things, but you can't stop how people feel about things. I don't know why Rogers didn't like me or why that man you work with thinks you shouldn't be with me, but we don't have to listen to them."

"Nina, you should do what I said. Leave here and I promise you'll want for nothing. You'll be taken care of for the rest of your life."

"I don't want that. What do money and things mean to me when the most important part of this life you've given me isn't there anymore?"

Pressing my lips to his, I kissed him tenderly, feeling his sadness. I didn't know why he was so tortured, but it tore me up to watch him like this. Those brown eyes that spoke volumes were crying out in pain, despite his ability to hold back the tears.

"Nina, are we just putting off the inevitable?" he asked in a voice barely above a whisper, as if merely saying the words scared him as much as they did me.

I leaned forward and pressed my forehead to his. "No. I'm not leaving you, no matter how fucked up you say you are. I love you, Tristan Stone. You better just get used to it."

He let out a huge sigh and I wrapped my arms around his neck, wishing that a hug would give him even a little comfort.

"Promise me something?"

"Anything, Tristan."

"Promise me someday when this is all over you'll forget all the bad and just remember I loved you."

Taking me in his arms, he kissed me, pulling me into him like he couldn't get me close enough. There was a desperation in him that I wished I could reach to prove that I loved him and vow that I would never leave, no matter what he tried to do to tear us apart.

When he was like this—so raw and vulnerable—I had a hard time reconciling the man who said so little and could be so cold. As we made love, we clung to each other, Tristan taking the strength I offered, as if nothing and no one could come between us.

I just prayed to God that was true.

TWENTY-TWO
TRISTAN

The low beat of a techno song from a room on the other side of Top reverberated through the building, making the floor beneath me vibrate as I sat staring up at the TV on the wall across from me. Some movie about a mobster played, but I wasn't paying attention.

I'd been at Top for two nights, unable to go home and missing Nina more than I could handle. I couldn't be around her, though. Not now.

Each night I laid in bed afraid to close my eyes, afraid of the nightmares. A new one had taken over my nights since coming back from Atlanta. I saw my face hovering over the body of a naked girl smiling up at me. She reached out for me, and my hands grabbed at her breasts, pinching and tugging until she cried out in pain. Each time, she screamed a single word over and over. Taylor. I knew that wasn't my name, but I couldn't stop myself from wrapping my hands around her throat and slowly squeezing the soft flesh until there was no more life left in her. Gentle brown eyes stared up at me in surprise that I could hurt her as I backed away into a someone who stood behind me.

My father.

He patted me on the back all the while wearing a smile. He said nothing but stared at me like he admired me for what I'd just done to the girl.

Pouring myself another glass of scotch, I leaned back against the leather couch and closed my eyes, letting the alcohol slide down my throat. I didn't know how much more it would take, but I needed it to make me numb. I didn't want to think anymore. I wanted to not care anymore. To not miss Nina like someone had cut out my heart and left a painful, aching hole in my chest.

Karl's announcement that morning that he'd gotten copies of Joseph Edwards' notes from Nina's sister had given me a second's peace and made me believe for a fleeting moment that all the terrible events put in motion by my father would finally end. That we'd finally be free to live without the past haunting our every step.

But Karl wasn't a man to let things go that easily. Kim's copies were just that. Copies. He wanted the actual notes Joseph Edwards took as he dug into the horrible world of Stone Worldwide and knew I had them.

You didn't think I wouldn't have you followed, Tristan? Did you? For God's sake, I had your father and brother followed, and I trusted them. I know where you've been and I know what you have. If you're smart, and I think you are, just give it all up and never tell her what happened and you'll be fine.

Are you threatening me now, Karl?

Son, I'm not the man to play with. This shark doesn't care if your father thought you were a piranha or not.

At least I now knew why Kim hated me from the moment she met me in Nina's hospital room. She'd judged me to be the same kind of man my father and brother had been. Could I blame her? Two Stone men nothing better than lying murderers. Who would want their sister to be involved with a man like that?

Was I truly any better? I'd brought Nina into my world believing I was keeping her safe, but it had been my own selfishness more than anything else. I was no different than I'd ever been. I wanted something and used my money to get it. Typical Stone behavior.

Out of the corner of my eye I saw the door to the private room open. "Get out! I told you I didn't want to be bothered, Chase."

"It's not Chase. It's me, Tristan," a woman's voice said quietly.

I turned to see Brandi standing with her back against the door, frightened by my barking. I wasn't in the mood to hear her sad stories about that asshole ex or current or whatever the fuck type of boyfriend Chase was to her now.

"I want to be alone, Brandi."

"I know. I just wanted to check to see if you needed anything."

She moved cautiously from the door as I turned back to stare at the TV. Taking a seat next to me on the couch, she touched my arm softly. "Are you okay?"

"I'm fine," I lied. "Just want to be alone."

"Sometimes when things are bad it's good to talk to someone. You've done that for me more than once. Maybe if you talk about it you'll feel better."

I drank the final gulp of scotch in my glass, enjoying the warmth as it sat in my mouth for a moment before I swallowed. "There's nothing to talk about."

Brandi shifted herself to face me and took my hand. "I hate to see you like this, Tristan. I can't believe someone who has so much could be so sad."

"Well, believe it."

I felt her squeeze my hand and looked over to see her grinning at me. "I have something that I think might make you feel better, at least for a little while."

"Brandi, don't," I said flatly as I pulled my hand away.

"You know you'd feel better. Just a little. Chase said it could help."

I knew what she meant and I should have told her to leave. I knew that. But as I sat there thinking about Nina and what I knew I had to do, all I wanted was some relief from the pain. A tiny reprieve from my sentence.

Brandi slipped a small box from behind her back and spread out three lines of coke on the coffee table in front of us. She snorted the first line and sniffing, flopped back on the couch and pointed toward the rest of it sitting there waiting for me.

"Your turn."

Leaning forward, I looked down at the white powder that had given me so many nights of good times. Clean since the crash, I hadn't even thought of getting high, but now as it sat there waiting to give me the relief it always had, I could think of nothing but the feeling I'd have in just a few minutes.

Blocking my left nostril, I inhaled a line and closed my eyes. A rush coursed through my head and instantly I remembered why I loved coke all those years ago. In minutes, I was on top of the world—powerful, free, and happy. Truly happy, like the way I felt every time Nina told me she loved me.

One more line and everything that had tortured my mind for weeks was gone, replaced by pure bliss. My heart raced and my body felt like it could run a marathon. Brandi was a novice, so it didn't take more than a line for her to be bouncing off the walls. She seemed to be talking a hundred miles a minute about how she wished Chase was like me, but I wasn't listening. I didn't care about her problems.

All I cared about was that mine had vanished, at least for the moment.

Brandi's hand fastened on my crotch, and she licked her lips in an attempt to be seductive. "Tell me you don't love fucking when you're high, Tristan. Nobody would have to know. You know it would be great."

I didn't want to fuck Brandi. That would only make me feel worse. I had someone I loved already. It didn't matter that I couldn't be with her. I still loved her.

"Get your hand off your boss's cock, Brandi. If Chase doesn't fire you, I will. You're ruining this."

She wasn't going to be that easily convinced. Sliding her palm up and down my zipper, she cooed, "You're not my boss, Tristan. You only own the place. I guess that makes you my owner. Oooh, I like that."

"You know he's got cameras all over this place. Look around. At least smile for your boyfriend as you try to fuck someone else in front of him," I snapped, already hating how this was turning out.

Brandi rubbed her body up against my arm like a cat in heat. "Mmmm, that would be hot. Come on, baby. It will help you forget whatever's making you so sad."

Her lips pressed against mine, and all I could taste was the flavor of her spearmint gum. She jabbed her tongue into my mouth as her hands attempted to pull my shirt out of my pants, but I didn't want any of what she had to offer. I pushed her off me, and she fell back against the arm of the couch, her legs wide open.

"You know you want it, Tristan. Just let it happen. Don't fight it."

The door flung open before I could repeat that I didn't want her, but it was too late. There in the doorway stood Nina watching Brandi rub her pussy through her shorts as she did her best to convince me to fuck her.

"What the fuck is this?" Nina asked, her voice full of hurt.

Brandi leaped off the couch and began explaining how she had just wanted to help me feel better. It only made things worse and made me look guiltier.

Nina turned to face her and put her hand up in front of Brandi's face. "I so don't want to hear another fucking word from your mouth. Get the fuck away from me right now before I totally lose my cool."

Brandi was cheap, but she wasn't stupid. Nina had barely finished speaking and she was running from the room, nearly getting her four inch heels stuck in the door as she slammed it shut behind her.

"Tristan, what is this? Why haven't you been home in two days? What's going on here?" Nina rightfully demanded to know.

I leaned forward to pour myself another drink. "Nina, go home." I couldn't explain to her why I was sitting there with a woman I didn't give a damn about instead of lying in bed with the woman I loved more than anyone or anything in this world.

She wasn't going home, though. That wasn't her style. My mind was still racing as she sat down next to me, but my high was quickly fading, leaving the reality of what I had to do pressing down on me like a weight on my chest.

"I'm not going home. I know we've been dealing with some things, but I can't believe you're just planning on never coming home again. Have you been here every night?"

I looked away, unable to face her when I saw the tears in her eyes. First, I'd been a selfish prick and fallen in love with her, all the while telling myself I'd been keeping her safe. Now, I had to tell her the truth. It didn't matter if she left anymore. Whatever I'd thought I could give her was over now.

"Have you been with her?" she asked quietly.

I shook my head sadly. "No. I wouldn't do that. I never meant to do any of this, Nina."

She took my hand in hers and held it to her heart. "Tristan, what's going on? Why would you stay here instead of coming home to me?"

I couldn't continue like this. I'd kept what I'd found out about her father's death and my family's part in it a secret for weeks, and I couldn't do it anymore. Every day I worried that her memory would finally return and she'd know the ugly truth and leave me again. At least now, I knew that she was safe from Karl and his friends on the Board.

It wasn't her they wanted out of the way. It was me.

"I'm sorry, Nina. I have something to tell you. I can't keep it from you anymore."

She touched my chin with her forefinger and forced me to look at her. "You can tell me anything. I love you, Tristan."

Bowing my head, I kissed her palm. "It's time you knew everything. Come with me."

I led her upstairs to the apartment above the club that I'd been staying at. It was nowhere as nice as our house or the penthouse, but it didn't matter. Telling her the truth as we sat on expensive furniture wasn't going to change what I had to say.

"What's this about, Tristan? Why are we here?" she asked as she looked around at the place where I'd been hiding from her.

"Sit down. I need to get his off my chest before it crushes me."

She sat on the edge of the grey sectional that took up most of the living room and looked up at me with eyes full of worry. I knew what she thought I was about to say—that I'd met someone else and didn't want to be with her anymore. Maybe she thought that I'd lied about Brandi and was actually cheating on her.

At least I wasn't that man.

I took out her father's notebook and held it in my hand as I finally confessed what I'd held in for far too long. "Before I tell you what I need to say, I want you to know that I never meant for things to get to this point. I wanted to tell you every day, but it just never seemed the right time. No matter what you think after this, I need you to know that I've never loved anyone like I do you."

Nina reached out to take my hand and squeezed it in sympathy, not knowing what I had to say would likely turn her away from me forever. Her blue eyes were begging me not to break her heart. "I know you love me. If you're going to tell me you've been with someone else, don't. I'd rather not know. Just let me go on thinking it never happened. I can live with that. I can."

I shook my head and dropped her hand. "I wasn't with anyone else. I wish it was that easy. No, there's no one else. That makes what I have to tell you ten times harder."

"Tristan, what is it? Tell me."

"I thought you'd remember by now, to be honest. I dreaded that every day I might come home and you'd tell me you remember everything and then leave me. Maybe it's better that you didn't. I should have to tell you this. It's the least I can do as the last remaining member of my family."

Her face telegraphed her confusion, and I continued, pacing as I began the story that I knew would be the end of us.

"My father was Victor Stone. I was never close to my father, so I never really knew what he was like. By the time I was an adult, I was too busy stuffing the shit you saw downstairs up my nose to be bothered to find out what Stone Worldwide was all about. My brother was the one my father wanted to take over for him. Taylor was all about business and following in my father's footsteps, so I didn't care about that world. It was for people like them. I was too busy having a good time."

I knew this probably wasn't making much sense, but I needed to get it all out. It was as if saying it out loud might finally exorcise it from my mind and give me some peace. I needed to believe that I wouldn't always be covered in the layers of guilt that covered me now.

"When Taylor was twenty-four, he got a teenage girl pregnant. She was only fifteen. Her name was Amanda. I don't know why, but he abandoned her and the baby she was carrying. He wouldn't take her calls or see her, so she became depressed and when she was three months pregnant, killed herself."

"Oh, my God...I'm so sorry."

Nina's sympathy only made this worse. Shaking my head, I continued on. "The girl's father was a judge who my father's company ended up in front of for a sexual harassment case. It was a common civil suit that Stone Worldwide gets at least half a dozen times each year, but this one wasn't going to be one my father could win because the judge knew what Taylor had done. So my father had him murdered to be sure he'd win the case."

Suddenly, Nina's eyes narrowed to slits and she sat back with a heavy sigh. "Why does this sound so familiar? I swear I've heard something like this before."

My heart began pounding in my chest at the real fear that she was finally remembering. I wanted to stop, to push it all out of my mind and take her in my arms and never let her go. But I couldn't.

Now I had to say the hardest part. "No one would have ever known about all this if an investigative reporter hadn't begun checking into something about my father's company. I imagine he probably thought he was onto some real estate scheme or something like that, but he somehow found out about Taylor and Amanda Cashen, and from there it just snowballed until he had uncovered everything my father had done, including the murder of her father."

"Who was the reporter, Tristan?"

I stopped pacing and looked down into her face. "I never knew what my father and brother were doing. I had no idea, Nina."

"What was his name?" she said again, louder.

"I didn't know, Nina. I need you to believe that."

Her eyes grew wide, and she covered her mouth with her hands. Behind them, she said with a sob, "Oh my, God! I remember. I remember everything. You knew when you met me. You knew who I was and didn't tell me until that night."

I fell to my knees in front of her and stared up into all that pain. It tore my heart out. "Nina, I'm not asking for forgiveness. I know what I did was wrong. I didn't know what to do. If I told you when we met, you wouldn't have come to live with me. Karl and his friends were sure you knew about what your father had uncovered. I couldn't let them hurt you. I wanted to stop the cycle of pain that my father had begun."

"So you lied to me from the minute you met me? I fell in love with you!"

"I fell in love with you. That's the only part that wasn't built on a lie. I love you. I never meant to hurt you."

"This is why you've been avoiding me? You didn't want to face me with the truth," she cried as she recoiled from my touch.

"I'm sorry, Nina. Karl was threatening you, telling me that if you knew anything of what your father had found out that he'd kill you to keep you quiet. I didn't know about any of what Taylor and my father had done to the Cashens until I met with Judge Cashen's daughter in Atlanta. Until then..."

She cut me off as she jumped off the couch to get away from me. "Until then, all you knew was that your father had my father murdered execution style in a parking garage in Newark and you weren't going to tell me."

I slumped against the arm of the couch and hung my head. "I didn't know how to tell you without losing you. I couldn't lose you."

"So you lied to me every day and night."

"I convinced myself that it was okay because I was protecting you. I thought if I could make sure you were safe that someday you'd understand."

"I found out that night when I got into the accident. When were you going to tell me this time?"

I didn't know how to answer that. I'd never gotten that far. I'd been so concerned that Karl would hurt her that telling her the truth had been pushed aside.

"When, Tristan? When?" she screamed.

"I don't know."

"Look at me! At least face me now."

I turned around and looked up at her. "I'm sorry. I thought if I just had enough time I could solve this whole thing and you'd never have to know what my father did. I swear I didn't know about anything he did until right before I met you."

"You aren't to blame for what happened to my father, Tristan. Your crime was lying to me. We built a life together based on a lie. You asked me to marry you. Our entire life is a lie."

Standing, I grabbed her hands, needing to feel her touch on my skin, some small connection I could believe still meant something. "Don't say that. I know I lied and I know I hurt you, but we love each other. No matter what else happened, we fell in love."

"How could you do this? I wanted to believe we'd be together forever," she said in a sad voice as she looked down at our joined hands.

"I'm sorry, Nina. No matter what else, I need you to believe that I love you."

She yanked her hands from mine and glared up at me. Shaking her head wildly, she sobbed, "I can't listen to this. I can't. I trusted you."

Dropping to my knees, I wrapped my arms around her legs and held her tight. I needed to keep her there. I couldn't let her go. "Come away with me. We can go anywhere. Venice again. Wherever you want. As long as we're together."

Nina stared down into my eyes and I knew. I'd lost her. No amount of begging was going to work.

"I can't do this, Tristan. I can't," she said sadly and then pulled away from me, never looking back.

I watched her run out, knowing that I had to go after her. My feet took the steps downstairs by two, and I caught up with her just as she was reaching the street. Jensen stood next to the car looking over at me for what to do.

"Take me home!" she ordered as she opened the car door, but he stood still as a statue waiting for my orders.

"I want to go home! Take me home, Jensen!" she cried, but still he wouldn't move, his eyes focused on me to know what to do.

Silently, I nodded to let him know he could leave, and he sped away toward the house as I watched everything I loved leave me. I'd told myself over and over that I was willing to lose her if it meant she was safe, but now I couldn't do it. I couldn't let her go. I needed to know she believed I loved her.

I heard her cry as I stood in the hallway outside her bedroom door, knowing I was the only person who couldn't make her feel better. For an hour, I listened to her heartbreaking sobs as my hope that she'd understand why I'd done what I'd done faded away.

Sliding down the wall, I finally leaned against her door and whispered, "I can't do this anymore. I'm sorry. I never meant to hurt you."

I'd lost her. The one soul on Earth that I truly loved and I'd lost her because of who I was. That was the truth at the heart of it all. I was a Stone and because of that—because of what I was deep down—I'd lost Nina's love.

I was no different than my father or Taylor.

Closing my eyes, I pressed my cheek to her door and whispered one last time, "I love you, Nina. I hope someday you can forgive me."

I waited for what seemed like hours for her to say anything, but all I heard was silence.

TWENTY-THREE
Nina

My throat hurt because I cried so much, but the tears kept coming. I didn't know which hurt more—knowing what really happened to my father and that Tristan's father had been the one to take him away from me or that everything I loved had been based on a lie. I wanted to run away, like I did before, but I couldn't. Tristan had lied to me from the moment he met me, but I loved him. And he loved me. I just didn't know how we'd go on from here.

I'd heard him outside my door telling me he loved me. His voice was so sad that I couldn't face him. I pressed my ear to the door and heard him whisper that he hoped I'd forgive him.

I knew I shouldn't want to forgive him. He'd lied over and over for months. That should have been enough for me to never want to speak to him again.

If only it was that easy.

Exhausted from crying and thinking for hours, I finally fell asleep just as the first rays of the sun began to stream through my window. Not that I slept well. My body may have wanted to rest, but my mind raced the entire time so that when I opened my eyes at ten I was up and ready to face Tristan and our life together.

I couldn't just let this go. That had been the one thought preoccupying my mind. No matter how many times I told myself I couldn't forgive, it's the only thing I wanted to do. I knew what everyone would say. Kim would tell me I was stupid or being a fool. Once a liar, always a liar. Even Jordan would likely tell me to walk away.

My mind knew that was the smartest thing to do. My heart had an entirely different agenda, though.

For better or worse, my heart had won the tug-of-war, and I got out of bed prepared to tell Tristan how I felt. I could forgive him, but this would be his only chance. The man who'd been there for me when I was broken and hurt deserved at least that.

I spied an envelope sitting on the floor near the door, which was so typical of him. I hurriedly walked over to get it, noticing as I picked it up that it was far thicker than his usual notes. A tiny spike of fear ran through my mind at the possibility of what I'd soon find in those pages. Unfolding them, I began to read his words. As they flowed in front of my eyes, my stomach dropped and an emptiness filled me.

Dear Nina,

I can't say I'm sorry anymore and convince you how much I never meant to hurt you. I was a fool to believe that we could be happy. How could we be when I'm who I am?

You made my days happier than you'll ever know. Before I met you, I had never loved anyone. My life was empty. That was my fate, and I accepted it. I was a Stone, and it was better for me to be alone than to hurt people like my father had.

Then I met you and all that changed. I didn't want to accept my loneliness anymore. I wanted to believe I could make someone happy. I tried, but what I had to give wasn't enough. Money, trips, clothes—none of it made you love me. I didn't know anything else, and for that I'm sorry.

But somehow you made me understand none of that mattered and if I gave my heart I had a chance to have someone like you love me. I gave you my heart, and you gave me love. I know it wasn't easy to be with me. I'm all closed off and I need to have control more than other men. I don't know why I'm so fucked up, but you freely gave me your heart, and your love was the best thing of my life.

I'm sorry I didn't tell you the truth in the beginning. I'm sorry that when I had the chance to make things right when you came home from the hospital that I didn't. I know you may not believe it, but I never wanted to hurt you. That was the last thing I wanted to do.

I will always love you. I can't fix the mistakes I've made. I can only say I'm sorry and hope you'll forgive me someday. You can't accept my love after what I've done, but I hope you'll accept what I promised. Enclosed you'll find a legal document that will ensure you'll want for nothing. This house will be transferred to you, and I've made sure that each month money will be deposited in your account to ensure you have everything you can possibly desire.

I'm sorry that all I am is money and things. For a short time, I was more because of you.

I love you, Nina. Someday, I hope you'll believe me.

Yours always,
Tristan

Tears clouded my eyes so I couldn't read the words anymore, but I'd seen enough. I didn't need to read some legal document to know Tristan was gone. Instantly, I felt alone. I couldn't let him give up on us like this.

I tore down my hallway screaming his name, but I instinctively felt the emptiness of the house now that he'd left. I ran from room to room but found nothing.

"Tristan! No! Tristan!"

All there was in return was silence.

His room looked like it always had, like he hadn't even been there that night. Something in me said to check Rogers' room, and I raced there, stopping dead in the doorway at the sight of the bed. Neatly made the last time I'd been there, now the bedspread and blankets lay crumpled as if someone had spent a restless night there.

I checked the garage to see if Tristan's Jag was still there, but I knew better. He was gone. Jensen stood in the corner ready to take me wherever I desired.

"Where is he?"

"Miss?"

"Where is Tristan, Jensen? Where did he go?"

"He drove on his own, miss."

"Do you know where?"

Jensen stood silent as he stared at me. Tristan had likely told him not to tell me where he'd gone. I didn't care. I needed to find him and let him know I forgave him, even if I didn't understand everything that had happened. I needed to tell him I still loved him.

"I have to find him. Tell me where he went!" I yelled across the garage, shocking the driver.

"He's gone, Nina," a voice behind me said quietly, and I turned around to see a strange man standing there.

"Who are you? Where is Tristan? Tell me! I need to know."

"Come with me. We can talk inside."

I followed the large man with too much red hair and beard to a sitting room. As I took a seat on the couch, I remembered being in that room with Tristan. We'd first kissed right there after he'd taught me how to tie a Windsor knot. I remembered everything. Our first night together. How crazy I was in love with him just days later. Everything was back now.

"My name is Daryl Knight. I work for Tristan. I guess ordinarily Rogers would have had the job of telling you this, but it's fallen on me now."

"I hope you don't hate me like Rogers did because I need you to tell me where Tristan is. I have to see him."

"That can't happen, Nina. All I know is that he's gone. Karl and his friends on the Board want him dead now that your sister gave them her copies of your father's notes. Because Tristan wouldn't give them the original notes, they can't let him stay alive."

"I don't understand. What's so important about my father's notes? Tristan knows what happened with his father and brother. He knows what they did and why my father was murdered. Why doesn't he just give them to Karl and be done with this whole horrible thing?"

"I don't know why. All I know is that he's not done with those notes yet."

"Well, I don't care about that. I just need to see him. Where is he, Daryl?"

He frowned and shook his head. "I don't know. All I know is what he told me when he called. He wanted me to make sure you read the papers he left you."

I angrily waved the envelope Tristan had left me in front of him. "I don't care about the papers. I want Tristan, not things. Please tell me where he is."

"I can't."

Out of the corner of my eye, I saw two huge men who seemed to be hovering just outside the door to the sitting room. Pointing at them, I asked, "Then can they tell me?"

Daryl turned to look at the them and shook his head. "No. They're not here for that."

"Then what the hell are they here for? Who are they?"

He waved them into the room and they took their place in front of us like two giants eying their next victims. The one who stood on the left had very short, cropped dark hair with some streaks of grey, and his face said he was all business. He was enormous, like a bouncer at a club, and he looked as if he could pick me up with two fingers. The man on the right wore his lighter brown hair slightly longer and had no grey in his, but his eyes were the darkest blue I'd ever seen.

"Nina, these men protect you. They've protected you since your accident. When you leave this house, they're always nearby making sure you're safe."

"Do you mean every time I went out they were there?" I asked in astonishment.

I looked at the men as they nodded silently. My bodyguards looked down at me as I worked to process all of this. Two men had been watching me and obviously Tristan had hired them.

"Yes, and they'll be there every time you go out from now on."

"What if I don't want them to be?" I asked, feeling slightly irritated by Daryl's officious tone. It was one thing for Tristan to be all Alpha with me. I loved him. Daryl was just some scruffy guy sitting in what was now my house and bossing me around.

"I'm sorry, but you don't have a choice. They have their job, just as I have mine. Your safety is paramount to Tristan, so you'll just have to get used to having them around."

"I don't understand, Daryl. I thought that Karl and his thugs didn't care about me anymore because my sister gave them what they wanted. Why would I be in danger?"

"If Karl doesn't get what he wants from Tristan, he's not above hurting you. These men will make sure that doesn't happen."

"What? For the rest of my life?"

"I don't know the answer to that. For now, they'll be next to you at all times."

I looked up again at the men. "Since you're going to be my shadows, I should at least know your names."

Mr. All Business nodded. "Nathan West."

The corners of Blue Eye's mouth hitched up slightly, giving him a sort of scary-sexy look. "Gage Varo."

Both men had hollow, deep voices, adding to my anxiety about all of this. Turning to face Daryl, I asked, "How do they know when I'm leaving the house? Does Jensen call them?"

"They stay in the carriage house. When Jensen leaves, they leave."

I sat stunned at what Daryl was saying. These men lived on the same property as I did and I'd never even seen them. And they'd been following me for weeks. How is it I'd missed these two gigantic men near me at all times?

"Why haven't I noticed them all this time?"

The one named Varo answered, "Because you weren't looking for us. Our job is to be invisible. You would have never known we were there if you hadn't been told."

"What if I don't want to live here with bodyguards and a driver?"

Daryl seemed to think about my question and answered, "I think that would make Tristan unhappy. He wants to ensure you're safe, Nina."

"I want to talk to him. I'm tired of all this. Where is he?"

Instead of giving me the answer I so desperately wanted, Daryl simply stood to leave. "I can't help you with that. What I can say is that Tristan has taken care of everything to make sure you're safe."

Jumping up, I screamed, "Why do you keep saying that? I don't care about being safe. All I want is to see Tristan!"

"I'm sorry, Nina. I wish I could say more."

"Then there is more to say. Where is he? Why can't I at least see him?"

My bodyguards walked out, leaving me alone with Daryl. He smiled for the first time and said, "Nina, I can't say more because Tristan hasn't told me more. I don't know where he is. All I know is that in the middle of the night he called me and told me he needed my help to make sure what he wanted to happen happened. That's it."

"Did he sound..." I didn't know how to say it. "Did he sound like he was okay? There was coke and..."

Daryl smiled again. "He sounded tired."

"Would you tell me if you knew anything else, like say, if he said anything about me other than that he wanted to know that I'm safe? Give me something."

"I work for Tristan, but I know how much you mean to him, so yes, I would. He said very little, Nina. All I know is that his first concern was for your safety."

I hung my head in sadness. "Thank you, Daryl. Did he say anything else at about anything I should do?"

"One last thing. Don't try to contact your sister. She and her family are safe from Karl and his friends, but to make sure they stay that way, you can't speak to her for a while."

"Did Tristan do that?"

Daryl nodded. "Yeah. They weren't safe, even after she gave Karl your father's notes."

"When is all this going to end, Daryl?"

Shaking his head, he shrugged. "I don't know, but trust that Tristan won't let Karl and his buddies get what they want."

I wish I knew what that awful man wanted. So much of this was still a mystery to me, and with Tristan gone, I didn't have anyone to help me understand all of it.

Daryl handed me a slip of paper. "This is my number. Call me if you need anything. West and Varo will take care of your safety, and Jensen is here for you like he's always been."

Nodding, I pressed a fake smile on my face. "Thank you, Daryl."

It seemed like I had men everywhere to take care of me except for the one I truly wanted standing next to me. The memory of those pictures of Tristan came back to me as I sat alone, and I found myself in the attic next to the trunk that held those images from so long ago.

I sat down on the wood floor and lifted the lid. Inside were letters and pictures from years before. I recognized the large portrait that sat on the bottom of the trunk. Pulling it out, I propped it against the inside of the lid and studied it in the faint sunlight streaming into the attic. Instantly, my eyes were drawn to the left side of the picture where Tristan's father and brother sat. Hatred coursed through my veins as I stared at their faces. Even though Taylor was just a small child, I hated him. It was almost as if he wasn't Tristan's identical twin. Nothing about him reminded me of the man I loved. All I saw was the man who was to blame for that poor girl's death.

Victor Stone sat behind Taylor smiling and happy. I hated him even more. My hands began to shake as they clutched the sides of the picture containing the two people responsible for my father's death. Not just death. Murder. They'd murdered my father to save themselves. I wanted to scream—to find them and hit them until they felt like I did when I first heard my father was gone.

But I couldn't. Fate had punished them before anyone else could. They were gone, taken from this Earth, and I'd have to learn to live with how much I hated them.

I couldn't look at them anymore. My eyes filled with tears at the hatred inside me. This wasn't who I was, though. I didn't want to hate. I forced my gaze to the right side of the portrait where Tristan sat in front of his mother. Her face was placid, but something in her eyes made her look sad. She was beautiful, her eyes so much like Tristan's now as I stared at them. They seemed to speak from the silence of the image. Had she known what her husband was like? Did she ever find out what Taylor had done, or had she remained blissfully ignorant like many women in her position?

I understood wanting to be ignorant of the painful facts of life. I couldn't blame her if she had chosen to believe her husband and son weren't the monsters they were. I just prayed that she knew how good Tristan was.

Unable to look at the ones responsible for all this heartache anymore, I placed the portrait back in its spot in the trunk next to a stack of letters tied with a red silk ribbon that reminded me of all the notes and letters Tristan had written me. I ran my fingertips over the handwriting as I read the name they were addressed to.

Tressa.

Had they been love letters from Tristan's father to his mother? Tossing them back into the bottom of the trunk, I closed the lid. I couldn't think about Victor Stone being someone good and kind. He was a monster, and that was all there was to it for me.

I walked back to my room, still determined to at least let Tristan know that I forgave him. Grabbing my phone, I laid back on my bed and texted him a message, my fingers saying what my voice couldn't.

I wish you hadn't left. I wanted to tell you this myself, but I'll have to do it this way instead. I forgive you. Please tell me where you are so I can come to you. I don't want this house and the money if you aren't with me. I love you.

For more than an hour I waited for him to text me back and tell me he loved me too. He never answered my text.

EPILOGUE
TRISTAN

The sun was just setting as I watched the blue sky change to a deep purple shade I hadn't seen since my last time here. I'd only visited this place once when I was a boy. My mother had brought me here with my brother to see a hotel my father was considering buying. She fell in love with its old world charm, but he dismissed it out of hand, knowing full well how much it meant to her to play some part in the business.

The building had fallen into disrepair in the years since, and it was nowhere near as beautiful now. No longer a hotel, it was merely a home under construction. It was the first purchase I made after becoming CEO of Stone Worldwide. I bought it sight unseen and immediately set about reconstructing it. I'd always planned on bringing Nina here once the home was finished. I'd had this fantasy that this could be our summer house and we'd bring our kids here. They'd play in the yard while she and I watched them from the balcony.

As I sat in the livable part of the house admiring the darkening sky, I tried to remember that all those dreams were gone now. Nina had reacted just as I feared when she heard what I'd done. I didn't blame her. How could I? While my crime wasn't the same as my father's or brother's, it was still a betrayal and I'd knowingly committed it, no matter what my intentions had been.

Rogers had been right.

My chest felt like a weight was pushing down on it every time I thought about him. As much my father was Victor Stone, he'd been the one I'd turned to for so long I hadn't seen what he'd become. That he'd chosen Karl and the world I'd sworn to never be a part of over me and had tried to hurt the woman I loved hurt more than I could express.

But his death was as much my fault as the one who'd run him down that night. I wanted to kill him right there in his room in my home, my hands tightening around his neck until there was no more life left in him. I wished him dead for what he'd done—for his disloyalty when I needed him most. For threatening to hurt the one soul on this Earth I'd ever truly loved.

Nina.

My thoughts always came back to her. Thousands of miles separated us, yet I could still smell her perfume each time I inhaled, could still feel the touch of her hand on mine when I closed my eyes.

I wondered how she looked when she read my letter, her gentle blue eyes taking in my words like she had that first night home from the hospital. Had it made her happy when she found out that she owned that house she loved so much, or had she thrown the paper away from her in disgust, unwilling to listen to my apologies even in that form?

Looking around at the almost empty room I sat in now, I accepted how it all had ended up. I was supposed to be alone. I'd told shrink after shrink that, trying to convince them of the reality of who I was while they tried their damnedest to persuade me to believe that no person was meant to be alone, not even someone as fucked up as I was.

That all souls deserved love.

I'd lost my family, Rogers, and now Nina. Whether or not I deserved it, I was alone.

I looked down at my phone, a new one I'd gotten just days before. I knew it was impossible since she didn't know the number, but every so often I checked anyway to see if she'd texted to tell me she'd forgiven me, she loved me, or even that she missed me.

It was better this way. Nina was safe with West and Varo. She had Daryl looking out for her and Jensen at her beck and call. She had as much money as she'd ever need and a home she'd said she'd loved.

Pushing the phone away from me, it slid across the table and I told myself this was how it had to be.

It's better this way.

Even if it wasn't better this way, this was how it was.

I slipped one of the letters she'd written me out of my pocket and ran my fingertips over the words, imagining her hand holding the paper as she wrote the lines that I read and reread every night. I missed her so much my body actually hurt. I missed her voice as she asked me dozens of questions and her smile when she tried to bring me out of my shell. I missed the softness of her lips against mine when she kissed me and the feel of her cuddled up next to me as she drifted off to sleep.

How was I going to live like this for the rest of my life now that I knew what I missed?

I leaned over, pulling my phone toward me, and turned it on. I ran my finger across the screen, but it didn't change the picture. Maybe it was a sign. Staring at it, I tried to talk myself out of what I was about to do.

But it was no use. I had to try.

I lightly dragged my fingertip across the screen, bringing it to life this time, and pressed until the only contact I had saved came up.

Nina.

I miss you.

Pushing the phone away, I watched it, my eyes fixed on it for her text back. I hadn't told her who I was, so she might never reply. Maybe that's what was supposed to be.

I waited for what seemed like hours, although it was likely just a few minutes, before I gave up hope and closed my eyes, silently telling myself this was what I deserved. This was my punishment for my crimes.

Pulling the phone back, I opened my eyes and saw a message come in. *Please come home. Don't leave me here all alone.*

I didn't think it was possible for my heart to break more, but just seeing those words made it feel like someone was tearing it out of my chest. She forgave me, yet I couldn't go home now.

I love you. If I could return, I would.

Texting Nina had been a mistake. Wishing for something that couldn't be was bad enough. Wishing for something that could someday happen was worse.

My phone lit up with another text. *I love you, Tristan. I don't know why you left, but whatever it is, we can handle it together. Please come back to me.*

I didn't answer her. I couldn't tell her I wasn't coming back, as much as I wanted to. I couldn't hurt her again. As I beat myself up for wanting what only she could give me, my phone lit up again with her final message.

I'm not letting you go. I won't let you give up on us, Tristan. If you won't come to me, I'll come to you. Even if no one helps me, I'll find you again.

TRISTAN AND NINA'S STORY

CONCLUDES IN

GIVE IN TO ME

COMING SOON!

Be sure to visit K.M.'s Facebook page for all the latest on Tristan and Nina, along with giveaways and other goodies! Check out her **blog** and **Twitter** too! And to hear about Advanced Review Copy opportunities and all the news on K.M. Scott books first, sign up for her **newsletter** today!

Other books by K.M. Scott:
Crash Into Me (Heart of Stone #1)

Love sexy paranormal romance? K.M. writes under the name Gabrielle Bisset too. Visit Gabrielle's **Facebook page** and her website at **www.gabriellebisset.com** to find out about her books.

Books by Gabrielle Bisset:

Vampire Dreams Revamped (A Sons of Navarus Prequel)
  Blood Avenged (Sons of Navarus #1)
  Blood Betrayed (Sons of Navarus #2)
  Longing (A Sons of Navarus Short Story)
  Blood Spirit (Sons of Navarus #3)
  The Deepest Cut (A Sons of Navarus Short Story)
  Blood Prophecy (Sons of Navarus #4)
  Blood & Dreams Sons of Navarus Box Set

  Stolen Destiny
  Destiny Redeemed

Love's Master
Masquerade
The Victorian Erotic Romance Trilogy